WODE HOUSE

Rachel Howells

For Andy,

Who somehow managed to stay on this rollercoaster with me despite the fears, tears and tantrums. I'm forever in your debt. Thank you for your advice, support and encouragement but most of all, for being my muse.

And to Mum,

LYTTLSGO

...by the sweat of your brow you will eat your food until you return to the ground, since from it you were taken; for dust you are and to dust you will return...

Genesis 3:6-19

Chapter 1

Dyrac had already succumbed to his need for the day having drawn from the neck of his housekeeper Merril. Merril was a weak and feeble woman who believed she was totally inadequate; that was until she fell into Dyrac's service. Dyrac was brilliantly devious entrapping Merril by empowering her with responsibilities, managing his affairs and those of Wode House. He fulfilled her need for approval and acceptance. This provided Dyrac with someone who idolised him, and be at his every beck and call, someone who would be a willing donor.

Merril was slight in stature; she stood no taller than 5 foot. She had glossy, straight hair which had a chestnut hue that was always tied up in a tight bun. She was neat and tidy in appearance and wore the same outfit most days, black tee underneath a woollen grey pinafore dress that stopped just above the knee, black tights and polished black brogues. She wore a solid silver bangle on her right wrist. The only day she wore anything different would be her day off, usually a Sunday, when she would spend her day in a long and baggy smock dress wearing black Doctor Marten boots that had splatters of paint on them. This was also the only day she would wear her hair down. Only when it was down could you see that reached the small of her back. She was plain but beautiful. Make up had never tired her flawless complexion.

Dyrac always found the Sunday Merril very alluring and she would often catch him staring at her from the corner of her eye, but she never acknowledged him. She'd secretly smile and saunter on by, occasionally brushing against him as she passed him by apologising for not seeing him when she clearly and purposefully had. Each time she brushed against him she would tingle throughout her body and goose bumps would appear on her arms, her hairs would stand on end and she'd feel an electricity consume her.

Merril portrayed a timid exterior around anyone who visited, and she never set foot out of the house. All her needs were met by Dyrac. Anything that Merril, or Dyrac, needed to purchase was always delivered to the door. The only time Merril usually entered into conversation with anyone was when Kurt, from Bryson & Sons, dropped off the weekly groceries. Merril was utterly infatuated with Kurt. The infatuation was not reciprocated but, Kurt was compensated well by Dyrac on the basis he encourage Merril's infatuation. Despite the banal conversation that ensued at every drop off he always mustered a devilishly charming demeanor. The money he was paid by Dyrac exceeded the salary he received from his day job at the grocery store which helped finance his gambling addiction. An addiction which Dyrac had full knowledge of, and manipulated to his advantage.

Today was Saturday, it was 7.25am and Merril was beyond excited as Kurt would be due in five minutes with this week's delivery. It was the first Saturday of the month which meant Merril's time with Kurt would be longer than usual as the first Saturday of the month was always the largest delivery.

As well as the normal weekly groceries, once a month Kurt would also deliver other adhoc items that had been ordered by Dyrac. With the additional duties came extra perks. The longer schedule enabled Kurt to stop for a break in which time Merril would prepare and serve him a full English breakfast. Merril came to treasure those extra moments with Kurt and often sat with him whilst he ate. This annoyed Kurt but he never let it show, after all the deal with Dyrac was that he had to encourage Merril's advances so, he would always make polite conversation and entertain Merril with stories that he usually made up. Merril never ate in view of anyone else and whilst Kurt often invited her to take some of his breakfast she would always, with grace, decline.

Merril had gone to extra efforts this morning dousing her delicate skin with her favourite scent, Lovely by Sarah Jessica Parker. She recalled on one occasion that Kurt commented on how deliciously splendid she smelt so, since then she saved her perfume just for him.

Kurt pulled through the tall wrought iron gates at the entrance of the driveway and drove around to the side entrance. Ringing the old fashioned bell on a chain Merril raced towards the door, pausing momentarily to gather herself, brush down her pinafore and catch her breath. She opened the door with a slight grin.

"Good morning Kurt," she said nodding her head.

"Morning Merry," Kurt responded with the pet name he chose for her. "Something smells delicious, is that you?"

Merril quivered and giggled, that girly kind of

giggle women do when they are utterly head over heels.

"So, Merry, shall we get the groceries in; I can help you put things away before I sit down for breakfast?"

"Thanks Kurt, but I can manage," she politely declined his offer to help put things away as she wanted to delay his departure for as long as she could.

"Ok, if you're sure? I've got 14 boxes today plus the chest that Dyrac ordered under the strict instructions I was not to open it. Where do you want it?"

"Usual place for the boxes and the chest needs to go into the cellar."

"Roger that beautiful."

Kurt set the boxes aside on the vast kitchen table whilst Merril got to work putting it all away. The kitchen table was a large oak piece, approximately 3 foot wide by 12 foot long. The grain was beautiful and had the occasional natural knot. It had aged well with signs of use but that it had fulfilled its purpose

Kurt returned to his pick up and hauled the chest inside. Although he struggled, he managed to get it to the cellar door.

"This thing weighs a tonne," he said.

"What's it for I wonder?" asked Merril.

"You're guess is as good as mine, but I can tell you one thing for sure, I'll be glad to get this out of my sight. I picked it up Tuesday and since then I've had some kind of darkness overshadow me I'm sure of it and I've felt an unusual coldness set deep in my bones. It's got some odd marking on the top of the chest look."

Before opening the cellar door both Merril and Kurt took a momentary glance at the chest. The chest was made of old oak just like the kitchen table although it had become stained and darkened over the years. It had two wide brown leather straps that sat parallel from each other either side. The straps were held together with enormous brass buckles with a deep set lock sat dead centre. Irrespective of his compelling urge to discover the contents, the warnings not to by Dyrac and the fact that the chest was locked, there was no way of discovering what secrets lay within.

On the lid was a marking, it was engraved into the wood but had weathered with time. It looked like an unusual rune. Kurt had tried in vain to identify by scouring the internet however, nowhere in the ether of the web could he find anything that came close.

The marking mesmerized both Merril and Kurt; it was the whistling of the kettle boiling on the stove that startled them back into the now.

"Christ! My fucking heart!" gasped Kurt.

"Sorry, I forgot I put that on. I never understood why Dyrac wouldn't allow an electric kettle, or other normal kitchen items for that matter. That kettle catches me out every time."

In an instant both had lost all trace of thought for the marking on the chest and Kurt dragged it down the stairs, setting it to one side in the cellar. He was ambly walking back up the steps into the kitchen when he heard Merril humming away to herself. It wasn't a tune he recognised.

"Tea or coffee with your breakfast this morning Kurt?" she asked.

"Tea, three please Merry," Kurt replied indicating the number of teaspoons of sugars he wanted.

Merril made the most delightful cup of tea thought Kurt. She couldn't be more English if she tried. Her tea literally made you melt with comfort into complete relaxation. She was a great cook and ever providing. Completely selfless. Sometimes Kurt thought he could do worse but then he remembered that this was all just part of a deal.

"Two eggs, sunny side up; three rashers of unsmoked bacon; two sausages; one piece of black pudding; grilled tomatoes; mushrooms; baked beans; fried and toasted bread and the piece de resistance, HP sauce. Bon appétit."

"Woman, you are sensational" Kurt responded, drooling slightly as Merril placed the breakfast spread in front of him.

During breakfast Merril and Kurt exchanged stories from the week. Merril's, the same as always, were about the things she had been doing around the house. This week however, one thing that was different, Merril had begun work on a new piece of art. She rambled on about how the prepping of the canvas had used up most of her day off and that tomorrow she was going to start with the first paint stroke. She was always excited when it came to discussing art. And Kurt, whilst not entirely interested, encouraged her and praised her on acting upon her artistic urges.

"Sounds pretty amazing, I'd love to see it when it's done if you'll allow me?" he said.

"Seriously, you'd really want to see. It's not for everyone; I've an unusual taste in what I consider to be art," replied Merril.

"Seriously, I'd love to take a look," said Kurt. "Now, you're not going to believe the change in luck I had this week."

"Ooh did you win at The Lavender Lounge?"

The Lavender Lounge was a casino that Merril had only heard of through Kurt. Her images of what it looked like far outweighed the actual sight. Merril imagined a Vegas style casino all shiny and buzzing inside. Neon lights everywhere and the sound of the slot machines dropping wins. It was in fact more like a working men's club from the 80's but with a more upmarket branding. There were worn out sticky carpets that you risked leaving your shoes on if you stood for too long, burgundy banquettes with tears in the leather and foam hanging out where people had picked away at them over the years. Bevelled copper topped round pub tables with ripped beer mats and smoke stained wall paper. Since the smoking ban in public places came into effect the casino smelled sweaty, from body odour and bad feet, mixed with the stench of the deep fried food being cooked to ruin in the kitchen.

"Well yes, in a way I sure did. I was feeling lucky Monday night so, I took a trip over to The Lavender Lounge and played fifty G"

"Wait," exclaimed Merril, "FIFTY G, as in £50,000?" she added annunciating the words.

"Correct" said Kurt holding up his hand in an 'I know, I know it's a lot of money but I'll do with it as I see fit' kind of way. "So, there I was with my chips and I thought I'm going all in. All in on red 24."

"24? Why 24?" asked Merril.

"It's your birthday, is it not?" replied Kurt.

A sudden rush of giddiness tangled and knotted in Merril's stomach. "Well yes, how do you know, I mean you chose that because of me? Why? I mean that's, how do you?" she struggled to be coherent.

"Never mind Merry, I know a lot about you," Kurt said as he winked at her. "It seemed like the ball and roulette wheel were never going to stop. The continued rotation and the anticipation built to a disorientating crescendo. The tension inside was bordering on unbearable, then," Kurt paused for effect, "nothing. Time literally stopped. I stared and stared and looked up at the croupier and back down to the wheel. I'd won!"

"And?" asked Merril excitedly.

"And, well I almost passed out that's what! I had to grab the edge of the table to stop me from falling. I heard a 'WINNER' announcement and saw the croupier usher me to the counter to collect my winnings. I was in such a daze I had no idea how much I'd won. I staggered over to the counter where another croupier acknowledged me with a nod and then she handed me my winnings."

"How much?" Merril was intrigued "I mean you don't have to say but I'm dying to know."

"£250,000 Merry!"

Merril stood mouth agape!

"But..."

"But what?" asked Merril.

"Well, I left The Lavender Lounge and went straight home. I couldn't really sleep that night. I didn't believe my luck. The next morning, I collected the chest for Dyrac and decided to head straight over to The Lavender Lounge whilst my luck was still hot."

"Kurt?"

"Let me finish" he said. "Like I said, I went over to The Lavender Lounge whilst my luck was still hot. I waltzed in the place like I owned the joint. People were smiling at me, shaking my hands as I passed by. I felt like a celebrity walking the red carpet at a Hollywood movie premiere. I headed straight for the roulette table and place fifty on black. The wheel spun, stopped and the croupier announced 'RED'. Shit! I thought. Oh well, I've still got £200,000 left right so I hedged my bets and placed another."

"I can't look" said Merril "I mean I know that makes no sense but seriously my ears don't want to look."

"Well, this time I place £100,000 on red and "£100,000 on black. I thought, well I can't lose right? Wrong! I lost big time," said Kurt.

Kurt continued regaling of the story of how he blew £250,000 in twenty minutes.

"And, I left penniless," he ended.

The rest of Kurt's visit was sombre in nature, albeit the story had been highly exaggerated by Kurt as part of his ulterior motive to gain sympathy and more attention from Merril. *It's all part of the deal remember* he thought. Merril tried her best to make the end of Kurt's visit a pleasant one and offered some of her homemade Dorset apple cake but Kurt was stuffed from the mammoth breakfast he had just devoured.

"Are you sure you need to go right away Kurt?" asked Merril.

"Sorry Merril, other deliveries to do, if I don't get to old Mac's with his tobacco and whisky he'll have his hounds out hunting me down. But another time?" Kurt put on his plaid tweed hunters jacket, picked up his steel toe capped boots from by the side of the door forcing his size 11's into the 10½ fit. He gave a curting glance back to Merril and nodded.

"Bye Kurt," said Merril.

Merril could be heard singing away as Kurt walked across the gravel drive way back to his pick up.

"Kurt!" shouted a man's voice. It was Dyrac.

"Yes sir? Good morning," said Kurt.

"Yes, yes it is a good morning. Now, the chest, did you bring it?" asked Dyrac.

"I brought it, yes. It's in the cellar as you requested. May I ask...?"

"No. No you may not," interrupted Dyrac brusquely, forcing an envelope into Kurt's hand. "I trust you're still playing your part as instructed?"

"Yes," replied Kurt.

"And Merril has no idea?" asked Dyrac.

"None sir," came the reply.

"That'll be all," replied Dyrac, turning and walking back towards the front door of the house.

Kurt got into his pickup throwing the envelope Dyrac just gave him onto the passenger seat. He switched on the ignition and drove down the driveway. He continued through the gates before pulling over and stopping. With the engine still running he pulled on the handbrake and grabbed the envelope.

With some apprehension Kurt tore off the top edge and glanced inside. As well as the usual bundle of cash, payment for his extra services, he spotted a piece of paper with handwriting scribbled across it. He slid it out and read it:

> *You have played the game well and it's time to bring things up a notch. You've two choices:*
>   1. *Earn double you've earned so far with no questions asked and await further instructions*
>   2. *Reap the benefits you've been rewarded so far and make this your final*
>   *journey to the house.*
>
> *If you do not return, you're decision will be clear however, if you return to the house next Saturday then you must meet me in the study at 8:00am where I will have your next task waiting for you.*

Kurt pondered momentarily before taking a breath and setting off and continuing his deliveries for the day.

Chapter 2

A scrawny filthy and bedraggled looking boy scurried between the dustbins in the dark alleyway. Although he was silent, almost stealth like in his movements, his presence wasn't purposefully hidden. By the age of 6 years old, which is what he was now, he had learnt to blend into the background. To be that shadow in the corner of your eye that disappeared the moment you checked to see what was there. You could even look right at him and instantly forget about his existence. Initially the complete ignorance of his existence was painful. Now, he now felt nothing; nothing always.

The boy was so thin his cheekbones protruded unhealthily from his gaunt face. Skin hung off him like baggy, oversized clothing. His ethnicity was not distinguishable, no longer white in race as dirt, over time, had become so ingrained it greyed his appearance. No amount of soap would rejuvenate the natural colour of his skin. Not even that harsh carbolic soap mechanics used to remove oil from their hands after a hard days graft in the garage. Nor the spit of any mother on the corner of a snotty handkerchief; or scrubbing with a wire brush could remove the grubbiness from this little urchin.

It was dusk, approximately 7.00pm; the shop fronts had been closed down for a couple of hours and the staff long gone for the day. The alleyway was free of its usual comings and goings and that meant going through the huge rubbish bins out back interruption free. It was whilst rummaging in his usual survival instinctive way that he heard footsteps. They sounded distant initially but they were without shadow of a doubt heading in his direction. He froze, petrified that even the sound of his breath would reveal his whereabouts to the passer by.

The footsteps stopped, he held onto his breath, he thought *they will go soon surely.*

Nothing.

The boy started to feel light headed as he struggled to contain his breath any longer. He let out an enormous sigh, exhaling all the air from his lungs in a huge puff. In an instant the lid of the rubbish bin, where he had concealed himself, flung open.

Trying to remain still and urging every camouflage thought he could muster he tried in vain to remain hidden.

"You, boy!" beamed a deep and bone penetrating voice. You know the type of voice that is so deep it reverberates around your insides and momentarily makes you feel the need to empty your bowels.

The boy opened his left eye, peering through the corner hoping the voice was directed towards somebody else hiding nearby. Alas, the eyes belonging to that voice stared directly back at him.

"Yes you!" The figure pointed ominously and directly at him.

"..." he cleared his throat with a pathetic cough "what me?"

"Don't you mean who, me?" replied the mysterious man.

"Eh?" said the boy.

"Never mind. Get out of there boy I've something to discuss with you. Something that will change your fortunes, change your life forever," said the man.

Intrigue got the better of him and the boy hopped out of the bin landing on both feet, steadfast in front of this unusual figure of a man. The boy could see him clearer now, albeit not his face entirely. This man was enormous. Anything would be considered enormous to this waif of a boy but, the man appeared as wide as he was tall. The man wore a thick and heavy grey woollen coat with large wooden duffle buttons. A double breasted coat that went down to the man's ankles revealing only patent black oxford style shoes. They were so shiny the moon reflected off them as clearly as it was sat in the night sky. The man wore dark leather gloves and that was pretty much all you could decipher in this light.

The street lamp a short distance away blew out plunging the two into an eerie darkness. It was too dark to see but, too light to disappear into the shadows.

There was a click of a door handle and Dyrac was back in the now. He was sat in his oxblood red high winged backed leather, chesterfield styled chair still clutching the Glencairn crystal whisky glass in his right hand. Only remnants of ice and diluted whisky remained. Dyrac's flash backs had become more frequent since Kurt delivered the chest to Wode House, a connection that Dyrac had not yet made.

"Do you have any other needs before I retire for the evening sir?" Merril asked delicately and politely.

"Not tonight Merril that will be all," came the reply from Dyrac with a wave of his hand. "And please Merril, do call me Dyrac. As you were."

"Goodnight, Dyrac," said Merril.

Merril left the room through the same door she entered without turning her back to Dyrac; another condition of her service was that she would never turn her back on him.

Merril was walking along the hallway when she heard what appeared to be the sound of shattering glass from the study. Quickly turning on her heels she flung herself through the door.

"LEAVE!" bellowed Dyrac

"But..," said Merril.

"OUT! NOW!" Dyrac retorted.

Merril quickly, but reluctantly, disappeared from the study and headed towards the staff quarters.

Dyrac sat slumped in his chair, tears cascading down his sullen face. The whisky taste on his tongue slowly dissipated into the saltiness left by the tears seeping through the corner of his mouth.

Merril lay in her bed wondering what caused Dyrac to fly into such a rage and to be so dismissive of her. Her thoughts were exacerbated by her anxiety and the Sarah need for reassurance. She wondered whether there was something she may have done, or not, that had caused him to be so aggressive towards her.

The realisation of Dyrac's own frustrations towards Merril began to seep in and he felt an unusual pang of guilt hit him hard in the chest. Dyrac only ever had thoughts for himself and, with the self protective barriers he had worked hard to put in place, he didn't know what to do with this new found feeling of hurt for another individual. Dyrac questioned his feelings towards Merril as though there was an underlying connection between them.

He raised himself from his chair and walked over to his desk. It was an immense piece of oak furniture from the 1500s which he had lovingly restored. Standing heavy set lion paw feet with 3 drawers either side, green leather top bordered with a gold leaf design. Right in the centre, above where you tuck your legs, was a small keyhole. Dyrac inserted a key he kept on a pocket watch chain on his waistcoat. There was click as the locking mechanism was released and a small flap dropped below. Carefully, Dyrac pulled the flap revealing a hidden tray. To shallow to hold more than a few pieces of paper but it was sufficient for his needs. He removed a brown A4 envelope with a broken red wax seal. The envelope was torn and tatty in the corners. Inside was a parchment document, Dyrac slid the pages out. The cover page was stained yellowed over time. The following words were handwritten in black ink in old, and barely legible calligraphy:

tantum in oculis vestris

Dyrac traced his fingers over the words and turned to the first page taking in each word slowly, he read to himself:

In the name of God, amen. The 10th daye of the moneth of Aprill, the yere of our lord 1529, I Abimilech Gideon of the parishe of Monkewearmouth in the dyocese of Durham, beyng in perfytt remembrance, thanked be our lord God, never the lesse seke [and fearing the] danger of deth, I ordeyne and make my testament and last wyll in manner and forme folowyng.

First I bequeth my soule to God, to our lady seynt Mary and to all the holy seynts in heven, my body to be buryed in the church yard of St Peter's in Monkwearmouth aforesayd.

Also I bequeth for my mortuary [after the custom of the towne.]

I bequeth to my........

The document breaks of here in a substantial area where it has been eaten away leaving the text undecipherable in places. It continued on to a second page:

And also, the residue of all my goods not bequethed, [my detts payd, my body] brought to the grounde, my leagcyes [discharged and] payd, I gyve and bequeth to my sole survivor and daughter, Idysha Sarah Gideon, the which I ordeyne and make my [hole executors, they] to dispose for the helth of my sowll and...

The wording ends there incomplete.

Dyrac's eyes were drawn again to the words *'bequeth to my sole survivor and daughter, Idysha Sarah Gideon'*. Upon reading the words again Dyrac brought a clenched fist down onto the desk with a bang.

'Who does he think he is, or was? Sole survivor?' thought Dyrac.

Dyrac rose to his feet and headed over to the Chippendale cabinet in the corner of the study. He removed a fresh Glencairn crystal whisky glass and picked up the bottle of Johnnie Walker, the Blue Label King George V Edition, pouring an unhealthy measure into the glass. Before the alluring aromas had chance to form, or coat the sides of the glass, he scooped it up and downed the lot wincing as the heat hit the back of his throat. Dyrac immediately poured himself another glass through clenched teeth. The next glass was allowed to breathe before Dyrac took a sip allowing the smokiness to envelop his pallet.

Dyrac walked across the room crunching the remnants of shattered glass, which had been strewn across the enormous red Persian rug which adorned the intricate parquetry flooring, with every step. He walked out of the study leaving the door open and made his way along the hallway towards the cellar. When he reached the cellar door he composed himself, tidied his clothing ensuring his tie was straight, that the plain gold tie pin was placed correctly and horizontally one third of the way down his tie. He adjusted his matching cufflinks and made sure they sat neatly in the cuffs of his shirt. Brushing his hair with the palm of his hand Dyrac reached out for the handle of the cellar door. As it turned he pulled the door towards him revealing a black darkness. Dyrac reached for the pull cord to turn on the light. As the light came on he heard a feint, yet distinct groan from below.

With his left foot first, Dyrac stepped forward.

Chapter 3

Dyrac descended the wooden stairwell leading into the cellar. Turning right at the bottom he walked into a small square room with four doors leading into other chambers. One chamber, to the left, was used to hold a variety of wines. The wine cellar was vast in comparison to the other chambers in the cellar and held over four thousand bottles of wine from Dyrac's favourite vineyards around the world. A particular bottle was over three hundred years old and it had three hundred years worth of dust collating on it. The bottle bore no label and was sealed with a cork and then wax. Dyrac had no intention of ever opening it.

Directly ahead was a chamber that was used to store various antiquities. Dyrac frequented this room often to rifle through curiosities he had collected over the years. Some pieces in there could hold their rightful place in most museums around the world. There was a variety of taxidermy; specimens in jars; a sarcophagus from ancient Egypt; weaponry from the medieval times including maces, axes, swords and daggers; a cacophony of unusual architectural finds and, Dyrac's most revered piece was that of the mummified remains of a middle aged man. The man, still in the foetus position, lay on his side. The position he had remained in since the moment of his death.

The room to the right of this was a long, narrow space. Usually empty but, since Kurt's delivery, it now housed the chest.

Before entering this room Dyrac looked to his

19

right. This room was always locked. Despite Merril having no access to the cellar, which Dyrac also kept locked, the final room required additional measures of security to avoid inquisitive, prying eyes.

Beyond the locked door was a chapel of sorts. There was an altar at one end. A purple velvet altar cloth neatly adorned it. On top of the altar, in the centre, was a twenty four carat gold candelabra which held 7 church style candles. To the right was a vestibule for drinking from with a small gold carafe and goblet set in front. To the far left was a small book stand, also made of gold which held an old leather bound book. The book, like the chapel itself was also kept locked.

Dyrac diverted his attention back to the room containing the chest. He walked inside carefully placing each foot one in front of the other to avoid accidentally treading on any area of the floor that may omit a sound.

He reached the chest and stood momentarily pondering whether he should open it there and then. He reached out, but before he touched the lid he stopped turned sharpish leaving the room. Quickly he ascended the stairwell, pulling the cord at the top of the stairs turning off the light. He locked the cellar door and tucked the key back into the pocket of his waistcoat. Tonight was not the time, but as he tapped a flat palm against his pocket, he knew that time would be soon.

Merril hadn't slept since her encounter with Dyrac and she had been waiting patiently and silently for the ring of the service bell. Each evening Dyrac would activate the bell to confirm he was in his private quarters and that service for the day was officially over.

Suddenly, killing the silence around her, a single chime confirmed Dyrac had retired for the evening. Merril got undressed from her usual working day attire and changed into her night dress. This time, like the only day off once a week, was Merril's own time; until the bell rung again in the morning like clockwork at 6.00am indicating service had resumed.

Merril sat at her dressing table, a plain pine dresser with a freestanding, three part hinged mirror. She released her hair from the intensely tight bun and rubbed her head with her fingers, sighing in relief. Using a paddle brush, Merril counted each brush through of her hair until she had counted to one hundred. This was something her mother, taught her to do from a very young age.

"It will prevent snagging and knots," Merril recalled how her mother would say. Smiling at her own reflection and the memory of her mother.

Set to one side of her dresser, Merril picked up her sketch book and the yellow and black striped HB staedler pencil began to sketch furiously. Merril was no Picasso, but she was absolutely passionate and dedicated to her art and her desire to be an artist one day. She appreciated various greats like Monet, Renoir and Degas amongst her favourites and was more than appreciative that Dyrac has acquired some famous works over time. Her favourite, Monet's Water Lilies hung in the great hall. Merril never really understood why it was called the Great Hall because, there was absolutely nothing great about it other than the art on the walls. The hall was never used, except for Merril's occasional dusting. The room was enormous, dark wooden panelling adorned the walls with various masterpieces hanging from the picture rail on chains to help spread, and hold, the weight of the pieces. As well as Merril's favourite Monet, there were other various impressionism pieces.

Sketching, for Merril, was a cathartic mechanism for her in the evenings. Merril kept her sketches hidden away, never to be shared with anyone other than herself but she found art as a way to escape her mind. Her sketches usually reflected her childhood and she would store them away in an old worn out tin that once graced the well known Victorian scene. The Quality Street brand emblazoned these images on their enormous tins of chocolates. Sometimes, when Merril opened the tin she could remember the scent of the delicious treats it once contained. She would salivate as the chocolate aromas tormented her and she would immediately be transported back to Christmas time with her mother. They would unwrap the sweets slowly, each picking out their favourites first. Removing the coloured cellophane wrapper followed by the next layer of foil before exposing the deliciousness within. Placing each chocolate on their tongue the two of them would savour the velvety texture until it melted in their mouths. Merril recalled that memory so vividly.

Merril stored away her latest sketch carefully. The sketch was of no extraordinary quality and the shading was poor but, her subject, on this occasion, was dark and Merril suspected others would form a completely view of her. Merril had worked too hard to become the person she was now and she did not want to risk becoming exposed. Not yet.

Snapping the tin lid closed Merril returned her pencil to the dresser, straightening it once it was laid down so it was perpendicular to the edge. Merril was precise in everything she did and her obsessive tendencies sometimes led to her undoing.

Merril pulled back at the old patchwork eiderdown and snuggled into her welcoming bed. As she lay her head upon her crisp white cotton pillow case and closed her eyes she saw an image in her mind of Dyrac looming over her, as though leaning in to kiss her on her cheek. In fact as he lent in, he moved towards her neck piercing the flesh drawing blood. Merril groaned in sexual arousal. Moaning and smiling, Merril drifted to sleep.

Dyrac paced his quarters. He wanted to apologise to Merril for his outburst but, as he had already rung the service bell, he knew Merril was no longer at work. By now she would be settling, if not already dreaming. He made a conscious note to address her first thing in the morning and apologise for his behaviour albeit, he would still have Merril clear the shattered glass in the study and clean the Persian rug.

Dyrac lay on his four poster bed instantly falling asleep fully clothed. He slept right through until morning. He woke with a start and an uncomfortable chilling pain pierced through his back from sleeping in an awkward position, having not moved all night.

It was 6:00am and Dyrac promptly rang the bell.

He made his way to his private bathroom where he got undressed and showered. Standing in front of the vanity mirror he loosely pulled a towel around his waistline. He doused himself in Tom Ford Tobaco Oud Eau de Parfum, a woody spicy fragrance with a whisky top note. The masculinity of the cologne would always encapsulate Merril's senses when he walked by. He knew she loved it and he loved the hypnotic affect it had on her. He cleansed, toned and moisturised his face. Combed his hair with a sandalwood comb and applied a small amount of beard oil to his moustache and van dyke beard. He stood back narcissistically admiring his own reflection.

He made his way to his dressing room just off to the left outside of the bathroom. It was pristine and organised. There was an aisle running down the centre and directly in front was a fitted floor to ceiling mirror. Dyrac stood there naked glancing himself up and down noting each scar and remembering how each had been acquired and, how before the age of 16 he had none. The scars were not caused by abuse, nor from fighting. Each scar had been carefully and precisely inflicted by himself. The scars were a myriad of runes, Norse mythological symbols, ancient Egyptian hieroglyphs and tribal markings. Some provided him with protection or guidance, some were a penance of actions once taken, others a source of self flagellation.

To the right of his torso was a Mannaz rune standing approximately 6 inches high and 3 inches wide, it looked like the capital letter M with the arches more of a squared infinity symbol. 'Be in the world, but not from the world' was the basic definition. He recalled that this was the first scar he bore into himself. He closed his eyes and remembered. At the coming of age, Abimilech presented Dyrac with a Karamabit, a small curved blade, once known as a peasantry dagger. Abimilech gifted the Karamabit to Dyrac to make him feel like a man. The Karamabit was known for looking like a tiger's claw and would have predominantly been used for close combat. This was not a gift for battle however, more a derogatory reminder from Ambilech of what he felt Dyrac was worth and Abimilech knew that one day his gift would prove significant.

The ornate ivory handle had a smooth finish and the dagger sat neatly when it was housed in its plain brown leather sheath. The blade glistened, albeit it was slightly tarnished in parts. That same evening Dyrac took the blade to his torso for the first time. He understood the condescension Ambilechs gift represented and it echoed around his mind that he did not belong of this world, nor did he ever feel he came from this world. As such he gouged the Mannaz rune as a reminder to himself that he would forever be alone.

The Karamabit remained in Dyrac's possession and the blade, never washed, lay silent now in a small glass cabinet in a chamber in the cellar.

On occasion Dyrac would cut too deep and he would bleed out for hours. Still, this never prevented him from inscribing his next marking. Each held a meaning and had reason to be there. These were not a result of a haphazard addiction of self harm but poignant to the time. They were protective and prophetic. Over twenty years Dyrac had added more and more brands until no space remained on his torso. His legs were covered front to back, upwards from just above his ankle. He was careful to avoid his arms and neck as these markings were never meant to be seen by anyone other than Dyrac.

Dyrac turned his attention to a few of his other scars, tracing over them as he remembered and analysed them:

> *URUZ – The rune of termination and new beginning – It means that the life you used to live has grown out of its frame and needs to be left behind now, so that life energy can liberate itself like a rebirth, into a new one. In order to rule, you must first, serve.*
>
> *HAGALAZ – The rune of destructive forces of nature, elemental, hail – Indicates the existence of an urgent needing your psyche to free itself from the confines of identification with material reality, and to experience the world of archetypal thinking. The rune of elementary destruction and of things that are completely out of your control.*
>
> *YGGDRASIL – Norse Tree of Life – At the top of Yggdrasil, an eagle, lived. At the bottom, a dragon named Nidhug. Both hated each other and were bitter enemies. Depicting the events of Ragnarok, the doom of the Gods and the apocalyptic record of the coming comet.*
>
> *WEB OF WYRD – A matrix of fate that represents past, present and future events in a*

person's life. Norse people believed that everything we do in life affects future events and thus, all timelines, the past, the present and the future are connected with each other.

ANKH – Representing life and immortality – a symbol of union between men and women, particularly Osiris and Isis which was believed to have flooded the river Nile thus bringing fertility to Egypt, also known as the key of the Nile.

THE EYE OF HORUS – Representing protection, healing, good health and royal power – Also known as the symbol of the moon.

AVANYU – Symbolizes a benevolent but fearful creature – A changer of seasons and the bringer of sudden and violent change.

Removing a freshly pressed grey three piece suit, Dyrac lay the days outfit onto his dresser. He collected a crisp white cotton shirt and chose the tigers eye and silver surround cufflinks. He attached his pocket watch chain to his waist coast making sure the key sat neatly in the right pocket. He tied a Windsor knot in his royal blue silk tie and affixed the silver tie pin neatly two thirds up. Once dressed he again took a glance towards the mirror and left his quarters.

Dyrac sat nervously at the breakfast table in the breakfast room shifting constantly to try to find a position in which he would appear composed and confident.

"You're breakfast Dyrac," said Merril entering the room.

"Thank you Merril, do I smell Eggs Benedict this morning?" asked Dyrac.

"You're favourite breakfast. I took the liberty of crisping some bacon under the grill too," she replied.

"That's very kind Merril," added Dyrac.

Merril placed Dyrac's breakfast on the setting in front of him. As she leant over she inhaled him and tingled as she noticed that today he was wearing the Tom Ford cologne. She poured him an Earl Grey tea into the bone china tea cup to his right and next to it put a small silver milk jug and tiny silver plate with two pieces of lemon, small silver tongs rested on top. Dyrac was never sure whether he preferred it with milk or lemon so he took both each morning and always made the decision right before the moment he took his first sip.

"Before you go Merril," Dyrac cleared his throat nervously.

"Yes sir, sorry Dyrac?"

"About last evening..."

"No need to explain," replied Merril.

"Merril, please allow me to speak," Dyrac was making direct eye contact now, "about last evening. It was extremely unbecoming of me to address you in that manner and for that I apologise. I will not explain what caused my reaction but I will apologise for the inappropriateness of my retort. I expect that you will accept my apologies without further question and that this be the end of the matter."

"Of course," replied Merril softly, curtseying as she left to return to the kitchen leaving Dyrac to finish his breakfast in solitude as per his usual request.

Dyrac knew that he sounded a little insincere in his apology but he convinced himself to leave the matter there. He devoured his breakfast, melting away in the comfort of Merril's cooking. No matter what, she never failed to deliver mouth watering meals.

Merril paused outside the Great Hall. Carefully she turned the handle and stepped inside without making a sound. She walked over to the Monet and stood there admiring the piece. Merril knew this piece off by heart easily able to visualise it with her eyes closed but, she still felt excitement upon looking at the piece. She concentrated on each stroke of paint, the way the water lilies sat idly in the water. She transposed herself to the side of the water's edge in her mind. She imagined the day was warm, she could feel the sun warming her cheeks, a slight breeze occasionally brushing her skin and causing a slight ripple in the surface of the lake. She could hear animals in the background going about their day to day business as she felt a soft trickle. It wasn't the water in the painting; a single tear rolled down her cheek. She caught it and brought herself back to the room and promptly back reality. She left the Great Hall and scurried into the kitchen.

Merril wanted to believe that Dyrac's apology was sincere but she desperately wanted to know what had caused him so much pain. She knew that there was something in the study that had been hidden away and with apparent good reason. *How could she console him? How could help if she couldn't question or mention it again?* She thought.

An overwhelming need to find out what Dyrac was keeping secret consumed her. Merril needed a plan. She wasn't sure how, but she knew she would find a way.

Something inside Wode House was changing. But what?

Chapter 4

It was 7:00am on Saturday, Kurt had just finished loading this week's delivery. This Saturday would be no usual drop off. Scheduled to arrive within the hour, Kurt would have enough time to have the full English breakfast prepared by Merril, before making his way to the study for his meeting with Dyrac.

Over the last seven days Kurt often found himself pontificating Dyrac's cryptic offer. He'd played out a number of roles including heists, forgery (for this was a little known field of expertise of Kurt's), money laundering to name a few but did not rule out the possibility of "a hit," an actual murder! He recoiled as he tried to envisage himself taking another person's life. *It's not worth thinking about something that may not be*, he thought.

"Don't forget the Stinky Bishop," shouted Byron Bryson.

"Already got it and the pickup bloody stinks of it," replied Kurt as the tinkling of the shop bell announced his departure from Bryson & Sons.

Bryson & Sons was a local grocers whom Kurt was in employment with. He was not the most reliable employee and less so since he started the rounds at Wode House.

Byron Bryson was the fourth generation of owners of Bryson & Sons. Before Byron there was Brahms Bryson, Bradwell Bryson, Braxton Bryson and the Byron himself. Now, following in his father's footsteps was Byron's son and heir Bradley Bryson. Bryson & Sons was established in 1899 and had not grown much since the first tinkling of the shop bell with its very first customer. That same bell still tinkled the same now as it did on that first day. A small brass bell affixed to the frame of the door with a coiled metal ribbon spring.

Kurt had just shut the door to the pickup when Byron Bryson ran out from the shop holding something wrapped in brown paper tied with string. *Jesus, it's like something out of a book* thought Kurt.

Winding down the window he shouted "What did I forget?"

"Not you Kurt, I forgot, I forgot to ask if you could take this to Merril. It's not on the order so you wouldn't have known about it. It's just a few things she asked me to pick up for her personally when she rang through this week's order," replied Byron.

"Giz it here then," said Kurt holding out his hand. He took the package from Byron and place it on the centre seat next to him. "What is it?" he asked.

"Never you mind Kurt, just do your job, if you can manage that," replied Byron curtly.

Kurt drove away from the shop anxiously anticipating his meeting with Dyrac.

Merril paced up and down in the kitchen excited to be seeing Kurt again but more so for the package she had been waiting for. Rubbing her hands together, Merril patted herself down and composed herself. She waited until she heard familiar sound of the pickup pulling up in the gravel drive way outside and for the clunk of the driver's door closing, before making her way to the side entrance.

"Good morning Kurt?"

"Merry, looking beautiful as ever I see," replied Kurt.

Merril giggled and shyed herself away from Kurt leaving the door open for him to bring in the delivery.

"Got this for you Merry," he said holding aloft a package, "Bryson asked me to give it to you personally. What is it?" asked Kurt.

"Never you mind Kurt, it's personal," said Merril. She had nothing to hide from Kurt but wanted to retain a certain level of privacy and intrigue.

"That's what he said," huffed Kurt. "Usual place for this lot?" he added, nodding towards the week's groceries.

"Please Kurt. Breakfast will be ready in five, I know you're scheduled to meet with Dyrac in the study at eight o'clock. Please don't be late."

"How do you..."

"It's my business to know Kurt," interrupted Merril, "I take care of all of Dyrac's needs, his diary commitments and schedule are ingrained in my mind."

"Oh yeah, of course, how stupid of me."

"Quite," replied Merril.

Kurt noticed that Merril wasn't her usual flirty self today. *Was it the package that he brought, his meeting with Dyrac or something else that had Merril so off piste* he thought. It annoyed Kurt just how much it bothered him that Merril was not paying him the attention she usually showered him with. The thought quickly left Kurt's mind as more important matters were at hand and the pending meeting with Dyrac was looming.

Kurt snaffled down his breakfast like a fat kid had

just been given a free cake. He barely stopped for breath as food spilled from his mouth. He shovelled the next forkful in before completely finishing the morsels of his last mouthful. Merril looked repulsed as she watched him. There was absolutely nothing attractive about Kurt today and she let out an audible gag.

"Huh?" said Kurt.

"Nothing!" came the reply. "Carry on, please excuse me," said Merril.

Merril turned hastily and walked into the larder and let out a sigh. She thought how rude her reaction to Kurt's eating was and that it was rather unbecoming of a mere housekeeper. She hadn't worked this hard to be where she was now to have it all slip away.

Returning to the kitchen table Merril reached out and touched Kurt's shoulder, squeezing it delicately thinking to herself, *be careful in there today Kurt.*

"Get off Merry," Kurt shrugged away Merril's hand.

"Best be heading to the study Kurt. It's down the hallway, go past the cellar and take the third door on the left," Merril told Kurt using her arms the way an air steward would to indicate the location and direction of the emergency exits in a pre-flight passenger safety briefing.

"Thanks Merry, any sauce?" Kurt asked Merril pointing to his face.

Merril's eyes rolled "No sauce Kurt, you're all clear."

"Thanks doll," replied Kurt.

Merril watched Kurt move swiftly down the

hallway whilst visibly counting the doors beyond the cellar. Kurt was just about to turn right when Merril shouted "Left Kurt, left!"

Kurt didn't reply just raised one hand in a thankful gesture. He paused momentarily and knocked on the study door.

"Please come in Kurt," came Dyrac's voice.

Merril had been ordered not to interrupt the meeting but two hours had passed with Kurt's pick still parked next to the side entrance. Despite the instructions, Merril hadn't even been called upon to bring refreshments, not once. *What could they possibly be discussing for so long and, why was she not needed?* She thought.

"Thank you Kurt. You'll be reaping the handsome benefits of your loyalty before you know it," said Dyrac, "you'll find a little extra in here as compensation for your time today," he added pushing an envelope into Kurt's hand. "I trust that our agreement will remain strictly confidential? Whilst no written contract has been signed I can assure you that the consequences, should the detail of our agreement be revealed to another soul will be severe. And you will learn the true meaning of my indignation."

Kurt nodded in Dyrac's direction and gulped audibly, simultaneously understanding as clear as the Glencairn Crystal whisky glass in Dyrac's hand. Kurt left without further comment and hurriedly made his way back towards the kitchen. He caught a fleeting glimpse of Merril standing in the larder but chose not to say goodbye.

Merril heard the pickup start and the wheels spin in the gravel. By the time she reached the door to say goodbye, and hopefully catch a quick word in an effort to extract information about the meeting, Kurt was already leaving the gates.

Looking in his rear view mirror Kurt watched as the stone plaque engraved with Wode House distanced itself from view.

Dyrac stood staring at the closed study door. "And so be it," he whispered out loud. Turning on his heels he smiled a devilish grin, headed towards the Chippendale cabinet and poured himself another tot of whisky. This would be his third today and it was only 10:15am. He took a sip and put the glass down onto a silver tray housing a decanter and rubbed his hands together.

Kurt flung the door of Bryson & Sons open with the kind of power of someone who didn't know their own strength. The bell barely given the chance to tinkle.

"Sup?" said Bradley, Byron's son was leaning idly against the counter reading a comic.

"Nothing Bradders. Nowt," replied Kurt.

"Summat is wrecking ya," he replied.

Kurt waved him off and made his way to the stock room out back. "Bryson? You in here?"

"Aye, Kurt just round in the dry store," replied Bryson

"I need to get off, I'll make the hours up to you during the week but I've got an emergency."

"No worries Kurt, I'm guessing this is a no questions asked kind of emergency what with the tone of voice and urgency in your finding me."

"Yeah Bryson, thanks. I'll catch up with you tomorrow."

Kurt turned fast on his heels. Gently he gave Bradley a friendly shove on the shoulder as he walked back through the shop.

"Hey!" Bradley exclaimed rubbing his shoulder in an exaggerated response.

"Laters Bradders," said Kurt.

Kurt returned to the pickup and sat momentarily before starting the engine. He drove along the high street and turned right down Greenfield. He pulled up outside 232, he was home. He left the engine running and the door of the cab open whilst he ran in grabbed a pre-packed holdall having left it next to the front door that very morning, and got back into the pickup. He continued down Greenfield and turned left onto Ally View Road. At the end of Ally View Road was a T-junction. To turn left would take him towards Wode House and to turn right would take him towards Clifton, the neighbouring town.

Sitting at the end of the Ally View Road, Kurt stopped at the give way sign and waited longer than usual at a clear road with no oncoming traffic. Two options were in front of him. Right now, he seriously contemplated turning right towards Clifton. He could dump the pick up and get a one way train ticket to anywherebuthereville.

Kurt indicated left.

Chapter 5

The evening drew in. A thick fog billowed from the ground eerily surrounding Wode House on a black and cloudless night. The air was still and the fog sat stagnant, highlighted only by the glint from the new moon.

Merril set about her end of day duties. New moon end of day duties took longer than the usual end of day duties. Merril collected the new moon set of keys from the cabinet next to the larder. A bundle of keys held together with a heavy set iron ring. Each ground floor window, as well as being bolted as normal had a black out shutter. A thick, flat iron bar with an elaborate medieval lock sealed them when closed and could only be secured from the outside. The other floors had internal shutters and a more modest lock. Doors would be locked and bolted with the addition of a thick piece of timber that would sit horizontally across the door; and were held into place nestled in thick iron L shaped brackets. 218 windows and 6 doors later and the clunk of the final lock echoed through the entrance hall.

If there is one part of all this I hate, it's the banality of New Moon lockdown. Keeping people out should never be this exhausting thought Merril.

It was now was 8:50pm. Merril had one hour and 10 minutes to finish her duties, get back to her room and freshen up and change before meeting Dyrac in Chamber four. Chamber four was a guest room but every new moon it was used for the same purpose.

During Merril's service, Chamber four, nor any of

the other guest rooms, had ever been used for guests. There were never guests at Wode House. But, nonetheless this is how they were referred to.

Merril bathed and before towelling herself down smoothed lavender oil into her skin. The oil would leave her with a hypnotic scent but it also provided a beautiful sheen to her olive skin. She brushed her hair and rather than tie this back into its usual bun she plaited it neatly across one shoulder showing off its length but keeping it back, and away from her neck.

Her wardrobe was a majestic art nouveau piece carved with Charles Rennie Mackintosh's famous floral design. She reached inside for a sleek, silver grey satin sleeveless dress. The dress had a deep v front which enhanced her voluptuous bosom. She needed no bra as her pert breasts sat neatly and perfectly in the dress. The back of the dress plunged and ruffled down to the base of her spine. The dress appeared seamless as though it had been tailor made just for her. She looked sensational.

She sat at her dresser expertly applying her make up to accentuate her flawless complexion. She applied a small amount of gloss and pouted before blowing a kiss to her own reflection. Her lips were plump and inviting and her evenings look was complete. Before rising from her seated position she gave herself a second glance over and slipped on the silver bangle that sat neatly to one side.

As was usual on new moon nights Merril was barefoot. She left her room and made her way to Chamber four.

Dyrac sat patiently on the chaise longue nestled

neatly in the bay window of Chamber four. He hadn't changed, nor had he washed since this morning, but he was ready. He could feel adrenaline build inside him with an almost sexual intensity. He knew what was coming and he relished in the moment.

Situated on a small side table next to him Dyrac reached for a silver goblet of Chilean Malbec. He glanced into the goblet at the deep inky red hue of the wine inhaling the aromas of violets and plums, leather and tobacco and, the subtlety of vanilla. He took a sip and breathed it in allowing his palate to fill with its splendour.

He placed the goblet back on the table and closed his eyes.

The hustle and bustle of the market filled with traders and buyers, vagrants and misfits, the noble, the weak and weary enveloped Dyrac's mind. He could smell the putrid sewerage from the gutters. An unfortunate soul unable to afford such luxuries as a small hand held silver vinaigrette filled with perfumes and pleasurable scents often only afforded to those of some wealth, to rid offensive smells from the nasal passages. He hated them, all of them, as they passed him with blind ignorance, not even acknowledging his existence.

He watched as a gypsy lady selling jasmine and heather sprigs bound in a bow of purple and white ribbon approached a gentleman dressed the finest of attire. The man was rotund around the midriff but tall and donned a glorious white beard. He wore a pin stripped tailored three piece suit. You could see a glimpse of his pocket watch and chain neatly placed across his waist coat. A top hat sat perfectly on his head and his outfit was completed with polished boots that fastened with buttons. He had a pair of gloves which he held in his hand and a bright blue silk cravat poked through the top of his overcoat. The man tried to ignore the gypsy, to evade her with all his will, but the will of the gypsy will was greater. She had a tenacious persistence and she was either making a sale or, this poor gent, was going to be cursed.

No longer could he fight her off. Dyrac watched from a distance as the ma uttered something to her. She leant towards him and whispered in his ear. The shock on his face caused him to swiftly retrieve his wallet and pass the gypsy a silver coin. From where he sat Dyrac knew not of the value of the coin but it was sufficient enough to make the gypsy grin. She curtseyed and handed the gentleman a small sprig. Shoving the sprig in his pocket the man moved off in a hurry.

Dyrac's intrigue got the better of him and he followed the gypsy for the rest of the day. She made twenty sales that day, issued two curses and accepted a sexual favour as payment for one sprig.

"Dyrac!" bellowed Abimilech "You're needed boy."

Dyrac almost shat himself as Abimilech's voice reverberated around him. Dyrac quickly followed Abimilech down a back lane.

"Tonight boy you feast. All that I have taught you will be needed for this night. This will be your first taste and from herein you will be a man!"

Dyrac delighted at the thought of no longer being referred to as a boy. He longed for manhood and the life Abimilech had promised him. He wanted more than ever to be as strong, as powerful and mightiful as Abimilech.

Abimilech handed Dyrac a small piece of parchment. Dyrac, who six months previously had not been able to write or read his own name, took the parchment from Abimilech and read the words to himself:

> *You must find your donor and feast by midnight of the New Moon to transform into the man you need to become.*

"There's an address?" questioned Dyrac.

"Indeed boy, you will need to be there by 10:00pm. Idysha will be waiting for you," said Abimilech.

"Idysha?" asked Dyrac.

"Idysha. She is my daughter, and has volunteered to be your first donor."

The door of Chamber four opened startling Dyrac.

"Merril!"

"Dyrac," Merril nodded and curtseyed slightly, in almost the same fashion the gypsy did at the gentleman buying her wares.

"Please, take a seat," Dyrac directed said directing Merril to the chaise longue in the room.

Merril appeared to levitate as she glided across the room. She was mesmeric and Dyrac could not take his eyes off her. As she sat she breathed in deeply, knowing that soon she would be under Dyrac's full control. Holding his eyes for as long as she could

Dyrac walked around the back of the chaise longue taking her in.

As he walked behind her he stopped and held her shoulders with both of his hands. He drew his index finger down her spine making her tremble and shiver. Dyrac was intoxicated by her.

Dyrac placed his hand against Merril's face pushing her head to the side exposing her neck. He leant forward and, with the same motion of kissing her he placed his lips against her skin. It felt soft and fragile like a rose petal. He clamped his canines into her neck, across her jugular vein. As his teeth ore into her sweetness, piercing the flesh Merril felt the warmth of scarlet trickle down her neck. Dyrac drank, sucking the life elixir he had been longing for. It tasted sweet yet metallic and, as he drew away a crimson stain whet his lips. Merril sighed and squirmed in delight. As troubling as this may be to some Merril had been a donor for many years and had succumbed to the pleasure which it now invoked in her.

Dyrac never spoke as he made his way to the four poster bed falling into it exhausted but exhilarated. As he fell backwards he began to drift. It felt like he had been falling through a rabbit hole of never ending luxurious fabrics. Silks, cashmere, furs, velvets rich in colours of golds and reds until his body finally rested on the bed. He knew it wouldn't be long before he slept contently.

As he drifted he muttered in a hushed voice "Abimilech, show me."

Merril glared at Dyrac, got up from the chaise longue and moved quickly towards the door of

Chamber four. She thought about bidding Dyrac goodnight but chose against interrupting him and left holding onto the words Dyrac just uttered.

Arriving at the address on the parchment that Abimilech gave him Dyrac stood nervously in front of the vast oak door. There was an enormous lion head brass knocker on the door, but to the right was a long chain which Dyrac chose to pull instantly activating a door chime.

The door was opened by a butler wearing white gloves who, without speaking beckoned to Dyrac to enter and wait.

The butler walked down the hallway and entered a room to the right. Dyrac heard muffled voices but was unable to comprehend the subject of conversation.

The butler returned and announced "Lady Gideon will be with you momentarily. If you would kindly wait in the parlour, this way."

Dyrac followed the butler and, as directed he sat down and waited.

"Lady Idysha Gideon," the butler announced moments later.

In walked a beautiful young girl, no older than 16 years of age.

"That'll be all Gibson," she said.

"Ma'am," replied Gibson, nodding and closing the parlour door as he left.

"Dyrac? My father has told me all about you. You're new," said Lady Gideon.

"It is correct that I am new but I fear you're mistaken. Your father couldn't have told you all about me for he doesn't know all about me himself," replied Dyrac.

"Quite. But don't be so prudent," she replied.

"My apologies," said Dyrac.

"Please, come sit next to me, we have much to discuss before we get on to the feast and indeed the purpose of your being here," she said, "your beginning."

"My beginning?" questioned Dyrac.

"Yes, you're beginning. It will all become clear but know this, before you do go ahead with this life be sure. Once you have begun this life there is only one way back," she said.

Dyrac was dreaming and remembering. He remembered Idysha's scent and how familiar and present it was. He didn't recall how she tasted but he remembered the rush he got that first time. It was as though someone had attached a tesla machine to every nerve ending and switched them all on at the same time. He thought he was going to explode. He remembers how his heart raced and how he could barely catch a breath. He never wanted to stop. He was latched on and Idysha had to fight in the end just to stop him.

"STOP DYRAC!" she screeched as the colour drained from her skin. Her pallor was bordering on corpse like, lips blue from lack of circulation and she was beginning to feel faint.

Dyrac heard three knocks.

"Idysha? Are you ok?" asked Dyrac.

"I'll be fine Dyrac, now its..."

Dyrac heard three knocks again. He opened his eyes and realised he was lay on the bed in Chamber four.

He got up and opened the door.

Stood in the doorway was Kurt.

"Did you find it?" asked Dyrac.

"Nothing. It's not there. Not that I know what I'm looking for but it's definitely not there. Just her wardrobe with clothing; dresser with vanity set and usual women's make up and perfume; an old sweet tin with some rough, but brilliant, drawings in it; a bedside unit which had only one drawer containing a bible with post it note tabs highlighting certain passages and her bed. And before you ask no, there was nothing under the mattress, in the mattress, in the bed or anything."

"Hmmm," Dyrac was rubbing his beard, "It's got to be there somewhere. I'm going to need you to go back. I'll get you more time," said Dyrac.

"Jesus, really. I mean Merry is so private. What am I even looking for? If you can give me an idea that would bloody help," asked Kurt.

"I don't know myself Kurt but, I know she has it," came the reply.

Merril opened the door to her room and noticed that her hair brush next to the tin on the dresser was horizontal and she knew perfectly well that she left it vertically every single time she placed it back.

Merril ran over to the dresser, picked up the tin and ripped off the lid. The drawings were still in there and hadn't changed order. Carefully she removed the pile of drawings and traced her finger over the bottom of the tin. There was a slight dent in the base. She pressed the dent and it popped up. She pushed her fingernail down the side in the gap that had appeared and pulled it up lifting the base of the tin. It didn't reveal a hole which is what you would expect to find when lifting up the bottom of a tin but in fact a hidden section. Inside was a small velvet bag. She removed the bag. The top was closed with two cords which she carefully pulled in opposite direction to loosen. She put in her hand and pulled out a small curved blade, a Karamabit.

Placing the Karamabit next to the components of the tin on the dresser Merril slipped the straps of her dress from her shoulders and it fell to the floor. On the top of Merril's right thigh was a scar. The scar was the symbol of Valknut, the heart of the slain often associated with a warrior's death in battle.

Chapter 6

The ensuing days saw no unusual activity at Wode House. Merril continued going about her duties as normal, serving Dyrac and his needs. Dyrac went about his daily business spending most of his time between the study, library and cellar.

Dyrac had endured a lot over the years and he often drifted into memories from 'that' time when Abimilech was his mentor, a force that controlled him and directed him. Dyrac's insubordination would not be tolerated and as such Dyrac found himself a slave to Abimilech's service.

The Abimilech Dyrac first encountered was a formidable character. He was impressively large and intimidating, Hades like and oppressively stifling. In time Dyrac would also learn he was foreboding and malevolent. He stood 6 foot 6 inches tall with broad shoulders that had carried many burdens. His face was pock marked and scarred. He had a bulbous nose with a long bridge and strewn across it was a deep and penetrating groove, the remnants of an old wound inflicted by a war hammer during one of Abimilechs many conquests.

He thought of himself as an unprincipled, ambitious ruler often engaging in wars with his own subjects over the years and, like his biblical namesake he had slaughtered his own siblings in an effort to become the sole heir to the Gideon family's estate which he believed was his birth right. In doing so he fulfilled his inner desire to become an untouchable and powerful force.

When Abimilech spoke his tone would drill fear and dread into you. Boring through you as you felt the vibrations from his voice reverberate throughout your bones. Hairs would stand on end and you could well imagine the power of his voice alone instigating the butterfly effect and somewhere in the world, at that precise moment and as a result of his retort, would cause a cataclysmic natural event to unfold. A storm, earthquake, volcano, tsunami even, killing masses and devastating whole populations.

The true age of Abimilech is not known exactly however, when Dyrac met him he guessed he would be in his fifties. Unbeknownst to Dyrac, Abimilech was in fact over 900 years old. It would be years before the realisation of Abimilechs so called mortality would be revealed, comprehended and understood.

Dyrac repositioned himself in his chair as he sat in front of the open fire in the study. The fireplace was something to behold. It was an impressive stone structure, a masterpiece and carved by master stonemasons when the house was built in the early 1500s. The fire roared furiously as Dyrac reached towards a lever situated near the base of the leg on the left side of the hearth. This activated a set of hidden bellows increasing the oxygen that fed the flames and also opened the flue allowing smoke to escape through the chimney. Dyrac felt the heat warm and comfort him. He raised his feet and rested them on an antique oak and leather rocking footstool.

Dyrac stared into the fire thinking back to the meeting he had with Abimilech after his first encounter with Idysha. As he watched the hypnotic flames dance across the grate he entered into a trance like state.

"My boy, I hear you fed well last evening?" Abimilech asked Dyrac in his guttural tone.

I wish he wouldn't call me his boy thought Dyrac as he replied, "It was exhilarating."

"Be careful not to over indulge too soon for there is much to learn and much to understand. But, all in good time for we have many obstacles that trouble our path and forces beyond your imagination right now that will try to stop us from succeeding."

"I'm not sure I..."

Abimilech interrupted, "In time Dyrac you will see and you will foresee."

"Foresee?"

"Envisage, expect, forecast, predict. Be patient but be ready."

A loud snap, crackle and pop spat out from the fire as the steam and vapour building inside the logs, where water and sap had surpassed boiling point, suddenly gave way splitting the wood and releasing the pressure. Dyrac jumped from his chair startled and poised ready to defend himself instantly realising he was alone in his study.

Dyrac made a decision in that moment to move Abimilech's will. He released the flap in the desk as he had done previously on many occasions. Removed the envelope with the broken wax seal and checked the contents were still insitu. He placed the envelope under his waist coat into the back of his trousers. Carefully he locked the flap back in place and neatly tucked the key back into his small pocket tapping it as he did so.

Leaving the study Dyrac had a quick look up and down the hallway for signs of Merril, she was nowhere to be seen. He walked down the hallway towards the kitchen and stopped outside the cellar door. A second glance around gave him the all clear and he entered locking the cellar door behind him. Consciously he left the light off, so as not to draw attention to himself as he knew once he got to the bottom of the stairs he could put on the respective wall lights isolated to the rooms he needed to use. On this occasion his aim was to make a quick drop off in the chapel and then head back to the study before tea at 8:00pm.

Dyrac entered the chapel and headed to the altar. He lifted the altar cloth to reveal a small casket. Taking the same key from his waistcoat that opened the flap in his desk he unlocked the casket and removed a large iron key. This key unlocked the leather bound book that sat on top of the altar. He opened the book and flicked through the pages stopping and back tracking two pages until he found what he was looking for. The page contained Latin text:

Ego, consecro
Et benedico istum circulum
Per nomine Dei Altissimi
In hec scripta
Ut sit mihi et omnibus
Scutum et praesidium Dei Fortissimi
Elohim, Invictus, potestatis
Gerum contra malignos spiritus.

In Nomine Dei Patris,
Dei Filii, et
Dei Spiritus Sancti,
Amen.

The text translated into English as:

I consecrate
And bless this circle
In the Name of the Most High
In these writings
In order to have everything
Shield and protection of the Most Powerful
Elohim Invictus, power
Bump against evil.
In the Name of the Father;
God the Son, and
God's Holy Spirit;
Amen.

Dyrac inserted the envelope into the pages he opened of the book then closed and locked the binding. He locked away the key in the casket and neatly placed the altar cloth back into place.

He left the cellar and turned off the wall light. As he headed to the stairwell he stopped and turned to look into the long narrow chamber. He walked into the chamber and up to the chest.

He whispered into the chest "The time of the Gideon's is coming to an end." The chest rattled in response and a hushed painful scream echoed as though it was coming from a deep and isolated well. The scream was barely audible to Dyrac but he smiled pleasurably and walked away.

Chapter 7

Merril woke on her day off early and didn't bother tying the laces on her docs before she left her room. It was a fresh autumn morning and the weather forecasted a clear day. Merril had asked for Dyrac's permission to leave Wode House for the first time in her fifteen years of service. Dyrac's refusal didn't faze her and came as no surprise so she decided that she would venture into the grounds.

Wode House was built in the English Renaissance style with the principal facade distinguished by its gables, pediments and classical statuary. The large, mullioned windows gave the appearance that the facade was built entirely of glass. Niches on the second storey were complete with statues which had become disfigured with time. The frontage was perfectly symmetrical.

The house stood in 104 hectares of lavish grounds having had a number of famous landscape gardeners and architects influence befall upon them over time. The most recent of which was that of Capability Brown, a famous landscape architect who was rightfully accorded England's greatest gardener of his time. His style still revered and endured. Many of the decorative outbuildings were designed by him, the gothic stable block, arches in the courtyard, two follies and many of the garden statues. His conviction led to changing many years of formality in the gardens of Wode House.

Cedars of Lebanon sat on an island in a small man-made lake which you could reach via a classical stone bridge and was to be the place Merril would spend most of her morning.

Before leaving her room Merril packed a brown leather satchel with her sketch pad, and drawing materials, and removed a small tobacco tin from the draw in her bedside table. On her way out she would stop at the kitchen to make a small lunch, retrieving a braeburn apple (grown on the grounds) from the larder; she cut off a wedge of red Leicester cheese from the enormous block in the cold store; grabbed a small kilner jar from the kitchen cabinet by the Bristol sink filling it with homemade pickle, a lump of fresh bread from the cob made yesterday, a cheese knife and teaspoon. She wrapped her lunch in a piece of red and white checked gingham, very quintessentially English of her. She stowed it away in the satchel and retrieved a small thermos flask and filled it with tea, not too milky and with two sugars. She was ready.

Merril breathed in the warm autumnal air as she left the side entrance of Wode House. She headed left away from the driveway and walked along the gravel path that ran around the whole outside of the house. At the end of the building she veered right, past the sundial and down a small slope in the grass toward the lake. As she reached the stone bridge she paused momentarily looking back at Wode House. She recalled a time when she was much younger and would look back at the house from this very same spot.

Merril crossed the familiar bridge and onto the small island. Standing, just off centre and shrouded by the cedars of Lebanon was a small, stone, turret styled folly. From the house you would never know it was there and in all the years Merril had been in service at Wode House she doesn't recall Dyrac having ever had crossed the bridge so doubted he even knew of its existence and as such, the secret it held within.

You could enter the folly through a small archway and it looked like a pointless stone tower. There were no rooms leading off and if you looked straight up you could see the sky. To any layman it looked like a large sculpture set in place for aesthetics only. However, Merril knew otherwise and traced her hand around the wall inside until she reached a stone plaque.

The plaque had the signature of the architect Capability Brown carved into it across the bottom. Sitting neatly atop was an engraving of tree. To the unseeing eye it looked like the architect had just signed his work of art like any artist would. Merril traced the roots of the tree and with a slight push moved the trunk off centre. Behind the trunk was a keyhole. Merril took the tobacco tin from her satchel and opened it. Sat in the lid, held in place with a small metal clasp was a key. She removed the key and put it inside turning the key left, as opposed to the normal right turning of a key to unlock something. There was an audible click and a small puff of escaping air blew away some of the dust around the plaque. Carefully Merril pushed the plaque to the left revealing an opening. It was dark and musty. Merril reached inside and picked up a small torch and illuminated the opening. It went back only a few feet but when Merril shone the torch downwards the opening dropped and an iron ladder could be seen descending into the abyss below.

Merril stopped and smiled.

Meanwhile back in his study Dyrac preceded about his business as usual. He just finished writing a letter addressed to a Cornelius Blackshot Esquire. Placing it into a brown envelope he laid it face down on his desk. He opened the top drawer to his right and removed a small red wax stick. On his desk was a small iron figure of a raven perched on the side of a box with a pin in its beak. Dyrac pushed the birds head down and the pin speared a match from the box retrieving it. Dyrac removed the match and struck it along the back of the bird between its wings lighting it. Melting the wax stick at one end Dyrac watched as the drips of wax dropped over the corner folding edge of the envelope. He promptly took his left hand and placed the signet ring on his middle finger face down hard into the wax instantly sealing the envelopes edge and leaving behind the decoration from the rectangular signet ring. The initial D sat in the centre of a diamond with the Latin words *Omnes,* sitting across the left upward edge of the diamond, *Morimur*, sitting underneath the right upward edge of the diamond. This translated into English as *All Men Must Die*.

Dyrac knew he couldn't wait until the following Saturday for Kurt to collect and deliver the message so, he decided he would leave Wode House later that day, hopefully unbeknownst to Merril that he wasn't in residence, so that he could post the letter to Cornelius himself. The nearest post box was located just outside Bryson & Sons however, to avoid being seen he would take the road leading into Clifton where, at the 'Welcome to Clifton' sign was a second post box.

"One more thing to do before I leave," Dyrac uttered to nobody walking out of the study. Dyrac was careful to lock the study as he was leaving to prevent a wandering Merril from haphazardly making her way into the study and seeing the envelope on his desk. He'd taken to locking the study since finding Merril in there one Sunday morning rifling through the books on the shelf looking for something "different" to read she had said. Dyrac informed Merril that the library held sufficient books for which she had unlimited access to and that she should only be in the study when he was. At all other times the study was to remain off limits.

Turning right out of the study Dyrac headed to the cellar. Upon reaching the cellar Dyrac turned on the wall lights of the second room making his way to the chamber of curiosities. He walked over to the mummified remains of the man lay in the foetus position and, confined in a glass case of sorts, visually examined him. The man's right hand was clutched tightly in a fist, something Dyrac had never really noticed before. Dyrac looked at the man's face noting the groove that lay strewn across the bridge of his nose. He reached out and opened the hinged lid of the case, placed his hand on the fist of the dead man and spoke, "So, Abimilech, still keeping secrets I see!"

Chapter 8

Merril descended the ladder with her satchel sitting across her body. Stepping off the bottom rung Merril stood tall and cast her torch around until she located a switch and dial to her right. She pressed the switch and turned the dial a quarter turn. The switch clicked liked the ignition of a cooker hob and suddenly gas lights illuminated a passage way in front of her. She released the dial and the lights remained on. The old gas lighting system that had been in place for over a hundred years never failed her.

Merril stared down the tunnel; the lights provided an omniscient ambience of an infinite awareness as to where the passage led. The tunnel was gray and foul yet somehow cosy with the smoky backlight provided by the Victorian lighting system. It was a vast and serpentine, mysteriously with a high vaulted corridor. Sufficiently so, Merril was able to walk through it without having to crouch.

After walking for some time Merril approached a slight and stepped incline. She remembered counting steps like this as a child and counted 1, 2, 3 ... 32, 33, 34 before levelling out again. Merril looked straight ahead and directly at a plain four panelled oak door. She grasped the handle and pulled it downwards. Opening with a groan the door creaked. Merril stepped through to a gloomy, badly timbered, secondary passage. Merril crept along the passage way and stopped at the break of daylight through a vented grate in the wall. Merril peeked through into the kitchen of Wode House. She could see it was how she left it and could see just through the kitchen to the cellar door and a small break of orange pearlescent light glowed from behind. *He must be in the cellar*, she thought.

She continued along the passage and didn't stop until she reached two handles on the wall. One was head height and the other, waist height. Before she reached for them both simultaneously she pressed the side of her face to the wall, brushing away cobwebs and thick dust. She listened intently. No sound broke through so she guessed the coast was clear. She pulled the handles pushed against the wall. A section broke free on one side as a latch released and there was a slight murmuring from the hinge. From the other side a fitted bookshelf irked forward.

Merril appeared from behind the bookshelf and made her way into Dyrac's study towards the door, leaving the hidden doorway behind the bookshelf ajar. Turning the handle she ensured the study door was locked, knowing that it would be.

Merril took in the whole room admiringly. It was a beautiful study with a feel of masculinity about it and was full of fascinating objects, antiquities and antique furniture. There was the feint undertone of a smokiness that echoed within its confine along with the musky residue of the Tom Ford cologne worn by Dyrac.

Merril sat in Dyrac's chair, removed the flask from her satchel and poured herself a cup of tea whilst cheekily placing her feet on his foot stool. She sipped away at the steaming hot tea and decided against eating in the study so as not to leave any visible clue in the form of crumbs indicating that she had been there.

Dyrac stood over Abimilech's mummified corpse smiling. He reached for Abimilech's clenched fist and as he tried to prise his fingers open he stared at his face, a small house spider crawled out from Abimilech's left nostril and across his face up into his sunken eye socket. Dyrac heard a crunch and he looked back to Abimilech's fist. Dyrac had inadvertently broken the index finger, snapping it backwards the light from inside the chamber reflected off something in Abimilech's hand.

"What have we here," said Dyrac "What was so important that you held it so intently at the time of your death?"

Dyrac tried in vain to release Abimilech's other fingers but he couldn't shift them. Not with his bare hands and not in the time he had right now. This was something he needed to return to. But, for now he had to get that letter to Cornelius.

After finishing her tea Merril repacked the thermos and placed the satchel next to the opening of the hidden doorway. She walked over to Dyrac's desk and rifled through his drawers carefully memorising the location of the contents within so that she could return them exactly how she had found them. Her OCD tendencies gave her reassurance that she wouldn't leave a thing out of place. She found books containing details of various accounts, purchases and orders in one drawer; nothing but stationery and a very beautiful calligraphy set in another; one drawer held a variety of hanging files which had tabulated tops describing the contents but nothing was worth noting there; two other drawers had different personal affects; the top right drawer had a small wooden tray in there for organising small stationery items such as paperclips, treasury tags, post-it notes etc and right at the front were three wax sticks for sealing documents. Merril noticed one of the sticks had been melted at one end and she pressed it with her finger, it was still malleable from being used recently.

On the desk Merril spotted a brown envelope with a wax seal securing the contents inside. *Damn it* she thought, *why would he leave it here sealed?*

Merril lifted the envelope, turning it she noted the unfamiliar addressee. Merril had never heard Dyrac talk of a Cornelius. She held the envelope towards the light in the hope she would catch a glimpse of what may be inside but, no luck. She let out a frustrated sigh and placed the envelope back in the exact location it had been left. Before pulling her gaze away from the envelope Merril noticed the seal on the top, it was Dyrac's.

She sat in Dyrac's office chair contemplating where else he may hide things away from prying eyes. Moving her focus Merril spotted a keyhole in the centre of the desk, just under the lipped edge of the top. She didn't have a key and couldn't see a key anywhere that would fit such a small keyhole, nor could she see what it unlocked. Merril went back to the top drawer on the right of the desk and picked up a paperclip. She straightened it out fashioning a 90-degree angle leaving enough space on one end of the clip to grip and act as a handle. She inserted the paper clip carefully into the lock's keyhole feeling a little resistance indicating the wire could go no further. She twisted the wire left and right, wiggled it back out and re-tried on a number of occasions before suddenly feeling the lock bolt inside move and click releasing a flap in the desk.

"Huh," she said out loud in astonishment, "it actually worked."

Merril looked inside and found nothing but emptiness. *Clearly something had been here; otherwise he wouldn't bother locking it surely?* Merril heard a door close from outside the study and footsteps echoed throughout the hallway. Quickly she closed the flap and fumbled with the misshapen paperclip to lock the flap back into place. The footsteps grew ever nearer. She put the chair back into place and grabbing her satchel slipped out of view behind the bookshelf. Carefully she grasped the handles on the wall inside the passage and pulled the hidden door closed. She made sure it was secure by giving it a slight shove with her shoulder just as she heard the door of the study unlock. She held her breath and took two side steps to her left; she pressed her nose against the wall and peered through two small holes. On the other side of the wall there was a tapestry hanging on the wooden panelled wall. Merril could see through the tapestry albeit the view was not clear she could certainly see it was Dyrac who entered the study. He had something in his right hand. He walked over to his desk and picked up the envelope. He left the study and Merril heard the door lock. The sound of Dyrac's footsteps suggested he was heading to the front door. Merril raced down the passage way tracing Dyrac's steps. She stopped as she heard the front door of Wode House open.

Dyrac headed off down the gravel driveway on foot, it was 10:30am and whilst he knew there would be no post collection today there would be a collection at 7:30am the following day which meant that Cornelius should have the letter by Tuesday morning. Dyrac knew Cornelius would act straight away upon receiving his word.

Merril headed back along the passage, from the direction she came. She raced past the secret entrance into the study and turned off descending into the corridor leading the ladder. She crept up the ladder and back into the folly. She stopped and turned pushing the stone plaque back into place. She didn't know how long Dyrac was going to be but she decided she was going to try and get into the cellar. She knew there was something of significance down there, as well as the chest that Kurt dropped off a couple of weeks ago. What she didn't know was how long Dyrac was going to be so she had to move fast.

Leaving her satchel on the island, Merril decided she would come back to this spot to eat her lunch once she had satisfied her other hunger of discovering what was in the cellar.

Merril ran along the side of Wode House and through the side entrance into the kitchen. She didn't bother to close the side entrance door and walked straight to the cellar. She had to figure a way to unlock the cellar and thought the picking of this particular lock would be more difficult than the lock on Dyrac's desk.

Pacing Merril thought. She trawled through the kitchen drawers and cupboards looking for inspiration then it dawned on her. She raced to the knife block and withdrew the fillet knife. All the knives had ivory handles and the fillet knife blade was perfectly thin and long. She ran to the cellar door and inserted the knife pushing against the locking mechanism. Applying just enough pressure she moved the knife in one direction then the other and miraculously heard a click. She reached for the handle and the door opened. Merril wasn't even hesitant upon entering the cellar. She got to the bottom of the stairs and fumbled around for a light switch, not realising a pull cord at the top of the stairs would've illuminated the cellar entrance.

The lights eventually came on and Merril found herself in a room with four chambers leading off. She wasn't sure what she would find but she chose a doorway and found herself in a room full of all sorts. She gasped as she looked around at the volume of collectibles, taxidermy pieces, oddities and antiques. *Why is all this down here and what on earth was the smell?* She thought.

Merril pinched her nose as the throat-grabbing pungent smell hit her like a brick wall and her eyes began to burn as she breathed in. The smell was formaldehyde. A number of jars and containers held various human specimens. Merril looked at a number of jars in front of her and, intrigued she shifted one from side to side to see if she could get a glimpse of what was inside. A complete human brain. "Well that's gross" she expressed out loud trying not to breathe whilst at the same time her throat felt like it had a huge concrete block in there ever expanding and restricting her airways. The formaldehyde was stifling her.

Moving the brain to one side, she reached for the next. It contained the head of a human. However, the face looking back at her had no face. That was the skin had been removed exposing a network of muscles intertwined and carefully weaved forming the basic structure usually not ever seen in real life. The eyes, as blue and alive as they once were, seemed to pop from the sockets staring straight back at her. She turned the jar away from her still feeling the eyes on her. After a few more jars containing many more human parts in various forms Merril decided enough was enough as she began to feel queasy.

She moved away from the unit containing the jars and headed towards the dark, cob web ridden corner. Something was drawing her there. Sub-consciously Merril slowed her pace and stopped, turned away from the corner and back to face the door. If she had looked down in that moment she'd have seen the fingers from the left hand of Abimilech's mummified corpse poking out from under his head, cupping his own face.

Merril couldn't take the smell from inside the chamber any decided she would look in the other chambers.

Merril walked into the wine cellar astonished at the sheer volume of wine that lay resting before her. Immediately to her left and fixed to the wall was a thermometer reading 55 degrees Fahrenheit. The chamber had a delicate balance of humidity and Merril decided to have a look through the selection.

The bottles were all tinted green or brown to avoid any spoilage from harmful lighting.

The wines were stored in sections according to their types and reeling off the list in her head she saw an array of wines, Cabernet Francs; Cabernet Sauvignons; Gamays; Grenaches; Malbecs; Merlots; Mataros; Nebbiolos; Pinot Noirs; Shirazs; Zinfandels and so on and so on. It seemed endless, *there must be thousands of bottles here* she thought.

And then Merril noticed a particular bottle sitting on its side on its own with a thick coating of dust now encrusted around it, consuming it. The bottle was sealed with wax and, despite the dust Merril could see it bore no label.

Merril lifted the bottle. It felt heavy and as she moved the bottle the liquid inside seemed dense, *too dense for a wine* she thought. Maybe it's got sediment inside it? Merril felt a cold shiver rush down her back. She placed the bottle back exactly as she found it and decided to leave the wine cellar for whatever she was looking for, even though she didn't know what it was, she knew it wouldn't be in the wine cellar.

Merril turned and walked out of the wine cellar leaving the sole bottle back in its rightful resting place not noticing her thumb had lifted away some of the dust exposing a small print against the fresh glass now peeking through.

Merril was back in the central room when she felt the same cold shiver again, this time lingering and making the hairs on her arms stand up on end. She quickly turned and was directly facing the long narrow chamber containing the chest. She stood, agape, glaring into a thick blackness.

"What the fuck was that?," Merril asked herself trying to reassure herself that the sound she just heard coming from the chamber was her mind playing tricks on her. "It's nothing," she answered herself, "Get a grip woman."

Taking a deep breath Merril walked into the long narrow chamber. She walked over to the dark mass towards the end, taking each step slowly and placing her feet so delicately on the ground you'd think she was walking across thin ice and was terrified of penetrating it falling into the icy cold waters below. She reached the mass and gulped as she looked down. "THE CHEST!" she shouted instantly clasping her hand over her mouth to shut herself up.

"I...D...Y...S...H...Aaaaaaaahhhhhhhhhh," came a distant cry.

Merril screamed and raced out of the chamber and up the stairs, out of the cellar not bothering to close the door behind her. Still running she left the kitchen and ran alongside Wode House, past the sun dial and across the stone bridge back on to the island. She paused by the folly entrance gasping for breath. Her heart thudded deeply and hard against her sternum. *What the fuck was that? What is in there? Who is in there? Why was I in there? What do I do now? Fuck! Fuck! Fuck!*

Chapter 9

It took Dyrac an hour and a half to reach the post box. He slid the envelope through the letterbox and tapped the side of it uttering the words "see you soon old friend."

Cornelius Blackshot was an unusual man. He was a fixer. A fixer of problems. He knew people, he could acquire anything you needed and, he was a cleanup man. But most of all he was also a prolific anthropophagist, an advocate of cannibalistic attitudes who feasted on the flesh of other human beings. Like Dyrac, he had a thirst for blood and understood how the next hit would rejuvenate and energise you, and of the immortality that gorging on the soul of another would provide.

Dyrac had known Cornelius for almost 50 years. They first met by sheer accident. Dyrac was in attendance at a large symposium celebrating the 100th anniversary of the publication of the first extensive English translation by Samuel Birch of the Book of the Dead. Dyrac's fondness of ancient Egypt and the spells contained within the book meant that this was an event he was not going to miss. It was 1967 and Dyrac back then looked just as he did now.

Dyrac had been quaffing on Dom Perignon, a prestigious champagne named so after the monk who founded it. He had also been holding on to a canapé of blini topped with smoked salmon and caviar. Dyrac had just turned to peruse the crowd and accidentally collided into a well dressed man knocking the canapé out of his hand and down the front of the double breasted blue pin striped jacket he was wearing.

"I am so sorry sir," Dyrac apologised.

"Young man, no need to apologise, the fault is all mine," came the reply.

"No, no really, it's my fault," Dyrac wasn't too sorry for he detested caviar and seafood and the smell alone from holding it for so long was making him wretch. He was merely trying to look the part by using it as an accessory of sorts.

"Honestly, its fine, I'll have my dry cleaning bill sent your way if you remain so insistent," replied the man.

"By all means," Dyrac responded bowing his head to the man.

"Cornelius Blackshot," the man held out his hand to shake Dyrac's.

"Gideon, Dyrac Gideon." Dyrac hated using the surname Gideon but having not known of his own origins he was left with no choice other than to adopt the surname of Abimilech.

Dyrac and Cornelius spoke to each other for over three hours to the point where the conversation moved on from the polite etiquette of champagne and canapés, to that of bearing each other's soul over a whisky and cigar at the local and exclusive gents club (some would say strip club but still). They found each other fascinating and intriguing. There were many similarities between them and by the end of the night they both knew of each other's thirsts and hungers and the need that these addictive habits conveyed deep within.

As days turned to weeks, then months turned to

years they became great friends and allies. Often targeting donors for each other, hosting dinner parties regularly to devour and demean their victims.

Cornelius never failed Dyrac, unlike Abimilech.

At their last meeting Cornelius expressed his concerns to Dyrac over the continued service of Merril. "There is something about her that feeds my uncertainty in a prophetically dark way."

Standing at the letterbox Dyrac was stuck in his thoughts. Cornelius was always called upon when Dyrac needed something.

Not knowing it right now, Dyrac's need was greater than he envisaged and it would not be long before a tumultuous change was to take place at Wode House.

Back at Wode House Merril had regained her composure as her heart rate plummeted back to normal and saliva was once again being produced in her mouth. She fell to a cross legged position letting out a huge breath as she did so. She picked up her satchel and took out the lunch and flask, she poured herself a fresh cup of tea and before it had chance to cool she took a swelteringly hot sip. She didn't feel the blisters that instantly formed on her top lip and she gulped down the hot, sweet and, reassuringly comforting tea.

She snaffled the food, barely tasting it. She shuddered and finished her lunch.

"Shit!" she exclaimed, "he'll be back soon, I'm sure of it."

Merril retrieved the remnants of her lunch and

fastened closed the lid of her flask repacking her satchel. In one swift movement she raised herself from her cross legged position and swished her satchel across her body. She needed to get back to the main house, she realised she hadn't locked the cellar.

Dyrac was on his way back to the house when a vehicle passed honking its horn. He raised his head in time to see Kurt waving out of his window as he turned left towards Bryson & Sons. Dyrac gingerly waved back hating that he had been spotted away from Wode House knowing also that he would likely face questions from Kurt during their meeting later that morning.

He walked leisurely, for he was in no rush, back along the road passing the turning Kurt had taken moments before. He could see Wode House in the distance and regretted that today was Merril's day off. He was famished and knew that he would need to prepare his own lunch when he got back which meant it would be something he could pick at rather than a meal he could sit down to enjoy.

Entering the gateway to Wode House Dyrac could see Merril walking along the side of the house having just passed the sundial. *I could just ask her* he thought, *no, it's her only day off*.

Merril spotted Dyrac from afar and swiftly threw on a pace. She hadn't noticed the vehicle parked by the side entrance its engine still warm. She entered the kitchen knowing Dyrac was seconds away. *How am I going to lock the cellar door?* she thought.

She reached for the cellar door and as she pulled it

closed she was startled.

"KURT!" she screamed.

Chapter 10

"Well, well, well," said Kurt "What have we here? Merry in a hurry is she?"

"Kurt, please, I need to get this door locked somehow before Dyrac steps through that front door any second," Merril replied frantically.

"Suppose this would help, wouldn't it?" he held aloft a key.

"Stop teasing Kurt, there is no way that you have a key to the cellar!"

Kurt inserted the key into the lock of the cellar door simultaneously closing it. He turned the key and the lock clicked into place. Merril dumbfounded stared at Kurt.

"But...how?" she asked.

"Well, you see after dropping off the chest a few weeks ago I forgot to return the spare cellar key to Dyrac and he trusted me to hold onto it until I next called round for a meeting in the study, which, from the look of your face, you didn't realise was today."

Before Merril got to thank Kurt she heard the front door close and Dyrac' familiar steps pacing down the corridor towards them.

"Kurt, hide," said Merril.

"Hide? I don't understand Dyrac is expecting me."

"Yes, that may well be but he will not be expecting you and me to be fraternising in the kitchen and me looking so, well, manic."

"You do look a little ashen and guilty. Fine, I'll go back out the side entrance and sit in the pick-up for five minutes before heading back in," replied Kurt.

"Thanks Kurt," Merril stepped to the side allowing Kurt to pass her. "Oh, and Kurt..."

Kurt cut Merril off mid sentence, "not a word," he said with a wink looking back at her.

Merril gave a thankful smile in response.

Dyrac was walking along the corridor and spotted Merril in the kitchen. "What brings you to the kitchen on your day off?" he asked as he entered.

"Just grabbing a spot of lunch," Merril lied.

"Ahhh don't suppose..."

"I could fix you something too whilst I'm at it?"

Dyrac sniggered "That would be very kind Merril. I can wait in here and take it to my study myself though. I can't have you a slave to me 7 days of the week now can I?"

Merril smiled and nervously shifted into the larder. She regained her composure and took in an almighty breath pushing out all of the disloyalty she had shown Dyrac this morning as she exhaled.

Grabbing a few small bits Merril put together a masterpiece of a sandwich. Nestled inside a small French baton which she spread thickly with salted President butter, Merril added pastrami, Bavarian ham, chorizo, roast beef and some honey glazed ham. She added a sprinkling of grated extra mature cheddar, some frisee and radicchio lettuce, thinly sliced cucumber and topped it off with homemade mayonnaise and a dusting of salt and pepper. She cut the baton in half and added a pile of tortilla chips to the side and a small pot of pickle which Dyrac could add if he chose to. She placed the sandwich on a serving tray alongside a small glass bottle with a swing top bottle top (like the stoppers that on trend kids of the late eighties would wear on the laces of their shoes). The bottle contained an old fashioned soft drink, Sarsaparilla. Dyrac adored the stuff but Merril didn't care much for it. Next to the bottle was a glass tumbler with a couple of ice cubes taken from the chiller.

"Merril, I don't know how you do it but you sure make a marvellous lunch. The Earl of Sandwich would most definitely approve," said Dyrac taking the tray. He headed off down the hallway, "Oh Merril," he bellowed backwards.

"Yes Dyrac?" she asked.

"Kurt should be here any second; if you do see him he knows where to find me."

"Yes Dyrac."

Kurt re-entered the kitchen and nodded to Merril as she pointed down the hallway towards the study.

"Speak soon," he said in a mysterious tone.

Kurt knocked on the study door and waited for Dyrac to beckon him to enter.

"Kurt, please take a seat," Dyrac gestured towards a chair opposite his next to the fireplace. "Excuse me whilst I finish my lunch wont you? I had to make an unplanned journey this morning, which is why you saw me down on the road into Clifton," pre-empting any questions from Kurt.

"Yeah, it's not like you to be away from Wode House. Must've been important?" asked Kurt.

Dyrac didn't respond to Kurt's rhetorical line of questioning. He simply finished the last morsel of his sandwich smacking his lips as he did so.

"Kurt, about our arrangement, I need you to do another search and it needs to be tomorrow. I can keep Merril occupied long enough however, it is imperative you find what I am looking for," said Dyrac.

"Err, Dyrac, not to be one to point out the obvious but, you don't know what it is I am meant to be looking for remember?" Kurt's response was blunt.

"Quite Kurt, however, the insolent tone isn't necessary."

"Sorry," replied Kurt.

"Now, inside Merril's room there is something that must be found. Check for hidden compartments in drawers, look around for secret writings or sketches, anything that will give me a clue as to what it is I need to find."

"Alright! So how are we going to play this?" asked Kurt.

"Tomorrow just so happens to be the anniversary of Merril's service to me and, in keeping with previous year's traditions I will be inviting Merril for dinner. I have arranged another service to prepare and serve the meal and this should give you ample, and uninterrupted time, to go about your business."

"Roger that and..."

"And" Dyrac continued Kurt's sentence for him "if you should so much as find anything you will call on me immediately and, I shall make my excuses and meet you back here. The study door will be unlocked from 7:00pm so you should be able to hide away in here locking it from the inside once you are in and therefore avoiding any interruption."

"How do I...."

"You will ring the service bell. It echoes throughout the house and I shall make a comment to Merril that the service help for the evening must've mistakenly activated the bell."

"Got it," replied Kurt.

"That'll be all Kurt, until tomorrow."

"Tomorrow," Kurt responded and left the study and headed back to the kitchen.

Dyrac rubbed his hands together in a wickedly devious way.

"Merry!" Kurt shouted.

Merril called back "I'm outside Kurt, I'm heading off to do some sketching," came the reply.

Kurt left the side entrance and jogged a few steps to catch up with Merril.

"Why were you so enthused as to have the cellar locked? Why was it unlocked? Have you been down there? What did you find?" Kurt bombarded Merril with questions.

"Kurt, Christ, will you just rein it in. Firstly, none of your business but I do now find myself in a predicament of sorts. I was hoping that I would have gotten that door locked and no-one be any the wiser however, fate had it be that you were there at the wrong time to catch me at a very improper moment."

"Well, you can say that again. Look Merry, I'm not a tattle tale so don't go worrying that pretty face of yours. Your secret is safe with me for now but, I would like to know whether you found anything exciting down there?" asked Kurt.

"You've been down there Kurt, when you dropped the chest off, remember?" quizzed Merril.

"Well yes, but I literally dumped the chest as requested and headed straight back up the stairs so, other than see four white washed walls with doorways leading from them I plonked that bloody great chest in the middle of the floor and promptly left. I did catch a slight glimpse of an epic wine cellar but couldn't really stop and appreciate it in all its splendour if you catch my drift."

"Hmm, ok, well to be honest Kurt I didn't really see much exciting," she lied. Kurt knew she was lying but chose not to press her further.

"Well, if it's all the same I shall leave you to your doodling. I'm going to head off, boss has a job for me back at the store so need to get that done before closing."

"See you Kurt, and thank you for not telling Dyrac of my little indiscretion," said Merril.

"It's no bother Merry," Kurt replied leaving Merril at the sundial on her way back to the bridge.

Kurt was wandering back to the pick-up deep in thought. *What was it he needed to find that Merril could be hiding that stirred such unrest in Dyrac? What was in the cellar that had Merril blatantly lie to his face? What could she have seen?*

What Kurt did know is that he had a hard lump sitting heavy in his chest. He was bearing a weight which he didn't understand but it was consuming him. Something wasn't right at Wode House and somehow, just a humble grocery store delivery driver (and gambler), had managed to find himself right in the centre of it all. Hiding secrets from both Dyrac and Merril.

This better all be worth my while he thought as he

climbed into the pick-up. He started the engine and suddenly remembered he still had that blasted cellar key he was supposed to return to Dyrac.

"SHIT!" he yelled, thumping the steering wheel. He jumped out of the cab, leaving the engine running, and ran through the side entrance and down the hall. He knocked on the study door and waited. There was no response?

"Dyrac," he said in a raised but polite tone, "You there?"

"Kurt?" Dyrac called from farther down the hall.

"Jesus sir, sorry," Kurt turned his head in a flash startled at Dyrac's response coming from elsewhere but the study. "The key, the cellar key I mean, I forgot to drop it off."

"Ah yes, thanks Kurt. I'll take that."

"No bother," quickly he fumbled the key into Dyrac's hand and left racing back down the hall.

"Kurt?" Dyrac called after him.

Kurt stopped dead in his tracks and without turning "Yes Dyrac?"

"Nothing, but just think how far you would've got if I hadn't called you," said Dyrac.

"Wanker" whispered Kurt to himself, "Ha, hilarious one sir," he replied.

Dyrac chortled to himself as he walked away. *That never gets old* he thought.

Chapter 11

"Another delicious feast for me I see," Dyrac said as Merril served him breakfast. "Merril, as you know it's the fifteenth anniversary of your service to me today and as usual, I have arranged for service help for the evening to meet my needs and to prepare and serve dinner. I would be honoured if you could join me?"

"Of course," Merril answered.

"You don't sound enthused?"

"My apologies Dyrac, I didn't rest well and...," Merril paused.

"Go on," said Dyrac.

"...and well, I shouldn't really dwell on you but, it had completely escaped my mind that my service anniversary was today."

"We can discuss why you didn't rest well over dinner," Dyrac placed a hand on Merril's forearm as she was removing the serving tray from the breakfast table.

"As you wish," she replied.

"Let's say 7:00pm in the dining room. Let's make this a casual evening Merril. Don't go dressing up, wear whatever makes you comfortable."

"Thank you Dyrac," replied Merril, bowing her head slightly.

"Seven o'clock then," he announced cracking the top off his soft boiled egg with a small solid silver egg spoon.

Merril was visibly shaking as she left the breakfast room. She could barely contain the rattling of the items on the tray as she made her way back to the kitchen. Once there she slammed the tray onto the extensive kitchen table. *Breathe Merril, count to ten. Sort that heart rate out otherwise you'll be setting yourself up for a whole world of bother. 1, 2, 3.....9, 10.* Merril exhaled. She took a seat at the table and poured herself a tepid cup of tea from the pot she brewed earlier that morning. She added sugar, unconsciously adding two extra teaspoons more than usual, and stirred whilst in some kind of daze.

She winced at the sweetness of the tea as it hit her lips but she continued drinking nonetheless.

Daydreaming, Merril thought about all she had seen in the cellar but her focus was mainly on the sound that she heard coming from, what appeared to be, the chest. She shuddered so hard the tea spilled over the edge of the cup in her hand. She grabbed the cup with her free hand to try to steady herself. *That voice, it was so familiar,* she thought to herself. But no matter how much she had tried since, she could not fathom the identity of the voice. One thing she knew for sure though was that, as clear as day, that voice uttered the name Idysha. A name Merril hadn't heard for many years.

Merril placed the teacup back into the saucer on the table and picked out a biscuit from the barrel next to the tea pot. She wasn't bothered which she pulled out but she was secretly hoping for a fruit shortcake.

"Custard cream?" she said out loud to herself somewhat disappointed. She ate it anyway and then decided to rummage for the fruit shortcake she needed to satisfy her craving.

Merril recalled a memory of her mother again. What was it she would say about the fruit shortcake again? "Merril, you know what they call those biscuits?" asked her vision.

Laughing to herself because she knew what was coming, "No mama, what?"

"Dead fly biscuits," Merril snorted a little of the tea as she chuckled having it go down the wrong way. Coughing bits of tea and biscuit out she was still smirking at the memory. You couldn't deny that they did indeed look like dead flies squished inside a delicious shortcake.

After a short break, Merril tidied up the kitchen and decided to set a menu for the service help to prepare and serve this evening.

"May as well serve me something I'm going to enjoy," she said out loud to herself.

After rummaging through the stores, chiller, cupboards and larder Merril retrieved a piece of paper and pen from the kitchen drawer under the butchers block chopping board next to the Bristol sink and wrote down the following:

Mr Gideon has requested that the following be served for dinner this evening. You'll find sufficient ingredients already within the constraints of the kitchen to ensure the menu can be served in the following order:

Appetiser:	*Pancetta Crisps with Goat Cheese & Pear*
Soup:	*Lemon & Orzo served with a poppy seed crusty cob*

| Main: | Rib eye with a garlic & shallot compound butter served with sautéed seasonal vegetables. |
| Dessert: | Strawberries & Cream Pannacotta, Chocolate and Cherry Torte and Spiced Apple Cake with Crème Anglaise |

Merril licked her lips at the deliciousness the menu foretold. She left the piece of paper in the centre of the table and held it in place with a small, but heavy morano glass vase containing the days freshly cut flowers.

Glancing around the kitchen Merril continued with her daily duties knowing she must be done by at least 5:30pm so she had time to get ready for dinner.

Fifteen years. I can't believe I've kept this up for fifteen years, Merril thought.

Chapter 12

The bell rang indicating dinner would be served in fifteen minutes. Merril had just enough time to give herself the once over and apply some clear gloss to her lips before heading down the warren of hallways and stairwells and reaching the dining room.

Wearing a black, off the shoulder, floor length dress Merril raised the hem chuckling at her feet. *Wear something comfortable*, she thought back to Dyrac's comments. Under the dress Merril's Doc Marten's sat completely out of place with the outfit, still she was comfortable. She picked up a black faux fur bolero to wear over her shoulders as she knew the dining room had a chill. No matter how much you tried to warm that room it never seemed to work.

Merril had fixed her hair into a loose, but neat, up do style. She wore no jewellery other than her silver bangle and gave herself a final glance nodding and smiling at her own reflection.

"You'll do," she complimented the image of herself looking back at her from the mirror.

Dyrac was already waiting in the dining room when Merril arrived. He cordially greeted her walking her over to her seat, pulling out her chair inviting her to sit down and carefully tucked her in. He inhaled her as he did so but let out an audible sigh. Merril blushed.

Dyrac had seated Merril at the head of the table and chose to sit to her left. The enormity of the table drowned them both but Dyrac had thought the occasion grand enough.

"Dinner will be served in five minutes," came the voice of hired service. She was slight in stature and frame. Barely 4 foot tall and, from where they sat, barely visible.

"How on earth is that little woman going to serve dinner? Her arms barely reach her waist," uttered Dyrac to Merril.

Merril tittered "Dyrac, you mustn't."

Dyrac smiled "But seriously, how, physics won't allow it surely?"

Five minutes passed by and the doors to the dining room opened. In walked Lauren, the hired service, baring two enormous serving platters lavishly adorned with unnecessary decoration with the appetisers sitting neatly in the centre.

Dyrac and Merril watched in awe and intently both secretly hoping that there would be a mishap and then both feeling somewhat dismayed when Lauren made it to the table and managed to serve the appetisers without flounder.

She left the dining hall and Dyrac and Merril stared at each other aghast. "Well, hats off to her," Dyrac said lifting his cutlery from the outside of the place setting. "Let's tuck in. If this starter is anything to go by I may have to rethink who provides my permanent service."

Merril smiled knowing she had selected the evening's menu and was pleased that Dyrac appreciated what was placed in front of him.

Dyrac had ordered Lauren not to serve the wine for each course as this was something he would do himself, unusual as it was. Dyrac had carefully selected four wines to perfectly accompany each course. He excused himself from his seated position and reached over to the assortment of wines to his left. He picked up a bottle and poured a little into two wine glasses placing one in front of both himself and Merril.

"This is a Sauvignon Blanc based wine, Sancerre which along with the chevré (goats cheese) provides a classic, and regional pairing given that both came from the Loire Valley in France," Dyrac said. "I bought this particular bottle whilst visiting the Loire Valley. You may recall two years ago I left for France to visit Le Château de Chambord, a most beautiful and if not the finest examples of French Renaissance architecture I have ever seen. Anyway, I digress, the wine was purchased from a vineyard not far from Loir-et-Cher and I have been saving the wine for the right occasion, tonight being it."

"Why thank you Dyrac, I'm not sure I'm deserving of your wines but I accept your gesture," and with that Merril sipped from the glass allowing the acidic yet waterfall like wine coat her palate. "It's perfect," she replied.

Dyrac nodded and they both enjoyed their appetiser whilst making polite conversation. When both had placed their cutlery in the twenty past four position on their plates it indicated that they had finished with their course and Dyrac rang a bell summoning Lauren to clear the plates and ready the next course.

Merril dabbed the side of her mouth with her napkin carefully placing it back in her lap once she had done so.

The next course saw Dyrac introduce a new wine and conversation began to loosen as both were starting to feel socially comfortable in the others company and less so of the relationship of employer and employee.

It was when Lauren was bringing in the main course that Dyrac remembered Kurt would have been in the house for at least an hour and a half by now and Merril noticed a shift in his relaxed face.

"Is everything ok?" she asked.

"Absolutely fine Merril, we are having a lovely evening aren't we?" something was fastidious in his response but Merril didn't push it and carried on regardless. "Smells marvellous Lauren, marvellous!" he announced.

"Yes sir," Lauren curtseyed. Both Merril and Dyrac sniggered and Lauren shot a petulant look towards Merril. Merril raised her hand apologetically.

After Lauren left Dyrac turned to Merril, "I think there should be more curtseying going forward."

"I think not," Merril replied too quickly immediately apologising "Sorry sir, err, Dyrac, I think I've had too much wine. I have forgotten myself."

"Nonsense Merril, all in good jest." He smiled at Merril picking up his steak knife, carving a slice of meat from the rib eye.

"All the same, I should still remember my place."

Dyrac hadn't heard Merril's last comment for the sound of his own chewing in his head drowned out any outside noises.

"The wine!" Dyrac shouted. He placed his cutlery

in the twenty past eight position on his plate as he had indeed not finished his course and stood to pour more wine.

"I really shouldn't," Merril said raising her hand in a no more gesture to Dyrac.

"Come on Merril, I'll let you have a late start tomorrow, the evening is young and you must simply try this Malbec. It accompanies this cut of beef beautifully. The heavy blackberry, plum and black cherry flavours along with a slight sharpness of raspberry comfort the palate. It's a combination that cannot be afforded to be missed."

Dyrac waved the bottle of Malbec over Merril's fresh wine glass. She cautiously nodded and raised her lip in a half hearted attempt at a smile.

"Very well, just the one more mind."

"Ok Merril, ok," replied Dyrac.

The main course was coming to an end and Merril was most definitely feeling the wine fuzziness filling her head. She desperately wanted to retire to bed to rest it off but she had been most looking forward to the next course and wasn't about to miss the opportunity to feast on the sweet treats.

Lauren cleared the main course leftovers away and, before leaving Dyrac asked for a short 15 minute break before she brought out dessert.

Well that's just what I need, a break. I want this night to come to an end at some point, Merril thought to herself.

Both Dyrac and Merril sat nervously. Dyrac was impatiently waiting for the call of the service bell indicating Kurt was waiting for him in the study. Merril was impatiently waiting for her dessert so she could devour it and get herself to bed. They looked at each other as though guessing what the other was thinking and at the same time addressed each other by name.

"You first, I insist," said Dyrac.

"Thank you Dyrac, I was just going to ask, I saw you leave the house yesterday? It's unusual for you to leave so I wondered if all was ok."

"Merril my dear, you need not worry yourself so, all is quite well I can assure you. I just had the desire to get some fresh air and, rather than walk the grounds of the house I confine myself to daily I chose to wander towards town." Dyrac was quick in his response and gave Merril no reason to disbelieve him had she not seen him hurriedly collect the letter from his study desk, from within the secret passage.

"What were you going to say Dyrac?" she asked.

"Well, I wondered what you did across that stone bridge on your days off."

Merril shifted in her chair pausing, but not too long, before responding, "I sketch. I draw. I create art. Well, I say art, I tend to sketch nonsensical images. It's not art really. I mean I barely..."

"Merril, you're wittering," he said.

"Sorry."

"I'd like to see some of your work someday, if you'll let me?" asked Dyrac.

"I don't usually allow people to see my work. Well to be honest, I don't think I've ever had anyone openly ask to see it before now."

Merril knew that the images she had created so far could absolutely not be shown to Dyrac so she had to think quickly on her feet.

"Also, I dropped my satchel off the bridge yesterday saturating most of my works and ruining them beyond saving."

"I'm sorry to hear that Merril. Maybe in the future, when you've created your next piece, I could take a look." Dyrac didn't want to push the conversation too much in the hope that he could leave and meet Kurt any moment.

"Sure," replied Merril uncomfortably.

There was an audible ring that echoed through the dining hall, and surrounding hallways and rooms. Merril looked perplexed and Dyrac tried to hide the excitement in his eyes with the same sort of perplexion Merril portrayed.

"That's the service bell?" Merril questioned.

"That Lauren must've accidentally pressed it. Please excuse me Merril, wait here, and I'll go and see what happened. I won't be long, feel free to help yourself to more wine."

The thought of more wine made Merril wretch and gag.

"I'll wait." She replied.

Dyrac left the dining room and instead of turning towards the kitchen he headed straight off to the study to meet Kurt.

"Let him have found something, please let him have found something." Dyrac spoke to himself as he reached the study.

Chapter 13

Kurt stood patiently in the study waiting for Dyrac, next to the service bell he had just activated. He couldn't sit as the exhilaration from his find seared through his body. He was shaking in excitement when the lock to the study clicked and the handle turned. With Dyrac walking in through the door Kurt couldn't contain himself any longer.

"I've found something. I found something and sir, you are not going to believe what I have found."

"Shh," Dyrac pressed his index finger against his lips expressing his desire that this meeting be discreet and Kurt's current volume was anything but.

"Sorry sir," he whispered back. "I have it here." Kurt put his right hand in his jacket pocket and pulled out a small velvet bag.

"What's in the bag?" asked Dyrac.

"Well, you will not believe what it is when you see it, especially given that Merril comes across all sweet and pure, as innocent as an angel almost."

"Hand it to me," said Dyrac. "Now Kurt!"

Kurt was hesitant. Something was pulling him away from Dyrac reluctant to let go but, he handed it over. Dyrac carefully opened the bag and caught a flash of light glinting from within; he instantly recognised the curved blade.

"Some sort of cutlass? Why would Merril have a cutlass?" asked Kurt.

"It's not a cutlass Kurt. It's a..." Dyrac paused looking down at the Karamabit in his hands, "never mind. Look I've got to get back to dinner before

Merril gets suspicious and before Lauren brings in dessert, I'm meant to be talking to her about activating the call bell and if Merril gets an inkling that I haven't been speaking to Lauren she will know something is afoot."

"Sure. Whatever you say Dyrac," replied Kurt. "And, payment?"

"Yes Kurt, I'll arrange your payment. You did well. You must never speak of this remember and under no circumstances must Merril ever find out. But, before you go Kurt, I need you to replace this exactly where you found it. You hear? EXACTLY!" Dyrac was firm in his latest instruction.

"Shit! Really? I've got to go back?"

"Yes Kurt and now. Dinner has almost come to an end and you must make sure this is back exactly as you found it and then you need to disappear without being seen by anyone!"

"All over it," Kurt replied.

Kurt left the study taking back the small velvet bag from Dyrac nodding in a bid of farewell as he left. Dyrac promptly followed locking the study behind him.

Merril was waiting patiently in the dining room and was daydreaming of her mother. Her reminiscence of her mother had become more frequent lately and, whilst she would fondly dive into her thoughts and indulge her memories, she wondered what could've triggered so many to the fore of her mind.

Merril was sitting in a pine rocking chair in a familiar, yet blurred kitchen. She was rocking back and forth watching her mother carefully measure out ingredients. She weighed and sieved the flour. Then, she would lop off a huge chunk of butter, pour the sugar from the sifter, beat the eggs to within an inch of their lives (albeit they were clearly already dead) and then peel and core the enormous cooking apples, chopping some roughly then carefully and perfectly slicing others for decoration a huge smile appeared on her mother's face.

"The final ingredient," her mother would say looking at Merril and placing her fingers on her lips as though this was a secret only bestowed upon her. With a wink, Sarah opened a small jar and placed it under Merril's nose, who sniffed at the contents, tingling and tickling her nose with comforting warmth. Merril would giggle and then lock eye contact with her mother's loving gaze. "And the most secret ingredient of all," Sarah continued, "Is always a sprinkling of love."

The secret ingredient, Merril now knew, was a combination of various spices mixed together. There was allspice, cinnamon, nutmeg, mace, cloves and ginger to name most of them. Merril never managed to recreate the flavour exactly as her mothers, despite adding numerous other spices in her experimental attempts and longed to find out what the 'sprinkling of love' ingredient actually contained.

Merril could taste the fresh out of the oven warm cake embracing her taste buds with a dollop of clotted cream coating her tongue with a thick silky richness.

The door of the dining room opened and Dyrac appeared, "Dessert is on its way," he announced waking Merril back into the current scene.

"There's really no rush," Merril replied secretly hoping that Lauren was in hot pursuit with the trio of desserts.

"Nonsense," said Dyrac "I've asked Lauren to hurry along as she is dragging her heels somewhat. She's not at all anywhere near as well timed as you Merril."

Merril nodded at Dyrac as he took his seat back at the table.

Moments later, as if on cue and staged, Lauren entered with a serving trolley. On the trolley were two three tiered cake stands. Each tier contained one of the trio of desserts. Lauren placed the desserts on the table and dealt side plates to Merril and Dyrac.

"That will be all Lauren," Dyrac ushered her away with the back of his hand.

Lauren curtseyed carefully keeping eye contact with Merril locked in a death stare of 'just you dare laugh at me again for curtseying' way.

Merril smiled and nodded to Lauren reading her mind as she closed the dining room door.

"Mmmmm," Merril breathed in the sweetness from the final course. She took time appreciating the presentation and detail behind each dessert before collecting the respective cutlery from her place setting and diving right in. She chose the Chocolate and Cherry Torte to start with hoping that the richness of the dessert wouldn't lay too heavy on her before she had chance to enjoy the others. Then came the Panna Cotta. Merril was tempted to suck it right off the plate as she once did as a child but then thought this was not quite the occasion of such immature, yet fun, behaviour.

Merril left the Spiced Apple Cake for the end, wanting it so much to be every bit as good as her mothers.

Dyrac smiled at Merril as he watched her enjoy the dessert in silence. "Why Merril, you haven't spoken a word during this whole course. I often thought of you being sweet and innocent enough but clearly you've a secret and devilish side." Dyrac's comments contained a hidden meaning after seeing what Kurt had found in her room however, he worded it well enough that Merril didn't flicker at his comment and took it for her merely enjoying the dessert.

"It's just utterly sublime and heavenly," Merril said seductively lost in the delectable and enticing charm of the Spiced Apple Cake.

Dyrac chortled, "Quite," came his reply.

As Merril finished the last morsel of exquisiteness she let out a dismayed sigh.

"What's the matter?" asked Dyrac.

"Nothing really," replied Merril, "I'd have just loved a few more mouthfuls." She laughed.

"We can retire to the study and enjoy a small brandy whilst allowing our stomachs to settle? I've an excellent Remy Martin Louis XIII cognac you are welcome to indulge in with me?"

"I shouldn't Dyrac, I've had plenty of wine already and I should really be getting back to my room."

Dyrac nervously changed tact from politely asking Merril to join him to being more insistent in his tone, knowing that he needed to give Kurt plenty of time to finish his job for the evening.

"I insist Merril, now come."

"Yes Dyrac" replied Merril submissively.

Kurt placed the bag back into the hidden compartment of the Quality Street tin in Merril's room carefully making sure it clicked back into place securely and that her sketches were returned as he found them.

Standing back he examined the scene in front of him trying his hardest to recall how he found it in the first place. "I didn't realise I'd be having to the put anything back," he said out loud to himself.

"Seems fine," he gave himself a metaphoric pat on the back and left Merril's room and sauntered off with a pleased with himself gait and made his way back out of Wode House. He hadn't brought the pick-up as he knew it would make too much noise and Merril had no doubt got that particular sound securely locked into her mind. He huffed a little as he realised it would be a long walk back into town.

Just as he was leaving the gates of Wode House he stopped wide eyed in his tracks? He hadn't put the pencil on Merril's dresser back correctly. She was bound to notice but there was no time now to return and fix the position. He had no choice but to hope that Merril didn't notice. He knew in his gut though that Merril would absolutely notice and that he had messed up!

Chapter 14

Merril returned her empty, elaborately cut crystal brandy snifter to the side table next to her chair in the study. "Thank you for a lovely evening Dyrac however, I feel that the evening has now drawn to a conclusion for me and with your permission I would like to retire to my quarters?" she asked.

"Certainly Merril and thank you, it's been my pleasure. May I also extend my thanks for your continued service? I know of no other person who is as loyal to me as you," he replied with a cutting and trenchant tone.

Merril looked bemused but didn't alert Dyrac to her acknowledgement of the tone. She simply smiled and replied "The pleasure has been all mine Dyrac, I aim to please you and know that whilst our relationship extends beyond my service as housekeeper and maid on occasion" referring to her donorship, "I know that the loyalty between us is mutual and my trust in you is complete," she replied with prevarication raising herself from her chair.

"Oh and Merril?"

"Yes Dyrac?"

"Nice shoes!"

Merril's cheeks flushed and she looked to her feet. Her Docs were exposed. "You said to dress comfortably," she smiled "Goodnight Dyrac."

Merril left the study and was heading back to her room when she felt compelled to go to the kitchen and speak to Lauren.

"Lauren? Are you still here?" she said walking into the kitchen.

"In here," came the reply from the larder "I'm just putting some things away."

"Lauren, I just wanted to apologise for earlier, please don't feel I was belittling you. Dyrac just isn't used to such formality with the curtseying and..."

"No need to apologise. I work the same way as I do in all my houses. When I was learning the trade it was instilled into me and I haven't quite shaken the habit."

"Thank you," Merril said.

"Merril, there was a man here earlier walking around the grounds. I initially thought he was the grounds man but thought I should mention it as I don't know who Dyrac has in service here other than yourself. It was probably nothing but as it was dark out I thought best to mention it. I've instructions on how to lock up but as I won't be here after today well, just know I noticed."

"Oh that's quite alright Lauren; it was probably Yorick the gates man." Merril lied quickly on her feet trying not to let any concern reveal itself on her face. Quite why she felt compelled to lie so earnestly was beyond her at the moment but her instincts told her Dyrac was hiding something and she had a somewhat duty to protect Dyrac and any business that he may have at Wode House.

Indeed there was no Yorick and Merril knew that no-one else should be within the grounds. She also knew she didn't want Lauren to go gossiping to her associates and had every faith she would have no idea that Yorick was in fact a dead court jester from

William Shakespeare's Hamlet and that, despite the famed phrase whilst Hamlet was holding Yorick's skull 'Let me see. Alas, poor Yorick! I knew him, Horatio, a fellow of infinite jest, of the....

Lauren broke Merril's thoughts "if that will be all Merril I must get on?"

"Sorry Lauren, thank you for the delicious meal, you've been outstanding and admirable. I will be sure that my reference back to the agency states so."

"Why thank you," Lauren responded with gratitude.

Merril turned and made her way back to her room wondering; who was the man that Lauren had seen earlier this evening and, why were they in the grounds of Wode House?

She entered her room shortly after midnight and leant against the door as it closed behind her. Her gaze was immediately caught by something that wasn't right. She shot a look to her dresser. *The pencil, my pencil had moved! Someone has been in here. The mysterious man maybe? What was he doing in here and what did he find?*

Merril paced around her room noting where everything was positioned. Nothing else was out of place then she looked back to her dresser, the pencil was next to the tin. Her eyes widened and her pupils dilated.

"My tin!" she exclaimed.

She tore off the tin lid and flung her sketches on the dresser she let out a huge sigh of relief as she felt the secret compartment was still sealed. "Well whoever it was, at least they never found it." She said out loud.

Chapter 15

It was Wednesday morning before Merril realised that the tin had been tampered with. She was readying herself for the working day ahead when she knocked the tin off the dresser spilling its contents on the floor, including the false bottom and the Karamabit in the velvet bag. She must've knocked that old tin around a million times before but never had everything fallen out. *The bottom must've been loose and, with the weight of the Karamabit moving, the lid came off?* In all the years Merril had used that tin the false bottom inside had never accidentally come loose of its own accord. *I knew something was wrong but couldn't put my finger on it*, she thought.

"But that means...," she stopped herself from talking out loud further but her mind carried on her words, *that somebody found what was inside.*

She fumbled through the contents on the floor picking up the velvet bag. It hadn't been fastened back as she always left it. There was no doubt now in Merril's mind that someone had definitely found it.

She gathered up the remaining contents, rough sketches and notations and carefully put everything back as it should be. She carefully tied the cord of the bag the same way she always did, fixed the bottom back into place correctly, then filled the tin with its usual pieces and firmly closed the lid. She decided to test herself and dropped the tin to the floor. Nothing happened, all the contents remained secure and safe within.

"I knew it!" she exclaimed out loudly.

She put the tin back on the dresser and left her room double checking she had locked it before setting off for her mornings duties.

Merril was cutting some freshly picked flowers from the grounds and was in the middle of assembling them in a cut crystal vase for the hallway when the telephone rang, reverberating around the empty hallways. Merril removed her green apron, which was worn specifically for when she was flower arranging, and placed it over the back of one of the kitchen chairs. She dusted herself down and walked into the hallway.

There was no urgency in her walk to answer the call she merely took each stride casually and then, lifting the receiver cordially offered the caller her usual salutation.

"Wode House, please state your name and nature of your business."

"Blackshot," Merril's eyes widened, "Cornelius Blackshot, this is a personal call for Dyrac Gideon. If you could be so kind as to announce to the master of the house that I am holding on to the other end of the line."

"Yes, Mr Blackshot, right away." Merril gulped as she spoke, her mouth was dry and she desperately wanted to push further on the reason for his call but thought better of it right now.

Merril walked to the study and knocked.

"Who is it Merril, can't you tell them the usual I'm in a meeting excuse?"

"Sir, sorry Dyrac, a Mr Cornelius Blackshot is on the telephone and said he needed to speak to you regarding a personal matter?"

Dyrac's posture immediately changed as he sat bolt upright in his desk chair. "I'll pick up in here Merril, please return to the hallway and return the receiver back in to its cradle. Do not disturb me until I have rung the service bell. Understand?"

"Yes Dyrac," came the reply. But Merril didn't understand and she so wanted to eaves drop on the call but knew the risks were too high. She thought about making a run for it after placing the receiver down and legging it out of the side entrance, down the side of Wode House past the sundial, across the bridge and onto the island, through the hole behind the stone plaque in the folly....*It's just not worth it* she thought. By the time she made it through all that and down the secret passage the call could be over and then she'd have the problem of getting back in time for Dyrac signalling service was back in force.

Merril took a deep breath as she picked up the receiver, introduced that Dyrac would now take the call and waited for Dyrac to say "Good morning Cornelius, it's been too long..." before returning it to its cradle.

"Right Cornelius, that click means we are clear to talk and will remain uninterrupted. I take it you received my correspondence?" said Dyrac leaning forward onto his elbows on his desk. "We've much to discuss old friend and I'm afraid to say that favour you owed me, well, I need to call it in."

Merril tried to hear through the study door without pressing her face against the actual door itself so as not to cause it to rattle against the latch. She couldn't

104

hear a thing. She sighed and decided to get back to the flower arranging, if Dyrac became suspicious that she was faltering in her duties he may ask questions and she didn't want to betray his trust, not yet anyway.

Dyrac spoke continuously for nine minutes with Cornelius offering the occasional "uh-huh" and "yes" and the usual verbal nods you'd expect in a one way conversation.

"...and then Kurt, the grocery chap who I hired a few weeks ago..." he continued, "...went and found something which has corroborated my suspicion that she was withholding something. I mean, I was as surprised as Kurt when he showed me the contents of bag he found hidden in her room. It was a Karamabit Cornelius, just like mine. I mean, when I first wrote to you I was suspicious sure, but I literally didn't know what she was hiding, I thought maybe she was stealing from me and I was going to get you over here to interrogate her for me and push her to her limits, whilst we both maybe benefited from a hit at the same time but this has thrown me off, what does it mean? Why would she have the same Karamabit as me? I need your help. Please say you'll come?"

"You quite finished Drack?" Cornelius spoke addressing Dyrac with the nickname Cornelius gave him all those years ago.

"I wish you wouldn't call me that Cornelius but yes, I've finished"

"I mean you sure do witter on like an old housewife Drack," Cornelius snorted a laugh at his use of the hated nickname again, "I mean that's a lot of information to process and from your letter indicating the favour was to be a simple scare to oust a petty thief has now escalated somewhat. I mean initially I was looking at maybe two days away at your place with a quick resolution for all, albeit it may have required you to hire in new service going forward. But now, now we're looking at a longer stay and I won't want that bloody shit hole room you housed me in last time. I want that Chamber four."

"Chamber four?" Dyrac asked.

"You know very well which chamber I'm referring to Drack! Your new moon room, remember?"

"Yes Cornelius I remember, ok, so you'll come?"

"I'll come on one more condition, you need to gather together as much information you can on this Kurt and of course Merril. Note down any suspicion you have, even if you think it too trivial or elaborate. Oh and make sure you've plenty of that Johnnie Walker, the Blue Label King George V Edition in. Ever since I tried it during my last visit I've become quite partial."

"Understood Cornelius. You still practice?"

"Yes I do, why?"

"I've a chapel set up now in the cellar. I've something I keep down there I'm going to need to show you but I can't discuss it over the telephone, comprendre?"

"Je comprends," came the reply.

"Good. How long before you arrive?"

"Well, I've to tidy up here first then I'll head straight to you. Should be with you sometime Saturday if that suits?

"Suits just fine and, Cornelius?"

"Drack?"

"Jesus," Dyrac sighed, "thank you."

"Say nothing of it." Cornelius hung up and Dyrac was left listening to the constant dull tone indicating that the conversation was over.

"And for now I wait," he uttered to himself.

Merril heard the service bell ring. It had been forty minutes since she took the call from Cornelius Blackshot. Merril knew that she needed to be ready should Dyrac call on her but for now she carried on with her work.

Within minutes the service bell rang again. Merril stopped in her tracks and felt a cold shiver tickle her spine. She shook it off and headed for the study.

"You called?" she announced opening the door to the study.

"Merril, I've a guest coming to stay with us for a little while. Can you make sure Chamber four is ready for Mr Cornelius Blackshot. He is due to arrive on Saturday."

"I'm sorry Dyrac, did you say Chamber four it's just we..."

"Chamber four Merril," he said bluntly.

"Yes Dyrac."

"Oh and Merril, make sure that you speak to Byron at Bryson & Son's he is going to need to make contact with the distillery for a special order. I'm going to need four bottles of the Johnnie Walker, the Blue Label King George V Edition to come in with Saturday's delivery. Tell Byron that no matter the cost to make it happen."

"Yes Dyrac. Anything else."

"Lunch would be good?"

"But it's barely past ten o'clock Dyrac."

"Well, in that case brunch or whatever it is they call it these days. I'm famished."

"Certainly Dyrac. Tea?"

"Earl Grey Merril, no, make it Ceylon."

"As you ask."

"Merril, could you also ask Byron if we can keep Kurt back a half hour extra on Saturday's delivery I need to speak to him."

"Yes Dyrac. I'll get on with your brunch." Merril looked puzzled. Why would she need to see Kurt again. She decided she was going to apprehend Kurt this Saturday and would press him for more information not taking no for an answer this time. She gave a little, one sided wicked smile as she closed the study door.

Chapter 16

Byron had just hung up the telephone and turned to Bradley "Go find Kurt will you son?"

"Sure thing Da," he replied.

Byron was rubbing his forehead massaging his right temple as he thought how best to approach the distillery with Dyrac's request. I mean four bottles, in the timescale he'd given. He'd have to have a private courier bring it all the way down from Kilmarnock. This was going to cost Dyrac a pretty penny and on this occasion Byron decided to add a little extra to the bill for himself for going the extra mile.

"You summoned?" Kurt flamboyantly announced waving his arms in a display indicating the magnificence of his arrival.

"You great fool. I've just had a conversation with that housekeeper at Wode House, Myrtle or whatever her name is."

"Merril," Kurt corrected him.

"That's the one," Byron replied pointing at Kurt, "anyway, she has an extra order for Saturday but also Mr Gideon has asked if you can give him an extra half hour during the delivery. Any problem for you?"

"No boss," he replied solemnly.

"Why so glum then?"

"It's nothing. Go on."

"There's nothing to go on with Kurt, just that and the extra delivery of four bottles of that whisky he favours. Well, that'll be all. Back to it."

"Yes boss," he said saluting Byron as he walked back through the doors to the shop front.

Kurt was pacing behind the counter of the shop front when Bradley, who was restocking tinned soup, called over to him "Hey Kurt, sup?"

"Nothing's up. Why do you ask?

"Well you've been wearing the floor out behind there for the last ten minutes and you haven't made any witty comment about me stacking shelves."

"Well, if you choose to have a day job working for your Dad stacking shelves so be it," replied Kurt.

"Ahh funny man, you're hilarious. You know full well I hate working here but I don't have a choice."

"We all have a choice Bradders. It's our choices that define us. We can never obtain peace in the outer world until we make peace with ourselves," said Kurt in a sarcastic and philosophical tone.

"Alright, who are you the Dalai Lama?"

"That's exactly right. That's who said it," a shocked Kurt acknowledged.

"Whatever, was just showing some concern bro."

"Seriously though Bradders, I'm grand. Nothing can get to the mighty Kurton," replied Kurt.

"Wow, Kurton, you never use your full name. Well, here if you want to offload anytime."

"Cheers Bradders. I'm clocking out now, half a day is quite enough for me. I'll see you Saturday."

"Yeah, Saturday, yeah," Bradley replied not looking up from the shelf in front of him.

Kurt left Bryson & Sons and drove home whilst static ridden music blared from the worn out stereo in the pick-up.

When he arrived home Kurt kicked off his work boots

before the front door had closed. He headed straight to the kitchen and opened the fridge. He looked at the contents and closed the fridge having not taken anything out, a habit he'd had since he was a boy. He took out a shave of bread from the thick, white sliced loaf sitting in the bread bin and spread a thick smattering of brown sauce across the top with his finger. He licked clean his finger of the remaining sauce and bit a chunk out of the bread.

He jumped over the back of the sofa landing in a lounging position and grabbed the remote with his free hand and flicked on the TV. The news was on and the newsreader was presenting a story of untold chaos and misery at some place in the world. It was always the same thought Kurt. He flicked through the channels annoying himself at the amount of rubbish TV broadcast nowadays. He stopped and flicked back two channels after spotting a nature documentary, he recognised the familiar tone of Sir David Attenborough and thought anything with that guy narrating was good enough for him and his brown sauce open sandwich.

Two hours later Kurt jolted himself awake having fallen asleep exhausted from his hard day's work. He laughed to himself as he knew he'd never done a hard day's work in all his life. He wiped his Bryson & Sons embroidered polo shirt after spotting a dollop of brown sauce just beneath the three buttons leading to the neckline and smudged it making it worse. "Ahh shit!" he exclaimed out loud, "I'll definitely have to put a load in the washer now," he scolded himself as he had a particular detest laundry. "Great!" he bellowed to nobody.

He hauled off his polo shirt and peeled himself from the sofa. He walked over to the washing machine in the kitchen and flung it in. He grabbed two liquid tablets, those ones that you desperately want to squash to bursting every time you reach for one, and threw them in too. He turned the machine to the quick wash setting and headed straight back to the sofa, immediately nestling back into the Kurt shaped mould that had formed in the cushions. "Ahhhhh," he sighed. *Now, let's see what's on.*

Kurt's attention was immediately drawn to a show on the History Channel, and he sat up rubbed his eyes and focussed. It was something he wouldn't usually watch as he considered anything to do with history dull and boring and was absolutely not his cup of tea but he watched with intent. The broadcaster was holding something he'd seen only a few days earlier. He was talking about some West Sumatran traditions and lifestyle and was describing the use of the claw like dagger in his hand. "...is a Karamabit" came the voice from the TV.

"A Karamabit?" Kurt replied.

"The Karamabit, according to folklore, was inspired by the claws of the tiger and was originally an agricultural implement designed to rake roots, gather threshing and plant rice."

Kurt watched the rest of the program with deep concentration. As the credits rolled he spoke out loud, "why the hell would Merril have a Karamabit?"

Kurt sat back in the sofa. His imagination was running away with himself. *Maybe she has it for self defence. No, she'd had a girlier knife surely? Maybe she was given it as a gift, but then why would she hide it away? Maybe Merril was some kind of secret assassin, yeah maybe, she kept it as a memento from her last kill and that she felt so bereft after that last kill she couldn't take on anymore hits and entered a life of service as a form of punishment to herself. Yeah that's more like it, I mean who would choose to work in that house for Dyrac Gideon out of their own free will.* Kurt laughed at his own ridiculous deductions, *or it could just be a souvenir Kurt.* One thing was for sure he felt compelled to know why Merril had the Karamabit dagger but for now, he wasn't quite sure how he was going to find out.

Chapter 17

Dusk had settled in for the evening and Merril had finished her main duties for the day, all that was left was to prepare Chamber four for the mysterious Cornelius Blackshot. There was no time known for his arrival tomorrow but Merril wanted to be ready this evening just in case he turned up in time for breakfast. There was more to do this Saturday than usual, especially with Wode House expecting a guest so Merril wanted everything to be set.

Chamber four didn't need much preparation but she was meticulous in the finer detail and would even go around the room inspecting her own work with a white cotton glove, getting in all the nooks and crannies to make sure there was no sign of dust anywhere. It was a hard job to maintain given the age of the property and the amount of debris that settled each night as the house creaked and groaned to rest.

The pleats in the drop of the curtains had to be equal and the placement of ornamental items precise. Soft furnishings had a particular way they had to be placed. Cushions always plump and zip facing downwards and Chamber four was not short on cushions. The silks and satins and velvets on the bed had to be carefully brushed in the same direction with a soft brush, like the type you'd use to brush a baby's hair. She made sure the candelabra on the dresser had seven new candles in place, the hurricane candle was replaced despite being used only once, she couldn't bear to see the burnt wick poking out of the top of the wide cylindrical wax column.

There was a particular painting that hung on the wall above the dresser. It stood 6 feet tall and 4 feet wide and was a beautiful oil painting by an unknown artist. The scene was familiar, it was of the folly on the island but there were no trees surrounding it, just the folly itself standing alone amidst a lake with the morning mist rising from it. Merril climbed the wooden step ladder she brought up from the housekeeping room under the stairs and, once she reached the 7th rung she stopped and concentrated on the window of the folly. Using a sable bristled paintbrush she carefully brushed the folly window and using a cotton bud she swabbed her mouth of saliva. This was an old trick she picked up as saliva contained enough enzymes to break down dirt and grime, but not so much that it would damage the painting. There used to be an old wives tale about how you could use bread or potatoes to clean an oil painting but this was not a good idea given the estimated value of the painting as they can leave behind a residue damaging the painting for good.

Once her saliva had been wiped away she blew against the window and instead of dust particles blowing back towards her off the painting they disappeared. Merril stepped down the steps of the ladder, looked up at the picture and smiled.

In her housekeeping trolley she had all the usual items you'd expect for general cleaning but additional items she liked to keep included a spirit level, to ensure that furnishings, mirrors and pictures were balanced; a small and thin fine bristled brush, to catch any dust that would collate in grooves on the furniture and ornaments; a razor blade to scrape away any difficult residue that appeared on windows from time to time (oh the thought of using it set her teeth on edge as she could hear the squeal of the blade pulling at the glass); and then there was a small can of WD-40, that stuff got rid of most things and was Merril's secret weapon.

Merril took a final glance around the room before re-inspecting every inch. "Perfect," she said.

She retrieved a spray bottle from her trolley and spritzed the room with her own room atomiser. It was made from witch hazel, lavender oil and water. She indulged in the familiar and calming floral scent of the lavender which would last for a few days.

"Chamber four all ready for you Mr Blackshot, I look forward to making your acquaintance," she said to the empty room.

She curtseyed, chuckling to herself, collected all her housekeeping paraphernalia and bowed as she backed out of the room.

"Dyrac!" Merril almost backed straight into Dyrac as she was leaving Chamber four. "Sir, I'm so sorry I didn't see..."

"Well you were walking backwards Merril so I doubt you'd have seen anything."

"Yes, well, sorry. I'm just finishing up here and will put everything away," she was looking at the ladders and trolley as she addressed Dyrac.

"That's quite alright Merril, I was coming to find you to inform you that Cornelius, I mean Mr Blackshot has sent word to say that he will be arriving at noon tomorrow. As such please can lunch be served promptly at one o'clock?"

"Yes Dyrac, and do you have any particular

request? Do I need to be aware of any dietary requirements for Mr Blackshot?"

"No request Merril and no fuss, that man literally would eat the heart of his own brother." Dyrac smirked.

"Oohhh – kkaaaay," Merril replied in a long and drawn out, that's a little bit twisted, kind of way.

"Obviously I don't mean literally Merril," Dyrac quickly noting the look in Merril's eyes. "What I mean to say is that he isn't fussy. Just serve one of your usual splendid meals and all will be quite well."

"Yes Dyrac," Merril sounded reassured, albeit still a little uneasy.

"Oh, Merril, don't forget to send Kurt to me once he has finished packing away tomorrow's delivery. As soon as he is done send him to the study with one of those bottles of JW I ordered."

"Certainly, will that be all for the evening?"

"That will be all my dear, chin chin." With that Dyrac left Merril in the hallway and retired to his quarters.

Merril strapped the ladders to the side of the housekeeping trolley and headed towards the stairs. The trolley fit perfectly in the old dumb waiter but the ladders; she'd have to carry those down the stairs herself. She loaded the dumb waiter and slid the door closed pressing a button which activated the pulley mechanism. She heard it trundle downwards and then made her way, with the ladders, down the stairs.

In the hallway, at the back of the stairs she opened the dumb waiter; it had stopped a little too early and hadn't quite reached the bottom. Merril had to jimmy it to get it to come all the way down so she could get to the trolley to remove it.

"This god dam ancient fossil needs to be rid of," she said "I mean I have to work with this antiquated system and it would be just as easy to install a new one but nooooo," hanging on to the O, "Dyrac insists on keeping all that he can at Wode House as it was when it was first built. Well, that's all very well Dyrac but you don't have to go through the daily frustrations with this infernal contraption. Are you the one who has to constantly maintain all that goes wrong in this gargantuan house? No! It's me, Merril," Merril had a good old moan out loud conversing only with herself and the overwhelming silence that consumed the great hall.

Eventually the pulley gave way and the dumb waiter rested in its correct place. "Finally!" Merril scolded it. She returned everything back to the housekeeping cupboard and closing the door she said "And that is me for the day."

Looking around the hall she considered a life outside the grandeur of Wode House and wondered whether a simpler life was for her. She wondered what the town and townsfolk were like. Other than Kurt and Byron Bryson her knowledge of outsiders had been limited over the last fifteen years and for the first time during her service Merril felt trapped, claustrophobic even despite the vastness Wode House offered. She realised in that moment that she was never really in control of neither her own mind nor her own future. But in a snap that thought rapidly changed and Merril gave away a secret smile. "But that is all going to change soon isn't it Merril?"

She hummed as she walked back to her room. At

first there was no order to her humming but she soon hummed a tune her mother once taught her, Greensleeves. She remembered her mother would sing along whilst playing the harp. *Funny, I've never remembered that before* she thought. The melody stayed with her long into the night, falling asleep the song replayed on repeat around her head.

Chapter 18

BRRrriinnGG, BRRrriinnGG, BRRrriinnGG.

Merril reached for her alarm clock, a mechanical clock with two bells on the top and a hammer banging each bell in turn, and pressed the stopper on the top to deactivate the ringing. She glanced at the clock, it was 4:30am and an unusually early start for her. She rubbed the sleep from her eyes and threw the blankets off her noting a slight chill in the air.

She was up and ready and in the kitchen by 5:00am. She was multi-tasking preparing breakfast and lunch. At the same time she thought back to the world beyond Wode House. Wode House was as far away from the modern world as you could get. There was no television or radio, there was a gramophone in the great hall but that was used only once during Merril's service. She had no form of music other than when she sang or hummed to herself and the natural birdsong she adored of a morning.

Wode House was stuck in a time forgotten. She really enjoyed the atmospheric ambience of the house but longed to know what the outside world had to offer. She came to Wode House straight from another private house, a choice that she made as a way to get into Wode House. Before that she was boarded at a finishing school for ladies, boarding school itself and then beyond that her memory fails her.

Occasionally she'd ask Kurt to leave his radio on in the pick-up whilst he was doing his deliveries but it was never loud enough that she could catch the lyrics to any songs, nor fathom the mutterings of the radio show's presenter. And Kurt wasn't usually around long enough for it to last and, there was the fact it would drain his battery.

The service bell indicated it was now 6:00am and that Dyrac had risen from his sleep. "All hands on deck Merril," she said to herself.

Boiling on the stove was a copper saucepan with just water and a splash of white wine vinegar. She cracked in two eggs separately, carefully making sure that they didn't burst or attach to each other. Minutes later she was retrieving them from the pan and sinking them into a bowl of iced water. Setting it to one side she took a plate from the Aga Oven which was never turned off and taking three thin Cumberland sausages from the gas oven she laid them out parallel to each other on the warm plate. She grilled a short vine of cherry tomatoes and placed these across the sausages drizzling a little olive oil and balsamic vinegar on top. She dropped the eggs back in the water for twenty seconds before adding these to the plate.

She took the breakfast plate and put it on the silver serving tray covering it with a solid silver cloche (a silver dome shaped food cover). To the side was a small silver toast rack housing two piece of wholemeal toast, a pot of the usual Earl Grey and, a small carafe of apple juice with a clean glass tumbler upside down on a small doily. She covered the whole tray with a second, yet enormous cloche.

She picked up the breakfast tray and made her way to Dyrac's study where he would be taking breakfast.

Merril reached the study and the door was ajar. She peered in before calling out "Good morning Dyrac, breakfast is served."

No reply came. Merril pushed the door slightly with her foot. "Dyrac?" she called out, "are you there?"

"Yes I'm here Merril," Dyrac's voice seemed distant but it was definitely coming from the study. "Come in Merril put breakfast on my table will you?" he said referring to the table near the fireplace.

"As you wish Dyrac," she looked puzzled as she entered and couldn't see Dyrac at all. "Sir?"

"Dyrac if you will Merril!"

"Dyrac? Where are you?"

Dyrac appeared from behind his desk. "I've been looking for something, thought I'd dropped it back here Merril."

"Anything I can help look for?" she asked.

"Never you mind yourself Merril; I've got it all in hand."

"Yes Dyrac, if you'd call when you're finished I'd like to get back as I'm preparing lunch."

"Yes, yes," came the reply.

Dyrac got to his feet and walked over to his breakfast. He removed the giant cloche and dropped it onto the hearth so as not to scorch the carpet. He devoured his breakfast so quickly he instantly gave himself heartburn and, the hiccups.

"Dam hic, blast hic" he said.

He was holding his breath turning purple trying to rid himself of the hiccups when, out of the corner of his eye, something caught his attention. He puffed out all the air he had captured in his lungs and walked over to the desk. Just against the side pedestal he spotted a misshapen paperclip on the floor deep in the pile of the carpet.

"I knew it!" he shouted as he picked up the paperclip.

Merril heard the service bell ring informing her that Dyrac had finished his breakfast. As she reached the study door she stopped *the paperclip?* She remembered something from the day she went into his study via the secret passage way. She didn't recall taking the paperclip with her. Had she dropped it in her haste to leave before Dyrac found her? *It was too late now* she thought.

She knocked on the door.

"Enter," came Dyrac's voice, "it's on the table Merril, mind the cloche it'll be hot I left it on the hearth."

Merril's hands over the years had become accustomed to the heat; it was as though an asbestos barrier had formed on her skin. She picked up the cloche without flinching at how hot the metal had become and placed it over the tray.

"Don't forget to send Kurt in when he's finished with the delivery please," Dyrac spoke politely.

"Of course Dyrac, thank you," said Merril.

When Merril returned to the kitchen she heard the familiar sound of Kurt's pick-up pull up outside.

"Morning beautiful Merry. All well?" asked Kurt.

"Morning Kurt, I'm fine thank you for asking. Can you put the delivery away as quick as possible? Dyrac is waiting for you in the study."

"What, no breakfast today?"

"I'm afraid not Kurt, Dyrac was insistent that you meet with him as soon as you had finished packing the delivery away."

"Right you are sunshine."

Kurt spent the next twenty minutes packing away the delivery trying to put off the inevitable. He looked at Merril as he was putting away the extra whisky quota holding one of the bottles in his hands and said "Hey Merry, why don't we sack this off and just get slaughtered?"

Merril sniggered, "I'm not sure that is quite becoming Kurt. And anyway, it's not worth the wrath."

"Spoilsport," he joked.

"If you're finished can you head over to the study and, if it's ok with you can you stop off and see me before you go?"

"Sure thing lady."

Kurt got to the study hoping that Dyrac would be ready with his final payment his clenched fist hadn't even made impact with the door to knock before Dyrac's voice echoed through the door.

"Come straight in Kurt."

Kurt opened the study door, "morning Mr Gideon, I trust all is well?"

"Kurt, please take a seat albeit this particular meeting will be relatively brief. First, this is yours," Dyrac handed Kurt a brown envelope, "I can assure you it's all there," he continued.

"Thank you Mr Gideon," Kurt said taking the

envelope and putting it in his lap.

"Now, Kurt, I want to invite you over for dinner this evening, I hope that the late notice won't be a problem and that you will extend your acceptance."

"Err sir?"

"Dinner Kurt, it's quite a simple concept, you turn up, you eat, you drink, and you leave?"

"Yes but..."

"But what? Kurt listen, as a way of my thanks for your loyalty of late and for undertaking such a difficult task I'd like to offer you dinner, here," Dyrac said waving his arms in the air presenting the room to him, "at Wode House."

"Why sir, thank you but payment is enough."

"Nonsense Kurt, how often do you get to eat in such a refined setting? I can assure you, Merril's meals are just as delicious as her breakfasts."

"Ok?" Kurt accepted, nodding dubiously.

"Excellent. Now Kurt, when it comes to dinner I do expect a certain standard of dress and I imagine that your wardrobe does not contain a tuxedo? Black tie, white shirt, suit?"

"Correct sir."

"Marvellous well in that case here," Dyrac handed over another envelope.

"What's this?"

"Well you will need to be fitted and fitted properly Kurt. Inside that envelope are the details of a fine tailor in town, he has been given the heads up and knows you will be there later this morning. You'll also find ample payment to meet his bill and, well, if there is anything leftover please keep it as a, shall we say, bonus."

"I don't know what to say," Kurt was confused and was struggling to try and process all the information Dyrac was giving him.

"Say nothing dear boy. Nothing at all. Just accept the gift, as you have the invitation to dinner and be back here at Wode House for 7:00pm. Oh and the front door Kurt, use the front door when you come back tonight."

"Yes sir," Kurt got up and nodded at Dyrac and shook his hand before leaving looking dumbfounded.

As Kurt left Dyrac retrieved a handkerchief from his jacket pocket and wiped down his right hand that had moments before shaking Kurt's.

"You've what!" Merril shrilled, coughing to try to regain her normal voice "You've what?" she repeated in a much calmer tone.

"Invited to dinner, tonight! Listen Merril, I know you wanted to speak but I've got to see this tailor Dyrac is sending me to and....well...I've got to go."

"Kurt wait," Merril replied as Kurt walked straight out of the side entrance in a sort of hypnotised state and got in his pick-up. "KURT!" she shouted.

"I'll see you later Merry," and with that, and still in a daze, Kurt left Wode House knowing he'd be returning later that same day.

Merril slammed her fist into the kitchen table. "What the hell was going on and why was Kurt being invited for dinner along with Mr Bigshot," she spat the words out purposefully changing Cornelius Blackshots surname.

Chapter 19

The door bell chimed precisely at 12 noon. Merril sighed, "Here we go, don that smile of yours and remember be charming," she said to herself "And, stop talking to yourself, you're going crazy," she added.

Merril pulled the large front door open, "Mr Cornelius Blackshot I presume?"

"You presume correctly my dear. And you, you must be Merril," Cornelius held out his hand taking Merril's and kissed the back of her hand. Merrils eyes rolled in her head.

"This way please, may I take your coat?"

"That's quite alright I'll have Verne take it to my chamber when he's finished bringing in my personal effects," he replied.

"Verne?" asked Merril.

"Yes, my butler, did I fail to mention he would be joining me during my stay? He'll need to be housed in the staff quarters and will aide you as service whilst I am here. I assume there will be no problem?" Cornelius peered over his half moon spectacles perched on the end of his nose.

Internally Merril was furious and retorted unspoken 'No, no I didn't know your butler, Verne would be coming, if I did I'd have sorted out a room for him, as it happens, on my busiest day of the year, I'll have to fit that in to my schedule and make sure he knows the dos and don'ts of the house. I suppose I'll be made to make sure he feels welcome and have to feed him too?'

"Absolutely no problem whatsoever Mr Blackshot, I'm always prepared for the unforeseen," she replied biting her lip.

"Marvellous, Drack said you were a special one."

Oh did he indeed? having an internal conversation in her mind.

"He says too much," she replied.

"Ahh, Verne, this way old chap." Cornelius beckoned Verne like you'd expect a master commanding his dog.

"Indeed sir" came a voice from the doorway.

Merril smiled politely at Verne closing the door behind him as he stepped through the porch and into the hall.

"Now, where can I find that old friend of mine deary?"

Merril pursed her lips "Right this way. Verne would you please wait here for me to return and then I shall show you to Mr Bigshots, err, Blackshots'" she quickly corrected herself hoping no-one noticed the slip of tongue, "quarters."

"Certainly," replied Verne.

"Lead on," came Cornelius's voice and he hitched up his ebony walking cane from his left hand catching it halfway down. The top end of the cane was embellished with a solid silver lion's paw the body of the cane was plain, polished ebony with a silver ring footing was at the other end.

Merril instantly knew this was going to be a long visit and she'd needed all her wits about her to prevent her from stepping out of line. She already wanted to slap him across his face. *What a brazen and malupert man this Bigshot was*, she thought.

As Cornelius followed Merril down the hallway to the study he took in his immediate surroundings. "My dear, how long ago was it that Drack became so pretentious," he directed his question to Merril having just passed a full suit of armour tucked away in a niche in the hallway.

Merril chose not to respond as they arrived at the study. She knocked waiting for Dyrac's reply.

"Come in Merril."

"Mr Cornelius Blackshot," Merril announced standing to one side as she opened the door.

"Drack!" bellowed Cornelius.

"Dyrac!" shouted Dyrac. Both chuckled.

"Good to see you old friend," said Cornelius as he and Dyrac embraced each other with a manly hug and double shoulder pat.

"That'll be all Merril, I'll call if I need anything."

"Thank you Dyrac, I'll get on with showing Verne the ropes."

"Verne?" asked Dyrac.

"Yes, yes Verne, my Butler, stop fussing man," uttered Cornelius.

Dyrac glanced at Merril in a wide eyed apology. She raised her hand without speaking in a gesture that indicated, 'not your fault'. Dyrac smiled.

Merril headed back down the hallway kicking her shoes along the floor as she walked trying to let out her frustrations before arriving back with Verne in the hall.

"Verne, this way. I'll show you Chamber four where Cornelius will be staying in residence and then I'll need to finish lunch which is to be served at one o'clock. Once lunch has been served I'll show you to your room and give you a whistle stop tour of the grand Wode House."

"Please, could I just ask?" said Verne.

"Ask away ask away."

"What is your name?"

"Oh my, excuse me, I'm Merril," she said as she stuck out her hand in a gesture to shake Verne's.

"I'm Verne," he smiled bowing his head.

Merril looked into Verne's eyes. He was much older than her but his soul was gentle and she felt a certain warmth come over her.

"Well Verne, follow me."

They climbed the fluted stairwell onto the landing which split off to the left and right. They turned right. Chamber four was the second room along and was situated overlooking the front of Wode House. Merril opened the door allowing Verne to pass her.

"Wow, opulent." Said Verne.

"It's probably the most lavish and luxurious room in the whole house," said Merril.

"Are you happy for me to collect Mr Blackshot's belongings from downstairs and have them packed away on my own? That way you can get back to lunch and I can always find you afterwards. I'm sure it's not too difficult a place to find my bearings."

"That's quite ok Verne, I'll help you with Mr Blackshot's luggage."

"As you command."

"Oh please don't feel it's a command, we are equals here and I..."

"Merril, its fine, honestly," reassured Verne.

It took twenty minutes to relocate the inordinate amount of belongings one person "needed" for a single trip up to Chamber four.

"Does he really need all of this stuff?" huffed Merril, placing the last bag onto the floor of Chamber four.

"Every trip I swear there is more," replied Verne, "my back's had it."

They both chuckled. "Well let's get this stuff put away so we can get on with lunch," said Merril.

Chapter 20

Dyrac and Cornelius were deep in conversation in the study when they heard Merril and Verne passing by outside.

"And after lunch," Dyrac said, "we'll head to the cellar. I've got a few things to go through with you down there which will fill in some of the gaps."

"Excellent," said Cornelius, "as at the moment I've many questions however; I shall leave them until later."

"There's one other thing Cornelius," Dyrac was being more than ominous, "when it comes to disposal, we'll need to make sure our stories are set should any questions from outside the two of us crop up. Not just set but water tight."

"I concur," said Cornelius, "I've got it all in hand old friend."

Merril and Verne had all but completed lunch when Verne stopped having put the serving trays on the kitchen table. He looked at Merril "So, why did Dyrac summon Cornelius at such short notice?" he asked.

Merril didn't waiver and continued arranging the food on the plates to perfect presentation.

"I imagine they were overdue a catch up?"

"That's not it. I mean, after their conversation on the telephone Cornelius instructed me to cancel all of his appointments for the foreseeable future. He wouldn't do that for something as trivial as a catch up."

"Well then," Merril tried not to arise any suspicion in her voice, "it could be to do with an expedition Dyrac is planning." She shifted uneasily.

She was lying, and Verne knew it so he kept things as close to his chest as Merril was. "Yeah, expedition, come to think of it Cornelius did mention it briefly."

"Well there you are," Merril clapped her hands together. "Shall we serve lunch?"

"After you," Verne bowed allowing Merril to take the lead.

Dyrac and Cornelius had already made their way to the dining room and Merril and Verne followed moments later. "Lunch is served," said Merril cordially handing Dyrac his lunch whilst Verne served Cornelius.

"Why this looks impeccable," said Cornelius looking down at the plate in front of him, "Roast beef, rare just as I like it," he smiled at Dyrac, "caramelised shallots with horseradish all served on a bed of creamy mashed potato with what are these?" he asked lifting a peculiarly crispy vegetable off the top.

"Honey glazed parsnip crisps," replied Merril.

"They sound delicious and fun," said Cornelius.

Merril added a small gravy boat to the table in between them both.

"Thank you Merril, and Verne is it?" said Dyrac.

"Verne," replied Verne nodding at Dyrac.

"We'll call if we need anything, otherwise carry on as you are," said Dyrac.

"If it's ok with you Dyrac, I'll show Verne the rest of the house now?"

"That's fine Merril, be mindful to make sure he is

aware of the rules regarding certain prohibited areas," said Dyrac

"Yes Dyrac."

Merril and Verne left the dining room. "Come on Verne we'll start at the top, that way you can bring your belongings up to your quarters and then we can work our way down."

"After you Merril."

Dyrac and Cornelius didn't speak as the first few mouthfuls went down. Once the coast was clear Dyrac reignited conversation.

"So old boy, now we know we will be left alone for some time let's get into the finer detail. I'm going to be honest with you as always dear friend, this is going to become complicated."

"I'm intrigued Drack," said Cornelius stuffing a forkful of every component of his plate into his mouth, gravy oozing out of the sides of his mouth as he spoke.

"After I killed Abimilech I thought I had tied up all those loose ends with the Gideon estate. I was wrong."

Cornelius was captivated immediately, listening intently and hung onto every word Dyrac spoke. It was as though he was recording it all for review at a later time. He didn't want to miss a thing. He pressed Dyrac to continue with a wave of his next fork full of food.

"...after I brought his body here," continued Dyrac.

Cornelius interrupted him, "...you brought his body here? Are you insane man? I thought you had disposed of him after I gave you careful instructions of what to do?"

"I know, I know but, well, I just couldn't. Despite all he did to me, after all he did do, I couldn't do that to him!"

"But you could kill him?" quizzed Cornelius.

"He deserved to die!" Dyrac felt a pang of anger, "I mean to say," softening as he continued, "he deserved to die for what he did and how he changed my life forever in that way but I couldn't just dissolve him into nothing, he had a soul."

"He was never a living soul Dyrac, that's my point."

"Anyway, what's done is done."

Cornelius didn't eat another mouthful, despite how his taste buds danced as the beef melted away on his tongue, how his senses sang with the aromatic song from the marinade glaze that was the gravy. He was fixated on Dyrac and the information that he was spilling.

"Then when I read the will I knew. I knew from the moment, she couldn't be dead like Abimilech led me to believe all those years ago. How could she be dead? Abimilech wrote his will after the date Idysha supposedly passed away. And the nerve of the man to refer to her as his "sole survivor," what am I? Who am I? I've questioned everything since then and it made me paranoid but, I now believe my paranoia has some weight behind it. Listen to this..." Dyrac continued.

"You're in far more trouble than I anticipated Dyrac."

Dyrac noticed that was twice in a row Cornelius had called him Dyrac.

"If you think all that I've told you was insane, wait until you see what I've got to show you downstairs."

"No time like the present, those two will be sometime yet right? So, why don't we get on with it?" asked Cornelius hopping to his feet and clicking his heels together.

"Ok but first understand, there's no going back once you've seen, once you know."

"I've seen it all Dyrac, there's nothing you can show me that will be any worse from the atrocities, the demise, the misery I've seen before."

"Well, hold on to that because I guarantee Cornelius, you've not seen this!" exclaimed Dyrac.

And with that they both headed to the cellar.

Chapter 21

"After you," Dyrac gesticulated to Cornelius with his arm outstretched, pulling the light cord with his free hand, "I'll meet you at the bottom of the stairs, I'm locking us in to avoid any unfortunate interruption."

Cornelius headed down the stairwell, there was something about the cellar that unsettled even his nerves which, was no mean feat given his reputation and the roles he had played in the torture and dismemberment of others lives.

"Follow me, if you will," Dyrac stirred a slight jolt in Cornelius, "right this way, I want you to see the will first. It's in the chapel."

"The chapel? Why is it in there?" replied Cornelius.

"I keep it in the book."

"The book!"

"Yes, the book! Come on Cornelius I've much to show, and discuss with you, before we both get ready for dinner and our additional guest."

"Oh yes, Kurt is it?"

"That's right but more about him and his role later."

"I'll follow you then?" Cornelius said gesturing with a salute to Dyrac to lead the way.

"It's in here," said Dyrac.

They moved to the chapel and Cornelius put on the light inside, this was not an occasion for the lighting of the candles.

"Bless Cerebrus and Hades himself, you've done quite a job in here," said Cornelius.

Dyrac let out a little snigger. "I'm pleased with it but I don't practice as much as I once did."

"Well, it certainly is fit for purpose. And the chalice? Is that the same..."

Dyrac cut him short, "the very same one he used."

"And you've the gall to still..."

"...the gall to still," smiled Dyrac. "I'll show you how much I've got left, the bottle is easily sealed so still looks like it hasn't been opened but it's a thick lining of dust as I've not used it since..." he stopped himself from continuing.

"Understood," came the reply from Cornelius.

Dyrac took the key attached to the small chain from the pocket in his waistcoat and lifted the altar cloth. He removed the small casket and used the same key to open that. Retrieving the large iron key he moved over to the book.

"I haven't seen this book in almost fifty years," said Cornelius.

Dyrac didn't reply he simply opened the book and flicked through the pages until he found the envelope containing Abimilech's will. He handed it to Cornelius, "read for yourself what that insect bequeathed and to who."

Cornelius read out loud, "In the name of....blah, blah, blah...was it really that long ago?"

"Cornelius please, read on," said Dyrac.

"Sorry Drack. Blah, blah, blah I gyve and bequeath to my sole survivor and daughter, Idysha Sarah Gideon, shit Drack, Idysha could still be alive? She's out there somewhere? I mean I know you said so in the study but reading it from that man's own hand. I thought you must've just misread it or, maybe, well I don't know but here it is. Black and white, or should I say musty gray and tea stained yellow," he tried to lighten the mood commenting on the age of the document hoping he'd draw a smile from the concern showing on Dyrac's face. "I've noted the page you've saved the will in. Quite appropriate," added Cornelius tracing his fingers over the wording of the incantation.

Dyrac snatched the will from Cornelius's hand and put it back in the envelope and back into the book snapping it closed causing Cornelius to cough as dust hit the back of his throat. "Follow me Cornelius."

Dyrac tidied the altar having put back the key and casket. "It's time you were reunited with the man who took your life, as he did mine. He's this way."

Cornelius followed Dyrac having another look around the chapel before leaving the room.

"Fucks sake Drack! How much formaldehyde have you got in here?" Cornelius winced at the familiar smell as they entered the room opposite the chapel.

"Well, I've got quite a collection look," Dyrac directed Cornelius to the cacophony of human remains forever preserved in their final states. The head of a man stared directly out from one of the jars, his death mask would not have shown as much detail as the image looking back at Cornelius. You could still see the individual hairs on the eyebrows, eyelashes, and upper lip. You could see the final moments in that face boring into you. Cornelius pressed his lips against the jar puckering up and kissing the cold glass.

"It's been a long time Jarvis Brockheimer," he said gently patting the jar on the top as you would a small dog for fetching you the morning's paper.

"Remember that night well do you?" Dyrac asked Cornelius.

"Brockheimer was a good man, it's just a shame he..., well, let's just say it was a shame. I miss how he laughed."

They walked further into the room.

"Drack, you're running out of room down here, you're going to have to extend or stop collecting this stuff. Wait, is that....it is! Where the fuck did you get this?" Cornelius lifted a small, ancient Egyptian Pharaoh's crook "Is this one of the looted pieces from Amenhotep I's tomb? I mean not the original tomb seeing as though he was moved from Dra' Abu el-Naga to Deir el-Bari Cache because people," he said glaring at Dyrac, "were robbing him in his death. I mean, if they ever unwrap that poor guy he's going to look pissed, as well as pretty shit having been dead for eons"

"Yes it is Amenhotep's crook, his flail is there somewhere too but I didn't loot it, well not from his tomb anyway. Put it down will you this is what, sorry who, we've come to see." Dyrac pointed toward a glass case resting in the dark corner of the room."

"HOLY SHIT!" said Cornelius, "What did you do to him and why is he lying like that?" Cornelius walked up to Abimilech, "Hope you're rotting in eternal misery!" he gave Abimilech the middle finger. "No doubting it's him, not with that nose."

"It's him. I've had him all this time. I couldn't, as you delicately put it all those years ago, 'watch him melt in the hydroflauric acid, see him dissipate into nothing', I kept him because I found something out and needed him."

"Needed him?" questioned Cornelius.

"For the summoning of...." he stopped interrupted by Cornelius.

"What's that noise?" Cornelius could swear he could hear a feint groaning. "Is it him?" he pointed to Abimilech.

"No, it's not him, we'll get to what that noise is in a minute. But first let me tell you about the night Abimilech took his last breath."

Chapter 22

Kurt felt so uncomfortable, pulling at his collar he asked, "Is all this really necessary? I mean a bow tie?"

"Mr Ellis, a black tie dinner requires you to wear the attire I've selected for you. The whole ensemble is a perfect fit and whilst I appreciate you are not used to this dress code, if you are to impress Mr Gideon this evening you'll heed my advice and wear the whole outfit and with my guidance I'll ensure you leave here with clear instructions how to fit the cummerbund and bow tie yourself for when you change later. May I also suggest you fit in a trip to Farrows." Meryck Thornhill said.

Meryck Thornhill, of Thornhill & Cross, was the finest tailor Dyrac knew and he had been Dyrac's appointed and exclusive tailor for many years. Thornhill & Cross was established in 1912, initially they proved a popular service in town however, when the war hit they lost their usual business and found themselves hired by the state to help with the war effort making uniforms for the armed forces and were hired again when the Second World War hit. Since 1948 they have worked as an elite tailoring service having an international clientele as well as the dressing the finest houses nationally. Meryck was not about to let the grocery delivery boy diminish the reputation of Thornhill & Cross in one night.

"Alright Mr T, but I can't believe people wear this stuff all the time," replied Kurt.

Kurt was about to leave Thornhill & Cross with an

enormous suit bag containing a white dress shirt, a black bow tie and matching black cummerbund, a wool, midnight blue dinner jacket with contrasting silk lapels, matching trousers with the same contrasting silk braided down the seams. He was also provided with a shoebox containing black patent oxford shoes. Kurt made the comment, "They're so shiny I can see my face in them," when Meryck first brought them out. In addition to the aforementioned Kurt was given a separate bag containing a variety of accessories which included new underwear, socks, a tie-pin and cufflinks. Both the tie-pin and cufflinks were simple polished silver, and the cufflinks were oval in shape.

"Right, well I guess that's me then?" he asked Meryck.

"That is, as you so eloquently put it, is you then," replied Meryck rolling his eyes at the commonness of Kurt.

"How much do I owe you?" he asked.

"The bill was agreed with Mr Gideon and will be £2,450."

Kurt coughed so hard a lump of phlegm almost escaped his mouth, he clasped a hand over his mouth catching the mucus and wiped his hand down his trouser leg. Meryck rolled his eyes again in utter disgust.

"You chaps sure must rake it in?"

Meryck didn't answer. Kurt handed over a pile of notes settling the bill. He had a quick glance back in the envelope seeing there was still a fair bit leftover.

"Well, good day," said Kurt clicking his heels and tipping his head as though doffing his cap in a pedantic gesture.

"Good day Mr Lewis," came the reply.

Kurt turned right out of Thornhill & Cross and crossed the road. A few doors down was Farrows the barbers. Kurt did, as Meryck suggested, and paid a visit. He went for a full close shave with a cut-throat razor, he indulged in a full facial and had his hair attended to. He wasn't going to openly admit it but he actually enjoyed the whole ordeal.

Merril and Verne had finished the tour of Wode House and were discussing the menu for dinner. There was a little disagreement over what would be served but Verne soon realised that Merril's choice was in fact perfect and they should definitely go with that.

Merril knew Dyrac would find some of the menu difficult given the seafood selection but he always made the effort during formal dinners and she chose courses with elements which Dyrac would be able to digest without too much displeasure.

Dinner tonight was to be served at 7:00pm and as there were outside guests in attendance Merril had to put together a physical menu which would be displayed at the entrance to the dinner hall. Merril knew full well that neither Mr Blackshot nor Kurt would read it but protocol was protocol and she set it up all the same.

Standing atop an elaborate brass pulpit (which was probably used in a church at some point given the ornate and intricate detail and the giveaway INRI banner just underneath an eagle standing on an orb wings spread wide), was a deep red leather folder open with two pieces of parchment on each side. The menu was written in Merril's own artistic hand in beautiful calligraphy:

HORS D'OEUVRES
Seared Ocean Scallop with Garlic Curry and Ginger
Figs wrapped with Prosciutto and Roquefort
Rosemary Apricot Chicken Salad Profiterole
Beef Carpaccio on Herb Toast with Lemon Olive Oil and Parmesan

SALAD COURSE
Radicchio and Endive with Candied Walnut and Apricot

FIRST COURSE
Veal Stew with Garlic and Gremolata

MAIN COURSE
Classic Beef Wellington with Duxelles served with Honey Glazed Carrot, Sugar Snap Peas with Fresh Mint and a Rosemary and Burgundy reduction

DESSERT
Lemon Mousse in a Chocolate Cup with Strawberry Coulis
Tahitian Vanilla Bean Créme Brulee garnished with Whipped Cream, Fresh Berries and a Cocoa Nib

Merril took a step back admiring her work. She was satisfied and now, had a lot to get through to make sure dinner could be served on time. She headed back to Verne in the kitchen. As she passed the cellar door she noticed a spill of light coming through the bottom of the door. *So that's where they are?* She thought to herself. *I wonder what they are doing down there?*

Cornelius was waiting and his patience was wearing thin, "come on Drack! Indulge me?"

"Ok, Cornelius ok," and with a deep breath he began.

Chapter 23

"On the morning of 21st June 1529 I woke knowing that I would be taking a life that day. It was the day I would kill my father figure, the only man who had ever held any influence over my upbringing. The man who turned me into who I am now, giving me immortality by teaching me dark arts and instructing me on how to influence and manipulate. How to become the man he was and how, living a life for the purpose of yourself alone would give you an unforgiveable power. Abimilech Gideon stole me from the streets, a mortal life. A life which would've ended abruptly with a premature death probably by the age of 10, if I was lucky. Anyway, that bit you know, that life you understand having walked in the same shoes, and still walk in those same shoes as do I today," Dyrac spoke with a feeling of sunken dejection. He remembered how awful his early days were and how initially the desperate need to have a father, in fact anyone in his life that he could look up to, respect, love even was. He continued.

"I'd just turned 21 years of age and had finally become a man in my own right. I was a far cry from the child I was when Abimilech found me aged 6. I'd been moulded into a formidable man. I understood from around the age of 16 that I was now different but it took a further 5 years to realise the impact of living in Abimilech's shadow. And I now knew that the feeling that I bore every day was regret and contempt, contempt towards the father who adopted me."

Cornelius listened in complete silence, but gave the odd gesture to indicate to Dyrac that he was paying attention.

"This was the week Abimilech broke news to me that my sister, his daughter Idysha, had died. I hadn't seen Idysha since meeting her the night I first fed from her. My memory of her face was failing but I remembered an innocence to her. She was sent away by Abimilech to a finishing school where she boarded and she never returned. I always thought that one day, the three of us would be so powerful we could influence the world and we would want for nothing. I was wrong. During that week Abimilech became withdrawn, he distanced himself and hid away. For the first time since I was on the streets, and after learning of her death, I felt alone and during the seven days Abimilech kept himself hidden away I explored areas of the house I had never been to previously. I never ventured outside. Stepping outside of the house alone was not permitted and, although I didn't know where he was within the confines of the house, or even if he was there at all, I still respected this and stayed inside.

The needs of the Gideon's, being just myself and Abimilech now, were met by Grafton. He was a mortal man and whilst I never knew his true age, he was still light and thrifty on his feet but his face, hair and mannerisms indicated he must have been in his 70s. Grafton was kind hearted and I swear sometimes when he looked directly at me, when his eyes met mine holding my gaze they spoke to me apologetically as though he knew something I didn't.

Anyway, I digress but wanted to make it clear that

all the time I had was free time since Abimilech was otherwise engaged. What I found during my explorative period were secrets that had been withheld from me."

Cornelius interrupted, "it was then you realised what you had become wasn't it?"

"Yes," Dyrac replied, "I found the book and I found the bottle. Follow me."

Cornelius followed Dyrac into the wine cellar. He looked around in awe at the amount of wine Dyrac had stored. "That's a lot of grape Drack," he announced.

"It's one of my many hobbies, you can see from the other room I like to collect. It's this way," he answered.

Standing next to an all but empty, floor to ceiling wine rack Dyrac pointed to the one bottle sitting lonely right in the centre. It was covered in dust and cobwebs filled the majority of the gaps surrounding it. There was a distinct musty smell with a suffocating humidity throughout the whole cellar but standing in front of this particular rack the smell, the atmosphere changed. There was a putrid odour permeating the whole space, you could feel it instantly clinging to your clothing trying to find a freedom from itself. For anyone else spending any length of time there the smell would've incapacitated you into nausea however, Cornelius and Dyrac had been exposed death beyond obsession and this had become more of a fanatical sensory trigger to them and as such the gravitational pull of illness evaded them. The fermented, sweet putrification aroma stirred an unusual emotion in them both.

Dyrac reached for the bottle but before he picked it up he noticed a thumb print in the dust on the bottle. "Someone's been here! Someone knows!" his anger clear in his tone.

"Calm down Dyrac," Cornelius resorted to addressing him in his actual name, "finish the story and we'll get on to this later."

"Yes, right, but..."

"But nothing for now," said Cornelius, "I need to know everything about Abimilech and then everything else you know so together, *we*," he emphasised the we, "can figure out what needs to be done to contain this."

"Ok. You're right," he replied containing the rage that was bubbling away in his gut, "So, I found the book and the bottle. At first glance I thought the bottle was just a rare bottle of red wine, albeit it bore no label then, as it still doesn't today. The book rested open next to the bottle so I read the script to myself and felt a pang of dread, fear, terror actually consume me. It was incantation for deathlessness, a state of everlasting life. The perpetual timeless eternity that one could exist in so long as the rituals were routinely followed and a single drop from the pure, unspoilt blood of another soul suspended in anathasia.

It described how the blood needed to be ingested and voluntarily taken by an innocent and how, after 1,800 solar and lunar phases had risen and passed the transformation would be complete and mortal would become immortal until the imprisoned is banished to exile in the wretchedness everlasting fire of the infernal regions of Gehenna.

Abimilech had hand written notes in the leaves of

the pages of the books explaining how to mix the blood with particular red wines without leaving any sign or giving the recipient of such wine any indication that it had been tampered with.

There were diary entries regaling how the first glass had been taken and how he felt exhilarated that he had succeeded and how the, and I quote directly as I have memorised this since that day 'volunteer took the chalice and sipped at his first taste of wine, he winced at the bitterness of the alcohol at first but then willingly, and of his own accord, drank the wine as though a connoisseur'.

I knew, right then in that moment he was referring to me as that was my 16th birthday. I remembered it vividly then, it's more hazy now.

I left the room with the book and bottle as I had found it and isolated myself in solitude in my room trying to unravel the chaos tormenting my mind. I realised that in the time passed since my 16th birthday the solar and lunar phases described in the book had passed and I had indeed drank wine voluntarily every day with every evening meal since then.

I couldn't really at that point fathom the meaning of immortality but I knew something foreboding and grave had changed me. And I knew that it was in that exact moment a loathing consumed me and my hatred towards Abimilech rapidly transformed into a derision of wanting him dead. But how, if he, like me was immortal, what could kill him?

For two days solid I studied the books in the library and returned to that book of incantations, not touching the bottle standing proudly next to it but staring at it each time. I figured out how to reseal the bottle without raising suspicion that it had been tampered with and finally had my answer as to how to take the life of a mortal inconspicuously. So I set about my plan and on the seventh day I murdered Abimilech.

I knew that the amount I extracted from the bottle would be enough to kill him. He was never an innocent or pure soul and the book indicated what would happen should a tainted soul drink the contents of that bottle.

I watched as he drank the tampered with wine as he had watched me in all these years. I glared at him. The moment he removed the chalice from his lips he knew. He knew I knew and he knew that this was his end.

"So this is how you repay me?" he retorted.

"How I repay you!" I yelled at him, "repay you for taking my life, for making a decision that I was to become a servant of Beelzebub, Mephistopheles, Lucifer? The Angel of Darkness, King of Hell, Diabolous, Satan himself?" I questioned.

"Boy, you'd have been nothing without me, nothing. You were a sewer rat, vermin. A cretin that would've died before young. Died in the naivety of a world that can be great. That can become a haven to the worthy." Abimilech began to squirm and writhe in agony as his death began to constrict him. He fell to the floor embracing his stomach. He reached for his pocket and clenched his fist tightly aiming it towards me. "Boy, you'll never understand or comprehend without my teaching, you will never be able to..." then he took his final breath and his arm fell beside him. His face bore the look of agony but his body was resting in the same position he once was as an unborn child in his mother's womb."

Cornelius breathed deeply.

"I had little time before Grafton would appear to clear dinner so I moved him. I heaved his enormous and great body and lay him in a void in the wall behind the portrait of Sarah, his wife. The void was big enough to contain him for now but I would need to return after Grafton was asleep to move him and relocate him to where he could never be found again."

"What did he have in his hand?" asked Cornelius.

"I don't know, in the panic that set in almost immediately after I moved Abimilech to the void I instantly forgot he was holding anything. Well, that was until..." Dyrac stopped himself then continued, "Follow me."

Cornelius followed Dyrac back in to the room where Abimilech now lay in a glass case. He pointed again, this time to Abimilech's hand.

"This mystery seriously has a hold of me Drack!"

"So, what happens now depends on what help you can give me?" asks Dyrac.

"Look, I'm here to see this through to the end and first that means we need to see what's in his hand. After that we need to discuss who has seen that bottle and..." Dyrac interrupted.

"It's Kurt," he said with conviction, "I mean he had a key to the cellar, he had access, and he had also been in my study where I found this," Dyrac took the misshapen paperclip from his jacket pocket. "I found it on the floor by my desk, he must've been looking for the will but why, I'm not sure yet? This is why I've asked him to dinner. I wanted to confront him about the break in of my desk with you here but now, maybe we should interrogate him further and ask about the bottle and what he actually knows. Thoughts?" he asked Cornelius.

"I'll make sure my toolkit is in the study before we go for dinner to avoid him becoming suspicious but yes, a good old fashioned interrogation might just reveal some of the answers we need."

"Before we go back upstairs," Dyrac added, "there's one more thing."

"More?" asked Cornelius.

Dyrac left the room of curiosities with Cornelius close behind him. "That groaning you heard." They entered the third room in the cellar.

"Is that a..." asked Cornelius looking the chest laying before him.

"It is," replied Dyrac.

"And inside it, is it..."

"Yes, a pythos. The pythos!"

"Let's call it what it actually is Drack! You're telling me that inside this chest," he almost knocked on the chest but he stopped himself before making contact, "lays Pandoras Box?"

"And contained within the box," Dyrac replied delicately patting the chest from which a feint cry was heard by both.

"How sure are you?" asked Cornelius.

"I'm positive," replied Dyrac.

Both of them stared at one another and then both left the room, ascended the cellar stairs and stepped back into the hallway of Wode House in silence.

"I need some time Drack," said Cornelius, "can we reconvene in the study at say 6:00pm? It will give us an hour before your other guest arrives for dinner. I'm going to need to make a call and then, once I've got confirmation, I'll go through the plan."

"Until six," answered Dyrac with a nod of gratitude that not only indicated to Cornelius that he was grateful for him being there but that he was in his debt. For in Cornelius's last sentence, he had committed to seeing this through.

Chapter 24

It was approaching 5:00pm and Merril and Verne were just finishing the preparation for dinner.

"We'll have to get ready ourselves shortly," said Merril, "we need to make sure we are in our finest attire, well as fine as a housekeeper and butler can be on such an occasion. Dyrac likes to treat all dinners he hosts as a proper formal affair no matter the number of guests. Have you brought your server dress wear?" she asked Verne.

"I've got my tails with me, I'll be ready for 6:00pm and will meet you back here?" asked Verne, looking for approval.

"That's perfect, I'll see you shortly Verne and thanks for all your help. It's amazing how much lighter the work load feels with the extra pair of hands," said Merril.

"You did most of the work Merril, I'm sure you'd have managed admirably without me but I appreciate the recognition nonetheless. It's not often accorded in our line of service," said Verne.

Both Merril and Verne left the kitchen and Verne headed up the stairs to his quarters. Merril had one other job to do before she returned to her room to get ready. She'd already laid out her outfit ready so she could have a swift change. Once Verne was out of ear shot and clear from view Merril returned to the kitchen and left the side entrance. She ran down the side of Wode House past the sundial and headed to the folly.

Cornelius was in his room stroking his impeccably groomed Verdi moustache and beard, inspired by the Italian operatic composer Giuseppe Verdi from whom the style's and fetching look was derived. His salt and pepper colouring gave him a dashing appearance which attracted the attention of women, and men, with whom he became acquainted.

He was pacing the room in deep contemplation almost wearing through the enormous Persian rug that lay on the floor protecting the parquetry underneath. He'd occasional pause making gestures with his arms as though he was conversing with himself, arguing with himself, establishing solutions with an almost eureka look.

He walked over to his large brown leather doctors bag, tired with age and officially an antique now being over 100 years old, which was resting on a side table next to the chaise longue in the room. He unlocked the small brass lock and released the clip peering inside. He rummaged through the contents and smiled upon feeling what he was looking for. "I'm glad I remembered you," he whispered to himself. He left the bag open and continued pacing.

Merril had just opened the door at the top of the incline leading into the secret passage but instead of turning left she turned right, took four more steps and reached up against the wall in front of her. She fumbled around until her hand found what she was looking for. She pulled towards herself and down dropped a solid wooden ladder. She climbed the ladder and, once she'd reach the top stepped to her left, carefully judging her foot placement so as not to fall back down the shaft from where she just came. She walked along the passage way in front of her and stopped when she reached her destination. Next to the wall along the floor were two steps. She climbed them and slowly pulled at a flap which was now at eye level. She pressed her face closely being careful not to make any noise and peered through a small opening which was masked from the other side with some form of canvas mesh.

Cornelius stopped pacing and took a seat on the chaise longue, he reached for the telephone which was on the same side table where his, now open, doctor's bag was and lifted the receiver. It was a heavy set old rotary style telephone. He inserted his index finger in the first number rotating the dial until it reached the fixed stop position and continued to do so until finally the whole number had been entered. *It's a good job this is no emergency,* he thought, *it'd take forever to call 999 on this thing these days.*

"Ranulph? It's Cornelius. Remember the town of Rachel, Nevada? Well...shhh listen don't interrupt," he said to the person on the other end of the line, "I need to repeat the cleanup we did there...Ranulph please, let me finish first. As I was saying before I was so rudely interrupted, the job requires that sort of precision and timing however; this time it's a little more delicate. It's Abimilech, I've found him," he stopped talking allowing the recipient time to speak.

Merril looked down at the open doctor's bag moving her gaze to the top of Cornelius's head lost in her own consciousness. *Abimilech? Found him? How? Where?* She thought. She stepped down back onto the passage floor and seated herself on the top step. *If Abimilech is still alive?* Her thoughts continued to escalate, *then maybe he doesn't know?* She returned to her spy post and continued to watch the formidable Mr Blackshot.

Cornelius was now unpacking items from the doctor's bag and repacking certain ones after closely inspecting each piece. He was checking for imperfections and was taking his admiring each tool. He was precise in deciding which instruments were making the cut on this occasion. There were some modern tools in addition to the medieval and barbaric torturous ones which he kept more as a scare tactic than anything else, but also because he favoured them. The heretic fork, thumbscrew, tongue tearer, Spanish tickler and lead sprinkler to name a few. There was a small leather bound wallet containing 16 different types of blade and an unusual pair of pliers which were thin at the ends like a tweezer.

But Cornelius' piece de resistance was the diabolical pear of anguish. He used it less so these days however it held a sort of twisted sentimental value to him. He lifted it from the array of instruments and had a look of awe in his eyes as he examined it. It has a pear-shaped metal body which can be spread into a few spoon segments by turning a screw located on the handle of the device. It would be placed inside an orifice of a person and then gradually expanded. The kindest use was in a person's mouth where it would ultimately shatter the skull, causing death but Cornelius enjoyed a more sadistic use inserting it into the anus of the individual he was trying to source information from. It was a degrading violation and would cause grotesque physical pain.

The goal would not be to puncture the flesh but to stretch the orifice as far as possible stretching and ripping the skin overloading the sensitive nerve endings producing searing agony. This method was more gratifying to Cornelius as the participant, which is how he referred to the person being interrogated as, was usually quick at confessing or divulging the required information rarely proved fatal.

Cornelius had been holding the implement for longer than necessary enjoying the feeling that was consuming his body, an almost sexual exhilaration came over him, when he heard a feint but distinct sound.

Merril was watching intently and let out an audible gasp upon seeing the pear of anguish in Cornelius' hand. She clapped her hands over her mouth but it was too late.

Cornelius didn't react but he knew he was being watched. He placed the pear of anguish into the doctor's bag. Once satisfied he closed the bag and put it on the floor next to the door ready to take down with him to Dyrac's study on the way to dinner.

Merril breathed a silent sigh of relief when Cornelius didn't react to the sound that escaped her. She decided she would make her way back to her room hoping that she wouldn't encounter anyone on her return to the main building of Wode House. She left her spot and headed back.

After releasing the handle of the bag Cornelius turned on his heels as he raised himself back into a standing position completing a half turn in one swift motion. He looked up staring straight at the picture hanging above the chaise longue directly at the window of the painted folly. The same window that Merril had just been peering through and a furtively sly sneer appeared on Cornelius's face.

Chapter 25

Dyrac was in the study waiting for Cornelius when Merril knocked on the door.

"It's open," announced Dyrac looking towards the door as Merril walked in, "everything alright?" he asked noting Merril didn't appear her usual composed self.

"Everything is just tickety boo," she replied with a hint of sarcasm, "sorry Dyrac, please excuse my flippancy. Everything is fine thank you," she corrected herself adding a smile.

"Ok, if you're sure," Dyrac said unconvinced.

"Dyrac? I have a question about this evening."

"Go on," Dyrac replied.

"I know that the dinner is a formal black tie affair and that there are only three of you which I can easily manage alone however, would you have any objection to Verne being front of house so to speak with me holding the fort in the kitchen?"

"I'd rather have you out front welcoming our guests and being available to manage the three of us but I know that you wouldn't ask me if you didn't have a reasonable explanation and reason. So, if you wouldn't mind explaining further I will take your request into consideration," Dyrac answered.

Merril shifted her stance adding "I'm happy to be out front but you know how much of a perfectionist I am Dyrac and..." she paused, "...I was hoping that would be enough," she changed the direction her conversation was going.

"Very well, in that case I'll agree to a compromise.

You will greet the guests and, once the hors d'ouvres are finished with and my guests are settled Verne can take over the front of house duties however, you will be back out to serve the desserts."

"Yes Dyrac, thank you," she replied and made her way back to the door pausing.

"Is there something else Merril?" Dyrac asked inquisitively.

Merril thought about it for a moment and decided this was not the right time, "No Dyrac, that will be all."

Dyrac sat back in his desk chair with his elbows resting on the arms, his forearms almost vertical and his fingers and thumbs, touching at the tips forming a triangle with his thumbs and fore fingers. He was concentrating hard.

The door of the study opened suddenly startling Dyrac. It was Cornelius.

"Drack!" shouted Cornelius.

"I wish you'd bloody knock Cornelius," retorted Dyrac.

"Dearest Mr Gideon, you should know me well enough by now that I, Mr Cornelius Harrington Louis Percival Blackshot, never announces ones arrival. My arrival should always be expected and welcome."

"You're a terrible narcissist," replied Dyrac, "King Edward?"

"Need you ask?"

Dyrac poured two large glasses of the whisky he ordered from Bryson & Sons and set them on a small tray. He added a small jug of water and took four large pieces of ice from the ice bucket using a small pair of silver tongs and placed them into a separate tumbler.

"One man should never mess with another man's whisky," said Dyrac.

"Too true my friend, too true," came the reply.

"So, how did you get on?" asked Dyrac.

"I made the call and, if you're ready now, can go through the finer details of the plan. You may need to get yourself that bottle," said Cornelius pointing at the bottle of whisky Dyrac had just returned to the cabinet.

"Let's sit and run through it," Dyrac said.

Kurt was in his bathroom staring into the mirror looking disgusted with himself.

"You put this bit over here, then tuck that up to....twist this...put it down...fuck it," he said to his own reflection. "This bastard bow tie is going to be the death of me," he added looking at the two pieces of bow tie hanging either side of his neck.

Taking a deep breath he counted to ten before trying again and shocked himself, "YES!" he yelled proudly looking around for someone to share his joy as he correctly tied the bow tie, "it only took you an hour boy," he added, finding himself obviously alone.

He hoisted the jacket over his shoulders and, using the clothes brush he found in the bag from Thornhill & Cross he smoothed over the jacket as he'd been shown by Meryck Thornhill, being careful not to go in the wrong direction so as not to ruin the fabric fibres.

"You, fine sir, scrub up well," he admired his reflection giving himself a wink, "ready," he said.

In the kitchen Merril was talking to Verne, "you're happy with that then?" she asked.

"Anything you say Merril, I'll happily cover front of house the whole evening if you like?"

"That's quite alright Verne, thank you but Dyrac has given me explicit instructions regarding the welcoming of guests and my role during the early, and final stages of dinner. Shall we start?" asked Merril.

"Ready when you are," said Verne.

Merril was uncomfortable and nervous. It was the first time in her service at Wode House that she felt exposed and vulnerable. She didn't know why she felt this way but she was definitely uneasy. Like the calm before the storm a silence and stillness was setting in. A pressure cooker reaching its limit ready to erupt at any moment. Something was unsettling her and she had a feeling Mr Blackshot played a big part in it.

Things at Wode House were about to change.

Chapter 26

Kurt grabbed the keys to the pick-up at the same time he was pulling at the collar of his shirt. "Bastard bow tie," he said, "I mean what is the point? And this," he said looking down and pulling the cummerbund, "why?"

He left his house not locking the front door. He never locked the door knowing full well that if anyone was to break in they'd look around the place and realise there was nothing worth stealing. If anything, he hoped they'd leave stuff for him out of pity.

He contemplated taking the bottle of HP sauce from the cupboard but then thought of the shit fit Dyrac would have if he started pouring it over the caviar or whatever poncey food would be served up tonight.

"Why am I doing this again?" he asked himself getting into the driver's seat, "oh yeah that's right," he answered himself, "because of the money. With any luck this will score enough to fund a trip to Vegas where we can blow the lot! Isn't that right Kurt? Yes Kurt, fucking yes!" he said still talking to himself.

He started the pick-up and a huge gust of black smoke puffed out of the exhaust. "And maybe get a new motor? Only joking Corina, you'll always be my girl," he said stroking the steering wheel.

Merril and Verne were all set to go. "Mr Lewis will be arriving shortly. Upon his arrival I will take him to meet with Dyrac and Cornelius in the study where they will have an aperitif. After half an hour I shall be ready to greet them in the dining room where they will arrive between 6:30 and 6:45pm. Once they are seated I will take the wine order and return to the kitchen. You'll be bringing the wine whilst at the same time I will serve the hors d'ouvres."

"Ok Merril," replied Verne.

"Once the hors d'ouvres are served you will remain in the dining room and I'll return to the kitchen alone," Merril said firmly. "You will only return once you are certain they are ready for the next course. You've been in the service longer than me so I know I don't need to explain dining etiquette."

Verne chuckled, "Longer than I'd care to admit."

Merril smiled.

Cornelius pulled out a pipe from his inside jacket pocket and gestured to Dyrac, "any objections?"

"You'd still light up even if I did," replied Dyrac.

"How well you know me," said Cornelius. "So, you are happy with the strategy for the evening? Once we get back here Kurt should be feeling at ease after we've instilled a false sense of security during dinner and, after plying him with copious amounts of your fine wines."

"All good at my end, I've no qualms except for one."

"Which is?" asked Cornelius.

"It's the blood loss. I mean I know you've probably got this all covered but seriously this rug," he said pointing at another Persian. Wode House was full of them, each one selected by Dyrac himself and purchased legitimately in person. It was an unusual obsession to have but obsess over them he did. There wasn't one room at Wode House that didn't have one, not even the kitchen. Dyrac could recall where he was and when, he bought each one. "This carpet," still pointing at the rug, "was bought in Iran when it was still called Persia and I'll be damned if the blood of a simple grocery boy be its demise."

"I know your precious Dyrac but you insult me if you believe for one minute that I'd leave any trace," Cornelius replied, offended.

"You're right, accept my apologies, after all I've witnessed your skills first hand and you are indeed the consummate professional. Cheers." Dyrac raised his glass and downed the remnants of the whisky and ice. "Another?" he asked.

"Keep it coming," replied Cornelius.

Dyrac topped up Cornelius' glass and Cornelius exhaled a fog cloud of smoke straight into Dyrac's face smiling.

"Such a gent," said Dyrac and they both laughed.

The door bell of Wode House rang throughout the whole ground floor. Kurt was shifting uneasily, he contemplated buying a bottle of wine as he wasn't sure what the rules were for this sort of affair but then he remembered Merril mentioned Dyrac had a huge collection of wines and he didn't feel the selection at Bryson & Sons would quite cut the occasion. So he stood there waiting for the door to be answered feeling completely out of his depth and beyond his comfort zone. He'd much rather have walked in via the side entrance but Dyrac's instructions were explicit.

"Welcome to Wode House Mr Lewis," said Merril opening the door, "right this way."

"Hi Merry, thanks but why are you calling me Mr Lewis, it's me Kurt!" he said tapping his chest.

"As a guest of Mr Gideon I am to address you formally Mr Lewis. Follow me for aperitif's in the study with Mr Gideon and Mr Blackshot."

"What the fuck is an aperitif?" asked Kurt, "and who the fuck is Mr Blackshot?"

Merril smiled not saying a word.

"Merry!" exclaimed Kurt in a hushed voice.

"Mr Lewis, you and Mr Gideon are joined by Mr Blackshot this evening. Mr Blackshot is a guest staying at Wode House. Now, shall we?" Merril knocked on the door to the study waiting for Dyrac's invitation to enter.

"Mr Lewis," she bowed her head slightly and, with her left arm invited Kurt into the study, "dinner will be served at seven o'clock." She said.

"Kurt, meet Cornelius Blackshot. Cornelius, this is Kurt Lewis." Dyrac said.

"I've heard a lot about you," said Cornelius.

"I've just heard about you," said Kurt, "sorry, err...I mean to say pleased to meet you," and he held out his hand to shake Cornelius's.

Cornelius looked at his hand and back to Kurt's face, "there's really no need," he said with a look of contempt and disgust. He thought to himself *as if he, Cornelius Blackshot would shake the hand of a man who delivered groceries for a living.*

"Ok you two," said Dyrac, "Kurt, please join us." Dyrac handed Kurt a glass of whisky. "Let the evening begin."

Chapter 27

"Gentlemen," said Dyrac addressing Cornelius and Kurt, "shall we make our way to the dining room?"

"I'm Hank Marvin," said Kurt forgetting himself.

"Philistine," said Cornelius under his breath.

"What was that?" asked Kurt.

"Gentlemen please," said Dyrac, "can we be cordial to each other. The night is young and we've plenty to discuss whilst enjoying the delightful food Merril has undoubtedly prepared."

"Indeed," said Cornelius.

"I will if he will," said Kurt scowling at Cornelius having taking an instant dislike to the man who clearly felt the class system was still in play with himself being the epitome of nobility and Kurt being something you trod in ruining a pair of finely polished brogues.

"Well then, if you'll follow me," Dyrac invited them to follow.

Merril was waiting in the dining room when the three of them entered. "Good evening, please take your seats, dinner will be served at seven o'clock sharp. Will there be any additional drinks to the chosen table wine?" asked Merril.

"Thank you Merril, the table wine will suit just fine," said Dyrac.

"Hi Merril," Kurt lifted his hand in a buffoonery hello.

"Mr Lewis," she nodded and smiled in response.

Merril waited for them to be seated and vacated

the dining room heading for the kitchen. Verne had readied the hors d'ouvres and was poised with the table wine, the bottle centred on a silver serving tray lined with lace doilies. A crisp white cotton cloth draped over his left forearm.

"Nice gloves," Merril smiled at Verne's white cotton gloved hands. They were so white the kitchen light reflected off them and Merril squinted in jest, "bright," she added.

Verne let out a little snort, "I do try to look the part," he responded.

Merril double checked, re-checked and checked again the presentation of the hors d'ouvres adjusting the beef carpaccio atop of the herb toast, "the folds aren't right," she said moulding them into perfectly identical fans. "Ok, let's go," she said placing the cloche over the dishes and hoisting the enormous silver serving tray onto her left hand holding it aloft at shoulder height.

"Onwards," said Verne.

Merril served the hors d'ouvres whilst Verne poured the table wine, serving Dyrac first then pausing momentarily allowing him to taste and accept the wine for the table. They worked in unison flowing in a perfectly choreographed performance. Merril couldn't help but think a more permanent working life with Verne would be idyllic then she remembered her working life would soon be changing and snapped back into the present.

"Verne will wait in the dining room ensuring that you are all suitably comfortable. Please do not hesitate to call on him should you require," Merril said stepping back from the table.

"Thank you Merril," said Dyrac.

Merril gave a nod to Verne whilst her facial expression indicated a 'I'm sure you can manage but I'm not too far so call on me if required' reassurance.

Verne nodded back in a 'thank you'.

Merril heard some of the conversation between the three diners as she was leaving.

"...and you serve Dyrac in what capacity other than that of grocery deliveries?" Cornelius asked Kurt with a mouthful of beef and toast, spraying crumbs out in front of him.

Dyrac rolled his eyes but didn't make any comment. Kurt replied, "Mr Gideon occasionally asks me to do additional tasks and I'm more than happy to obligate him."

"You mean you're more than happy to oblige?" asked Cornelius smiling at Kurt's efforts.

"Quite," said Kurt raising a wine glass to his lips, pinky finger extended. He took a long lingering sip so that he couldn't involve himself in conversation further hoping that Dyrac would be swift in changing the subject.

"So, Cornelius, I've invited Kurt along this evening as a thank you for his loyal service. Kurt has become a valuable asset and this evening is about recognising his dedication and loyalty. You're visit is pure happenstance and made a dinner for two into a dinner for three," Dyrac lied.

"I'm impressed Kurt, I mean Dyrac wouldn't invite just anybody to his dinner table."

Kurt was slightly taken aback that Dyrac held such a high opinion of him, or so he thought.

"I've a feeling we'll get to know each other quite

well tonight," added Cornelius. Kurt noticed a slight smirk on Cornelius's face but put this down to him being a patronising bigot

"To making new friends," Kurt raised his glass in a toast.

"To making new acquaintances," Cornelius corrected him raising his glass slightly immediately taking a sip.

The food was devoured, the wine flowed and before long Merril and Verne were finalising the presentation of the main course.

"During the main course Verne you may find yourself struggling to maintain a stance at attention. They could take over an hour to finish the main, given Dyrac's previous track record. Please feel free to stand at ease. I mean be ready the moment you are called upon but stand at ease."

"Sure Merril, will do," replied Verne, "what are you going to do whilst I'm in the dining room?" he asked.

"Me, well, I will be finishing the next course and will use the time to start the clear up unless you feel like working into the early hours," Merril lied, she knew exactly what she'd be doing during the main course but there was absolutely no chance that she would share that information with anyone, not even Verne.

"Don't overdo it, I'm happy to finish whatever doesn't get done and let you get an early night if you feel time is getting on," replied Verne.

"Thank you Verne, that is sweet of you. Now, the mains!" she exclaimed clapping her hands together.

The main course was served and Merril ensured that there would be no reason whatsoever for Verne to return to the kitchen until the course had been finished with and the place settings ready to clear.

I'll have an hour if not more. That's plenty of time, she thought.

Merril watched Verne go out of eye sight and paused a few seconds before rummaging under pieces of wood, chopped for the wood burner situated in the corner of the kitchen opposite the side entrance door. She grabbed her satchel which she has purposefully left under the wood in the wicker basket next to the side entrance. She quickly looked inside acknowledging to herself that she had everything she needed. Another quick glance around, the coast was clear and Merril left the side entrance.

Chapter 28

The passageways were dark and musty. The fumes from the gas lighting were permeating the air as though waiting in the shadows for its victim, with a noxious stealth like lure. Merril hadn't noticed the smell before but maybe it was because on this occasion she was pressed for time and her senses were stood on a pin head, on high alert to everything around her. She rushed along the hidden hallway weaving her way through the maze of secrecy until she reached where she needed to be. She inhaled a slow and deep breath and unhitched the latch on a doorway carefully pushing it open avoiding the inherent screeching from the rarely used hinges. With her right hand she raised a finger to her lips pleading at the door to not make any noise, "shhhh," she murmured. There was no point in peering through the spy hole first to check all was clear because it was blocked from the other side, covered with something. Plus she knew that everyone else at Wode House was in the dining room, right? She opened the door she'd been longing to open since she discovered where it lead to.

Verne looked on as the three diners were jovial in their conversation. The level of wine consumption helped eradicate earlier tensions and, for now the conversation and body language suggested that the three men were in fine spirit.

"Another bottle of Dyrac's finest," hailed Cornelius in Verne's direction.

"Right you are sir," replied Verne.

"Kurt? Drack?" he asked.

"Fill me up if you will," Kurt replied.

"Keep me indulged," said Dyrac.

"Drack?" asked Kurt.

"It's Dyrac, Kurt or, Mr Gideon. Ignore the insolence of Mr Blackshot. Cornelius!" Dyrac was stern but was addressing Cornelius not Kurt in his response.

Cornelius raised his empty wine glass in acknowledgement.

"So, Mr Lewis, I hope you'll join us after dinner for drinks and a cigar in the study?" asked Cornelius.

"That's very kind Mr Blackshot," he replied looking at Dyrac for authorisation. Dyrac nodded, "I'd be delighted." Kurt suddenly felt acceptance. *Maybe this is the circle of people I was born to mingle with?* He thought. He definitely hadn't felt acceptance on this level before. A huge weight of trepidation rose from him in a glorified torrent of hallelujah. Finally, he thought.

Verne placed a full carafe of wine onto the table. He had just finished topping up Cornelius's glass when Cornelius leant over to him and whispered in his ear. "Yes sir," came the hushed reply, "right away."

Cornelius sat back, clapped his hands together proudly and picked up his cutlery, "I'm going to enjoy this," he said smugly.

Verne was about to step outside of the dining room when Dyrac called to him, "Where are you going Verne? Your duty is to serve here," he asked.

"Yes sir, Mr Blackshot has just asked that I

retrieve something from his quarters. I shall return momentarily with your permission of course," said Verne.

"Quite alright," said Dyrac looking at Cornelius with a this is my house my rules glare.

"It's ok Drack, I've simply asked Verne to bring that bottle of brandy to the study, you know the one we were discussing earlier?"

Dyrac knew instantly that it wasn't a bottle of brandy that Cornelius referred to but a bottle of chloroform. It was how they were going to sedate Kurt so that they could move him if he hadn't conformed later. This wasn't usually something Cornelius kept in his toolkit but he felt, what with Merril still likely to be pottering around until the early hours, they'd need a way to move Kurt without any vocal objection. It was the first indication to Dyrac that Verne had an awareness of the plan and he hoped Verne's loyalty to Cornelius surpassed that of the instant bond he had found with Merril.

"Let's hope Merril doesn't hear about the brandy or the evenings antics. I wouldn't want to damage the reputation of gentry," asked Dyrac incognito.

"I'm sure we can keep a certain level of decorum and secrecy right?" Cornelius asked Kurt.

"She won't hear anything from me," said Kurt.

"You're right there Mr Lewis, she won't," said Cornelius.

Dyrac was poised and steadfast but a stir of unease wrestled with his inside. A pang of guilt and sudden endearment to Kurt began to set in.

Merril stood mouth agape. She didn't know what to

make of the sight before her but she knew instantly it was him. She stroked upwards along the arm reaching Abimilech's face. She cradled his face in her hands and a single tear rolled down her cheek.

Moments before Merril stepped through the hidden door into the cellar, in Dyrac's chamber of curiosities. She was in the far corner opposite the actual door leading into the room and after emerging from the passage way she looked back at the door. She found an old framed picture of Wode House hanging on the door, the cause of the blockage to the spy hole. She took a brief second to appreciate the picture noting the facade of Wode House was different in appearance. There were doors which mirrored the locality of those in the hidden passage ways and windows where spy holes now were. The house must've been extended at some point to how it is now, she thought. Whoever, secured the services of the architect back then clearly gave them instructions to include the passage ways but not detail them in the blue prints for none of the floor plans Merril had seen previously showed any of the passage ways nor the original layout of the house.

For what purpose did someone want hidden passage ways? She thought briefly but almost immediately interrupted her own train of thought in a, no time for this now Merril way.

Merril was cradling the face of Abimilech examining his preserved state laying in the foetal position. She traced the groove across his nose from the incident involving a claw hammer so very long ago now. She leant towards him and, before she made contact, felt the coolness from him pierce her warm lips. She kissed his forehead and wept, "Papa," she groaned.

In an instant a grief stricken Merril changed. A torrent of rage consumed her. She looked down at her silver bangle and removed it from her wrist. She read the inscription engraved on the inside, 'My dearest Idysha'.

Merril had contained her secret for too long. She no longer identified herself as she was once known. Idysha had long gone but, deep inside she was waiting for the time to resurface. She needed to know for sure and now, she knew. She stared into the face of her father, remembering a time long passed.

"Papa, why do you have a funny face," a six year old Idysha asked her father.

"I fought a great battle my dear sweet Idysha, I was brave and strong. This," Abimilech replied pointing to the groove across his nose, "is a scar. It's a reminder that battles can be fought and won but there will always be a consequence."

"What's a con skew ant?" asked Idysha.

"Consequence, my sweet," he replied chuckling at her mispronunciation, "a consequence is something which means we will always remember, or something that happens because of your actions. Take for example the time that Mama made those madelaines and you couldn't resist taking one even after Mama said they needed time to cool. Remember how Mama was cross and she scowled at you. She told you to sit on your hands on the kitchen chair until she felt you had learned your lesson."

A sheepish Idysha looked at her father, "I

remember Papa," she replied.

"That, dearest Idysha was a consequence of your actions."

A sudden screech echoed around Merril's head startling her. She pressed her hands firmly against her ears but the sound pierced through them. "STOP!" she shouted out loud. The screeching stopped. Merril cautiously lowered her hands and looked around the room. She thought she heard someone call her name but dismissed it almost immediately. She was alone. She heard a feint murmuring coming from outside the room. With trepidation she tiptoed towards the door leading to the centre room of the cellar.

She followed the sounds which lead her into a long narrow chamber. At the end was the chest Kurt brought to Wode House weeks before. Merril crouched down next to the chest and as her face came within a whisker's breadth the chest rattled and screams echoed around her head.

Merril fell back onto her behind with a thud. She stared at the chest but felt no fear. She reached forward and placed her hand on the top and uttered "shhh, there there, I'm here now."

The chest settled and the sounds ceased instantly.

Merril set down her satchel and consciously tried to recall how long she'd been gone. It must've been twenty minutes at least. There's still time, she thought. She reached into her bag and removed a small pouch containing a set of lock picking tools. Merril had ordered the kit discreetly from Bradley at Bryson & Sons. She had made him promise not to disclose the order to anyone threatening the custom from Mr Gideon would be revoked if the order was leaked. Merril held no authority to do such a thing but Bradley didn't know and Bradley wasn't about to risk losing the gentleman's contract with Wode House as it brought in more than all of the other of Bryson & Sons customers combined. Bradley knew his Dad would freak out it if no future orders were place from Wode House so Merril had no doubt that his discretion would be honoured.

She pulled out two of the tools and began picking at the lock on the chest. She'd almost given up hope of unlocking the chest before her time ran out and she had to return to the kitchen before anyone noticed she was missing when she heard a click. The lock released and she gasped at her success. She lifted the clasp and placed both hands on the lid of the chest. She grasped at the side and heaved open the heavy lid propping it open leaning it back against the wall.

A luminescent atmospheric glow seemed to appear from the inside of the chest but Merril knew that this was her imagination. It was as though she had just discovered the holy grail with its heavenly iridescent light beaming from within. She looked down into the chest at the pythos that lay before her.

A huge smile spread across Merril's face as she whispered to the sealed urn.

Verne heard a disturbance coming from behind him, in the direction of the kitchen. It must be Merril, he thought, but he could swear it was a feint cry. He shook his head disregarding the sound and carried on, heading back to the dining room from the study. He paused and took a second look back. There were no shadows in the kitchen and he couldn't see Merril. He chose to have a quick look. Merril was nowhere in sight.

Verne was just about to return to the dining room when he heard a noise coming from beyond the cellar door. He listened intently. He heard the feint sound of someone's voice saying "stop!" He checked the door handle turning it left, and then right, it was locked. He called out to the kitchen "Merril?" but there was no reply.

Verne knew Merril had a hidden agenda for her needing to stay back and man the kitchen. The fact she was nowhere to be seen corroborated Verne's suspicions. *What was she hiding? Where was she hiding?*

Merril had closed the lid to the empty chest ensuring the latch and lock were both secure. She left the long, narrow chamber clutching her satchel tightly against her side. She patted it feeling the additional item she was returning to the main house with and scurried through the passage ways.

Chapter 29

"Where have you been?" asked Verne as Merril ran through the side entrance into the kitchen.

A startled Merril replied, "not that it's any of your business Verne but I needed some fresh air, the heat in this kitchen can get beyond ridiculous."

"Fresh air huh? And your bag?" Verne said pointing to Merril's satchel.

"Verne, what's with all the questions? How's dinner going?" Merril asked changing the direction of conversation.

"Well they're ready for their desserts. Are you ready for their desserts?" asked Verne.

"Ready as ever," Merril replied as she sauntered over to the walk in refrigerator appearing moments later with the desserts ready prepared and already plated. "Service," she said as though a head chef would beckon waiting staff as food was placed on the pass.

"Yes ma'am," replied Verne bowing his head a little.

"I'll help get the desserts out Verne," Merril composed herself and picked up one of the three large silver serving trays. Each tray contained the three desserts so one tray could be served to each diner. Merril always was efficient. Verne collected the other two trays and followed Merril to the dining room.

"Merril, that has to have been the most spectacular food I've ever eaten," said Kurt as Merril served him dessert.

"That's very kind Mr Lewis," she replied.

"Of course you've never eaten like this before I assume so, actually you've not got much to compare to have you?" said Cornelius with a sly smirk.

"What do you mean by that?" asked Kurt trying to stop every inch of himself from punching Mr Cornelius Blackshot's lights out.

"What I mean..."

Dyrac interrupted him, "Gents please, can we get back to finishing our meals before we retire to the study?"

Cornelius nodded. Kurt just glared at Cornelius imagining a whole world of pain that he wanted inflict on the man and forced himself not to smile a psychopathic smile as he did.

Merril and Verne were back in the kitchen when the service bell rang. "That's the three of them retiring to the study now Verne. No more service needed tonight, we just need to clear up here and then we can both retire for the evening ourselves," said Merril.

"I'll happily finish here if you want an early dart," said Verne.

"Many hands make light work," said Merril, adding "plus, after we have both finished I've got a nightcap that we can both enjoy."

"Amen to that," said Verne.

Dyrac kept the fire burning whilst at dinner so the study was warm and inviting. He'd already ensured that Merril had stocked the drinks cabinet with the Johnnie Walker, the ice bucket was full and fresh water was available should any of them choose to add this to their tipple.

"Don't mind if I do," said Kurt selecting one of three cigars from the humidor that Dyrac held in front of him. He smelled at the cigar because he'd seen that's what people do. Kurt snipped off the tip of the cigar with a silver cigar cutter placing it back into the humidor with the remaining cigars.

"These cigars," Dyrac said, "are Ghurkha Royal Courtesan cigars," Dyrac too inhaled along the side of his cigar, "you'll note they have a distinct aroma. At a cost of $1,000,000 each they are infused with Remy Martin Black Pearl Louis XIII, a bottle of that alone would set you back $165,000. Each cigar is rolled by hand and the artisans who create these pieces of beauty are blindfolded to heighten their senses so that their movements are natural with minimal distractions. The tobacco is a rare Himalayan tobacco that has been watered only with Fiji water." Dyrac was caressing his cigar now as though he was in a tender intimate moment with a beautiful naked woman. "Each opulent piece is wrapped in gold leaf and the band is embellished with diamonds. They are hand delivered by a messenger wearing spotless white gloves..."

Dyrac was interrupted in his flow, "Did you say ONE MILLION DOLLARS?" asked Kurt having not heard the rest Dyrac had to say describing the cigars. "ONE MILLION DOLLARS?" Kurt was now holding the cigar as though a new born baby, fragile and delicate and, in no way whatsoever could you drop it.

Cornelius laughed, "These are the luxuries you will get to enjoy Mr Lewis, now that we are all friends," he said slapping Kurt on the back.

Four glasses of whisky later Kurt was starting to feel woozy. He liked a drink but the alcohol he had consumed tonight was of a far greater volume than what he was used to. Dyrac and Cornelius were still composmentus and they exchanged glances silently acknowledging that the time had come.

"I'm going to have to call it a night soon gents," slurred Kurt, barely coherent.

"Don't be foolish Mr Lewis, the night is young," said Cornelius, "here have a another." He turned having first prepared another drink, handing a glass to Kurt. Kurt hadn't noticed that Cornelius had tampered with his as he took the glass.

"To a good evening and to revelations," said Dyrac raising a toast.

"Rel-av-ay-shuns," Kurt said losing control of verbalising words, "I means celebrations, no wait, relav, cheers," he said.

"Cheers," said Dyrac and Cornelius in unison as they both watched Kurt sip from his glass.

Immediately Kurt found himself frozen with paralysis and the glass fell to the floor bouncing on the rug spilling the contents. He could still consciously think and speak, albeit the effects from his alcohol consumption were abundant. His widened and his pupils dilated, full of fear. He wasn't sure whether he was so drunk and unable to move or, whether something else was preventing him from being able to move.

"My bag," Cornelius pointed instructing Dyrac to pass it to him.

Kurt moved his eyes to see what Dyrac was

bringing to Cornelius. He watched intently trying his hardest to move his head to get a better look but he couldn't. "What is that? What are you doing?" he asked.

Dyrac remained silent and placed Cornelius's doctor's bag next to the chair where Kurt was sitting. Cornelius opened the bag and pulled out some polythene sheets. He placed them all around Kurt's chair and covered a side table. He put on a pair of nitrile gloves and took out a roll of fabric. He unravelled it on the table. Kurt caught a glimpse of what was inside.

"What the fuck is all that?" he shouted.

"You'll find out," said Cornelius continuing to take out different items from his bag. He took out the pear of anguish consciously taking his time ensuring Kurt could see it in all its horrifying glory.

"Mr Gideon?" he asked looking at Dyrac.

"Kurt," Dyrac replied, "we need to ask you a few questions and depending on how forthcoming you are, Mr Blackshot is here to help me get answers to these questions."

"What the fuck? What questions?" asked Kurt.

"Let's start at the beginning. Why did you break in to my study?"

"Break in? I've not taken anything Mr Gideon. Please Mr Gideon, I don't know what you're talking about."

Dyrac nodded at Cornelius.

Cornelius ran his hand along the tools that lay before him. He stopped over a pair of small needle nose like pliers, except they were thinner at the ends, designed to grip very small items.

Merril and Verne had finished for the evening.

"Verne, grab two glasses from the cupboard will you?"

"Any particular type of glass?" replied Verne.

"Wine glasses will do," she replied holding up a bottle of Chardonnay. "Dyrac usually allows me a bottle of wine after a formal dinner as a thank you. Tonight however," she said holding up a second bottle, "he's allowed me two."

"Sounds good to me," said Verne.

"We have to drink it up in our quarters but we can sit on the landing between our rooms on the two old chesterfield armchairs."

"Perfect," said Verne dinking two wine glasses together, "cheers."

Merril and Verne retired to their quarters, out of view and ear shot of the study.

Cornelius placed his hand over Kurt's left wrist forcing it down into the arm of the chair. He took the pliers and gripped the end of the fingernail on Kurt's middle finger.

"DYRAC!" he shouted.

"I'll ask you again Kurt, why did you break in to my study?"

"I haven't," Kurt said panicked, "I wouldn't."

"Don't lie to me Kurt, my patience is wearing thin," Dyrac nodded at Cornelius.

Cornelius pulled the fingernail outwards prying it away from the root. You heard the cuticle give way as the nail ripped away from the nail bed exposing torn tissue and muscle. Blood flowed freely onto the polythene sheeting.

"STOOOOPPP!" screeched Kurt. Tears rolling down his face as searing pain penetrated his whole body.

"Another," instructed Dyrac.

This time Cornelius reached for a long thin metal skewer. Holding it at one end he put the sharp end into the fire and waited a few moments for it to reach the right temperature. Still forcing the same hand into the arm of the chair Cornelius raised Kurt's index finger.

Dyrac watched on as the skewer was driven into the flesh under Kurt's nail. Kurt screamed in agony. Unable to move he sat there helpless and defenceless.

The skewer bore through the skin like a hot knife in butter. Upon reaching the end of the nail Cornelius pushed hard forcing it to pierce through the nail. He removed it in one swift movement and picked up Kurt's ring finger repeating the process. The second time it wasn't as easy for Cornelius as the skewer had cooled. He forced the skewer against the resistance under Kurt's nail.

"Enough!" shouted Dyrac.

Cornelius didn't speak but immediately stopped and removed the skewer wiping the blood clean on Kurt's trouser leg.

"Please Mr Gideon," Kurt was sobbing. Dyrac glanced down to Kurt's groin as he noticed it saturate with Kurt's own urine. Unable to take the pain Kurt's flight instinct kicked in and he wet himself.

"Kurt," Dyrac leant in close to Kurt's face and whispered to him, "why did you break in to my study?"

Kurt cried. "I didn't."

"More," Dyrac was heinous in his tone.

Cornelius picked up a scalpel and walked around the back of the chair where Kurt was sitting. Kurt tried to keep his eyes on Cornelius but he soon passed out of Kurt's peripheral vision. Instead Kurt listened as he heard Cornelius's slow footsteps crackle on the polythene sheeting. He shifted his eyes to the other side catching Cornelius as he came back into view. Cornelius slowly knelt beside him and turned Kurt's right arm so his palm was face up. Cornelius placed the scalpel just below Kurt's wrist and pierced the skin. Blood immediately began to spill and Cornelius paused. With the scalpel still stuck inside Kurt's wrist he caught some of the blood on his finger tip and licked the gloved finger clean. Kurt engulfed in terror, his eyes reflecting what he was feeling.

Cornelius gripped the scalpel and again and drew upwards towards Kurt's palm. He stretched open the precisely cut flesh and held it back. He pushed his fore fingers inside a felt for what he was looking for. He gripped something but Kurt didn't know what it was.

"Clippers, if you will Drack."

Dyrac hand Cornelius a pair of surgical clippers. Kurt heard and felt what Cornelius was clipping instantaneously. A gruesome gristly snap and a shocking intense pain coursed up his arm. Cornelius removed the clippers having just cut through the carpal ligament which once lay across the median nerve. Cornelius pinched the nerve and released it over and over again. Continuously torturing Kurt.

After 5 minutes Dyrac announced a halt to the

proceedings.

"Not getting cold feet are you?" asked Cornelius.

"Not in the slightest. I want this piece of vermin to confess all and one way or another we will get the information from him tonight otherwise..." he stopped himself and looked at Kurt.

Kurt was exhausted, drained of energy, no longer able to cry. The effects of the rohypnol that spiked his drink was starting to wear off.

"We're going to have to strap him," said Cornelius, "or break his legs at least."

"We'll strap him for now and, once we have him secured how about another drink?"

Cornelius and Dyrac strapped Kurt to the chair. Even if he could move he physically he wouldn't be able to. They stepped away from the polythene lined torture scene and moved over to the drinks cabinet. Both of them were calm and collected, as though this was a normal day for them. Dyrac poured them both a whisky and callously they both raised their glasses towards Kurt and, again in unison, said "cheers."

Chapter 30

"I swear I heard something, listen," said Merril shushing Verne.

"I don't hear anything Merril?" Verne was lying. There was no doubt about it, the feint noise coming from beyond where they were sitting in the corridor was the sound of a grown man moaning in agony.

"Really? You don't hear that?" Merril was suspicious. She knew she had a wild imagination but she was absolutely sure that she wasn't imagining this. Merril chose to accept Verne's blatant lie adding, "I must be overtired, my imagination is running away with me tonight."

Verne looked at Merril avoiding eye contact knowing his gaze would give him away. "Sometimes these old houses make all sorts of strange sounds," he patronised her.

"Hmm," came the reply.

In the study Kurt was writhing in agony. Well, writhing as best he could for a man strapped to a chair. The wounds to his nail beds on his right hand had congealed with claggy and clotted clumps of blood and flesh. His left wrist still poured freely. He was battling with himself mentally. *Am I drunk? Is this happening? I must be hallucinating right? I've not done anything? Have I?* His thoughts cascaded in ever decreasing circles with a new thought almost immediately replacing the previous.

Dyrac and Cornelius were stood by the drinks cabinet, both of them propped against it facing the other.

"We're going to have to take this further, quicker," said Cornelius.

"Explain," said Dyrac.

"Well, if he has anything to hide then he's hiding it well and isn't breaking. If he isn't hiding anything then, well we've gone too far Dyrac to let him go now."

Kurt could hear only broken parts of their conversation but he caught the "conclusive end" crystal clear. His heart rate rocketed, it was chaotic and rapid. He struggled to control it. He felt his heart in his throat. He tried to deduce a way out of this mess to no avail. He was resolute, he was solemn and he was doomed. His pulse boomed throughout his body and with every beat he thought it would beat right out of him. His breathing became erratic and he felt faint. Panic stricken, Kurt passed out.

Fifteen minutes later and Kurt's eyes burnt waking him. His senses were overwhelmed as a thwack of ammonia hit him with full force. The distinct aroma from a small bottle of smelling salts held under his nose by Cornelius engulfed him.

"Welcome back Mr Lewis, you gave us a scare. For a moment there we thought we had lost you," teased Cornelius, "and before we'd finished with you. But, here you are, back with us. Are you ready to talk yet?" he asked.

"Talk about what?" blubbed Kurt. He'd tried his hardest to muster a stern, strong sounding voice but the feeble terrified child within him answered first.

"Mr Gideon," Cornelius smiled. As he rose to his feet he turned towards Dyrac and leant over his doctor's bag.

Kurt listened out for Dyrac's voice but kept his eyes fixed on Cornelius.

"Mr Lewis? Kurt," said Dyrac, "let's change direction." Dyrac stood directly in front of Kurt. He was holding a Glencairn Crystal whisky glass which was almost full to the brim of Johnnie Walker. His other hand was in front of him, his thumb tucked in to the pocket watch pocket on his waist coat, his fingers fondled the pocket watch chain that lay across his torso to the fourth button where it was affixed by a small hinged bracket through the button hole.

"A few weeks ago I asked you to bring a chest to Wode House correct?" asked Dyrac.

"Yes sir," Kurt replied.

"And, as instructed you delivered the chest placing it in the cellar, yes?"

"Yes, but you know all this, please sir I…"

Kurt was interrupted, "and immediately after placing the chest in the cellar you left and locked the door correct?"

"Yes but…"

"Don't' lie to me Kurt, what did you do in the cellar after you dropped off the chest."

"I left. I don't know what you want me to say? I dropped the chest in the cellar in the main room. You told me not to go anywhere else so I didn't I just dropped it there and left the cellar and locked it."

Dyrac nodded to Cornelius.

"PLEASE!" Kurt cried out.

"Merril, Merril!" shouted Verne bringing Merril back to consciousness.

"Sorry Verne, I drifted."

"You're telling me you drifted. You talk in your sleep, do you know that?"

"Talk? What was I saying?" asked Merril.

"Excuse me, when I say talk I use that term loosely. You make noises, you murmur and gurgle. Occasionally there is a recognisable syllable or word but it was mainly nonsensical. Who is Idysha though? You kept saying it again and again. At first I thought it was a little bit of garble but then I realised it must be a name. It's not a name I've heard before but intrigue got the better of me and I just had to ask."

Merril paused for a moment. She wasn't willing to give Verne any information so had to think quickly.

"I've no idea what you're talking about. Must be, like you say Verne nonsensical garble. It's not a name I've ever heard of either," she lied.

Verne didn't press further but changed topic of conversation. Whilst Merril was officially off duty and enjoying the wine bestowed upon her by Dyrac, Verne was very much on duty. His duties after dinner came with only one instruction, distract Merril at all costs.

Cornelius was rummaging in his doctors bag and Kurt wondered what he would possibly come out with next. Kurt thought hard about his time in the cellar. *Had he inadvertently entered one of the rooms and forgotten? Had he left the door open leaving it exposed.* Then suddenly, like an arrow hitting bull's-eye, like a scientist reaching that Eureka moment, like the cries of a newborn baby taking its first breath it hit him. Merril! He remembered she was fumbling trying to lock the cellar door. *What had she been doing and was this the reason he was being tortured for information. What had she found?* In the same instant that all those thoughts entered his mind he had made a decision. Kurt wasn't about to let Merril go through what he was going through now and he certainly wasn't going to divulge that he'd seen her looking suspicious that day. He was going to have to hold out as long as he could. Bare all that he could bare. Tolerate any tool of torment that Cornelius revealed. He inhaled a long, slow breath and held it for a few seconds. As he exhaled he composed himself as best he could and looked Dyrac straight in his eyes.

"I'm ready," he announced.

"What do you mean you're ready? Ready to talk? Answer my questions?" asked Dyrac.

"I'm ready. Ready for anything that Mr Blackshot takes out of that bag. I'm ready to sit here until I take my last breath."

Dyrac looked towards Cornelius. Cornelius gestured with his eyes *don't worry I've got this under control*.

"We'll see if you're ready," said Cornelius as he held out his next instrument of pain, "this is an old favourite. It's slow, it's barbarically tortuous and before I finish you'll be begging me to end you."

Dyrac gagged. He recalled a time that he had been working with Cornelius when he used it before but he remained steadfast and watched as Cornelius readied himself.

"I'll take all you have, I'll tell you nothing. And as for begging you, I wouldn't give you the satisfaction old man," Kurt was defiant and confident now, despite the physical weakness he began to feel.

"Then let's begin," said Cornelius.

Chapter 31

Kurt looked on as Cornelius knelt next to him and untied his shoes. He slid each one off and placed them next to the hearth. He removed Kurt's socks and as ridiculous as it sounds Kurt was embarrassed of his feet being exposed. He had been a prolific toenail chewer and his toes were hideous as a result. None of this mattered at this moment but Kurt couldn't help but feel shame.

"These feet look like they've been regularly tortured, so this should be a walk in the park," said Cornelius, "although you won't be walking after I've finished," he added.

Cornelius placed an unusual looking device in between Kurt's feet. The device consisted of one horizontal and three upright metal bars, between which Cornelius placed Kurt's toes. On top of his toes he slid a wooden bar across them pressing his toes into the bottom metal bar. Cornelius affixed a large threaded screw with a wing nut head and spun it around the thread with one finger until the torque became too tight to move without pressure. The screw pressed the wooden bar downwards and slowly Cornelius began twisting the nut painfully crushing Kurt's toes.

Kurt winced but didn't scream, he maintained control of his breathing and focussed on other things.

"Playing tough? That's fine with me," said Cornelius undoing the mechanism and swapping out the wooden bar for a metal bar with small spikes protruding from it. Cornelius had barely turned the wing applying pressure when Kurt yelped. The spikes pierced the flesh on the top of his toes. Cornelius tightened the screw further seemingly enjoying the sadistic game he was now playing.

Kurt panted and tried to hide the pain he was feeling in that moment. Cornelius tightened the screw further and almost instantly fell back as he was spattered with blood and fleshy shrapnel. Kurt's big toe on his left foot exploded at the end exposing shards of bone, mangled muscle, ruptured veins and torn ligaments. Imagine a limb being forced through a hand turned mincing machine and that image right there, mixed with scarlet fresh blood is what was staring Cornelius back in the face.

Kurt couldn't take it anymore and screamed in agony. As quickly as the scream escaped his mouth Dyrac had rushed over and clasped his hands over Kurt's mouth from behind him. Holding his head steady.

"The cellar Kurt, talk now, it's only getting worse for you," pleaded Dyrac.

Kurt defied Dyrac shaking his head tears pouring from his eyes, the water was stinging and biting. The tears seeped into his mouth and a salty taste filled Kurt's palette. That's how you know the tears are real, if they're salty they are real. Fake tears aren't salty.

Cornelius turned the screw again and a fresh heat of pain rippled through Kurt's body. As the spikes penetrated Kurt's nerves he felt referred pain in different parts of his body.

Leaving the device in place Cornelius reached in his bag again and withdrew what essentially looked like a ladle with a long handle. He opened the ladle head and poured in a small amount of oil keeping the contents inside by securing the lid. He put the ladle headed end into the fire and stepped back.

Next he took out a metal collar which had a horizontal metal slot at the front. The collar was placed around Kurt's neck k. There was an inscription *I recant, ital,* meaning I renounce. It was a heretic fork.

"Hold his head back as far as it will go Drack whilst I put this piece in place."

Kurt couldn't see what piece Cornelius spoke of as Dyrac forced his head back almost breaking his neck.

"Far enough," asked Dyrac.

"Far enough," came the reply, "Don't release him until I say."

Cornelius fitted a double ended flat fork through the horizontal slot carefully placing one end so it rested neatly on Kurt's manubrium, that v-shaped gap between where your collar bones would meet.

"Release his head," said Cornelius.

Dyrac released Kurt's head whose instinct was to immediately drop it forward as though looking straight on. Instantly Kurt flung his head back, the metal fork at the top had punctured the fleshy bit underneath his chin.

Dyrac pushed Kurt for more information regarding the cellar but he never wavered. Dyrac even got his hands dirty and tried to get Kurt to talk by forcing his head forward onto the forks prongs. Each time Kurt's head fell against it new wounds were created and the underside of his chin began to resemble a cannibal's collinder.

"Dyrac, it's clear he isn't going to talk, he's certainly not going to divulge anything now. We've gone so far there is no going back. Why don't we turn things up a notch? I can see your enjoying this just as much as I. There's exhilaration in your eyes; that animalistic hunt mode. That's the same look you get when you're feeding."

"Let's make this more fun," Dyrac replied, "the tickler?" he asked Cornelius holding his right hand out.

The tickler sounded more like death by feather duster but it couldn't be further from that description. The tickler, as they had both come to know it, was the Spanish tickler. An iron claw like object heavyset and clearly designed to inflict unfathomable devastation.

Dyrac took the tickler and forced Kurt as far forward as he could. The heretic fork drove straight through Kurt's throat narrowly missing the major artery still resulted in significant and rapid blood loss.

With a swift swiping motion Dyrac brought down the tickler across Kurt's back shredding his skin, chipping at bones and dislodging parts of his spine. Kurt was instantly paralysed from just one swift movement, a direct hit.

Even if he was to get out of this, he would most certainly never walk again. Despite the searing pain confusing his mind and causing him to hallucinate. Despite the gush of blood that was now pooling around his feet, Kurt felt a sense of relief for despite the intensity of the pain he felt in his throat, across his back, in his hands and wrist he could no longer feel his legs or the pain in his feet. For that little break he was getting, he felt a sudden second whim and surge of energy. It was more the lack of oxygen getting around his major organs that was causing this endorphic effect but nonetheless it gave him some gusto.

"You've got nothing," he managed to gargle through the blood collecting in his mouth, spraying reddened spit as he formed the words.

"I'll give credit, where credit is due," said Cornelius, "this man has got some massive cahonies that's for sure."

Dyrac was exhausted but he knew that Cornelius had more he wanted to get through.

"Shall we add some sprinkles?" Cornelius asked Dyrac who nodded in reply at the same time taking another swipe from the opposite angle with the tickler.

Cornelius picked up the handle of the ladle like looking object that had been sitting in the fire. Kurt noticed that the ladle head had holes in it. Cornelius twisted it and the holes opened. Cornelius began swaying it across Kurt's body like a thurible containing incense being swung during a Roman Catholic service allowing the smoke from the incense permeate the air around it. Instead of smoke, burning hot oil dripped all over Kurt instantly blistering his skin. Some of the blisters formed so quickly they burst immediately.

Cornelius was haphazard in his swaying but he hovered more over Kurt's groin and allowed a slower flow of the scorching hot liquid to scald Kurt over his genitals. Kurt felt like his penis was trying to recoil up inside him, his scrotum bubbled and crisped up like pork crackling. Kurt cracked.

"It was Merril!"

Chapter 32

"Well, that's it Verne. The last of it," Merril shook the wine bottle trying to get the dregs from the now empty wine bottle.

"Time to call it a night?" asked Verne.

"I suppose it is," replied Merril, "Thanks for joining me for the nightcap, a bit of company has done me wonders."

"Anytime, well, anytime whilst I'm here Merril," he replied.

"How long are you staying again?" asked Merril.

"I suppose whenever Mr Blackshot has finished the job he came to do?"

"Job?"Merril asked and Verne knew he'd said too much.

"Job, visit, it all blurs into the same thing for me," Verne quickly replied.

Merril's gut knew something was afoot this evening. *Does this have anything to do with Kurt?* She thought.

Verne coughed to break the uncomfortable silence and startled Merril causing her to jump and spill wine from her glass.

"I'm sorry," she said.

"Drifting again?"

"It's getting late, I'm going to call time on the evening and get some rest," Merril rose to her feet with Verne reciprocating the rise of her wine glass and politely bidding her a good night to Merril.

Merril had been in her room for at least half an hour

and thought, *surely he's dropped off by now and, if not surely I can creep past his door without stirring him*. Merril knew every creaky floor board at Wode House so had no doubt she could pass by Verne's room unheard. She left her room closing the door with precarious caution. A barely audible click and it was closed.

With a deep breath Merril walked a few steps before stopping and looking at the floor. She side stepped twice and, on her tip toes, walked along the wall missing the broken board in the floor right by where she had been sitting with Verne. After a little more zig zagging and delicate foot placement she was clear of the corridor and safe to walk freely without disturbing the house.

She scurried down the stairs and was just about to run towards the kitchen when she heard it. Merril stopped, dead still, frozen in fear.

"It was Merril!" she heard a voice that sounded a little like Kurt, albeit it was wavering and limp. Desperation echoed through the hallway.

What's me? Why does Kurt sound so strained? What the hell is going on?

She felt a sudden pressure on her shoulder, a hand pulling her backwards. She spun around and Verne was standing there stern and oppressive, foreboding almost. He had his index finger pressed against his lips and he shook his head.

Confusion filled Merril's face, "but I..." she stopped.

Verne titled his head to the right gesturing Merril to move to her left. They both remained facing each other as they side stepped to the side of the stairwell.

Once clear Verne turned on his heels and walked towards the housekeeping cupboard stopping just outside.

"Quiet Merril, they'll hear."

"Verne? What are you? What the hell is going on?" she demanded, fear clear and present in her voice.

"I'll tell you all Merril but first we need to keep clear of the study. We need a safe place where we can talk without interruption. There's a lot you're going to hear which you'll not want to hear and, some of it you won't understand straight away but I need you to listen to me until I finish. Do you understand?" he asked.

Merril nodded not really understanding.

"Where can we go?" asked Verne.

Merril swallowed trying to muster up some saliva to whet her palette, her mouth drier than sandpaper. "Follow me and watch where I place my feet," she said.

Dyrac and Cornelius stood back both aghast at the outcry from Kurt. Believing he wouldn't falter they were both equally surprised when he spoke out and more so at the revelation he just unveiled.

"Merril? My Merril? In the cellar?" asked Dyrac.

Kurt could speak no more, all his energy had been sucked out of him. There was barely anything left. His body went into survival mode concentrating on his major organs whilst at the same time suffering significant blood loss. Kurt mustered a single nod of his head before nothing.

"Kurt?" shouted Dyrac, "KURT!"

Kurt sat lifeless in the chair. The pool of blood around his feet ever increasing. His head was slumped forward being held up slightly by the heretic fork still in place. The insides of his left arm still exposed pumped the occasional spurt of blood. His back, now torn to ribbons from the tickler resembled something that had passed through a wood chipper. His toes remained bound by the crushing thumb press. Suddenly his body spasmed into a seizure. The heretic fork penetrated his throat and chest holding them together in an almost right angled fixed position. The fitting stopped and his back arched, he remained seated in the chair.

Verne followed Merril past the study. Merril held her hand up and then pointed to the floor. Verne could see a slight raise in the parquetry flooring where a piece had worked loose over time and took care to avoid stepping, or even tripping, on it. When they reached the kitchen Merril let out an almighty breath as though she had been holding it the whole time. Verne shrugged with his palms face up as though to ask, 'what now'? Without speaking Merril curled her finger back and forth in a 'this way' response.

Carefully Merril took out a key which was fastened to her chatelaine, a decorative belt worn around her waist from which she suspended keys, scissors, thimbles and other household appendages that housekeepers frequently used. The chatelaine was a very Victorian item however, Merril found it remained the best way to keep things close and used it often. The key was for the side entrance door.

"Merril," Verne whispered, "where are we going?

It's freezing out there?"

"You want to talk and I know a place we won't be disturbed. If you can't bear a little chill then it will have to wait until tomorrow."

"It can't wait Merril, let's go," he replied wrapping his arms tightly across his chest embracing himself hoping his own body heat would keep him warm. He followed Merril out of the door and along the side of Wode House. Passing the sun dial they crossed the small bridge to the folly.

"In here," she ushered him into the folly. It was no warmer inside but at least it was private, "I'm ready when you are Verne, what the hell is going on?"

In the study Dyrac and Cornelius stepped away from Kurt. "Well he's definitely dead," said Dyrac.

"Don't be so sure, the human body is a phenomenal thing and despite what we've put him through tonight he could still be alive," said Cornelius.

"Alive, after that? No way Cornelius. Look at him! Jesus what did we do to him. Did he deserve that?" questioned Dyrac addressing his own conscience as well as Cornelius's.

"Dyrac!" Cornelius shouted pronouncing his name correctly enforcing his seriousness. "Get a grip man, this was all planned out. You were all for it before when you wanted information."

"But he never…"

Cornelius interrupted him, "He gave us Merril. He was stronger than we thought he'd be and admittedly I never thought it would need to go as far as it did but you were prepared for him to leave the room in a body bag so don't waiver on me now. We've got to get him moved. We can't keep him here and we need to clear the place up so Merril doesn't suspect anything. After all, she wouldn't be expecting to see Mr Lewis again until Saturday's delivery."

"Yes Cornelius, you're right. I know you're right but, shit. Look at him, it's easier when you don't know the subject. Disassociation is a wonderful thing."

"Snap out of it Dyrac!" said Cornelius.

"I need a drink before we start. You?"

Cornelius replied, "agreed. We can both do with a large tot."

They both moved away from the body slumped in the chair and walked over to the drinks cabinet where Dyrac poured the last of the opened Johnnie Walker into their respective glasses.

Merril listened to Verne, hanging on to this every word.

"The day the letter arrived I was instructed to cancel all of Mr Blackshot's schedule. Usually an urgent matter called for the postponement or rearrangement of meetings, lunches, dinners etc however; this time I knew something was wrong. Mr Blackshot advised to cancel all future engagements. I did as I was instructed and Mr Blackshot requested my assistance in packing his things. There was an unknown urgency in getting everything together, booking the earliest flight possible and making sure we arrived at Wode House promptly."

"What did the letter say?" Merril asked intrigued.

"I haven't read the content but I knew, based on

the equipment I was packing, that this was more than a friendly visit."

"Equipment? What equipment?" asked Merril trying to extract as much detail from Verne as she could.

"I'll get to that shortly Merril, just bear with me," replied Verne.

"Ok, ok. I'm sorry," she replied pressing her fingers against her lips.

"So, everything was in order and ready and we began our journey to Wode House. As soon as we turned into the gates and drove the long tree lined driveway to house I felt a shiver. I had been on many a "work trip" with Mr Blackshot but nothing quite like this one. The employer on this occasion was known to Mr Blackshot and, from what I already knew based on what was in the luggage, this was a hired hand for a friend and would undoubtedly be a bloodier event than usual."

"Bloodier? Sorry?" Merril stopped herself.

"When I arrived and learned that dinner would include an extra guest to that of Mr Gideon and Mr Blackshot, I knew instantly that Mr Lewis was the intended target and…"

"TARGET! What does that even…"

Verne cut Merril short, "Merril!" he said sternly, "Please listen, I'll answer questions if I can when I've finished. Mr Lewis was clearly oblivious this evening at dinner and had clearly been brought to Wode House under false pretences. There was no way I could forewarn him, you don't understand how Mr Blackshot works, it wasn't just instructions I had but orders. And, if I didn't follow those orders it's not me, but my family that would be made to suffer."

Merril was engrossed and confused at the same time. She didn't know what to make of everything that was happening but she decided once Verne had finished regaling the story as he knew it that she would be going through the hidden passageway to see for herself what was going on in the study.

Verne continued. "We arrived at Wode House and after you had shown me to Mr Blackshots quarters, and after he had met with Mr Gideon in the study, but before dinner I was given my instructions. I was to act like I was in normal service and play along with the process. I was informed that following dinner the three of them would retire to the study where Mr Blackshot and Mr Gideon would extract information from Mr Lewis. This wasn't going to be a simple Q&A type affair Merril. Mr Blackshot's field of expertise was extraction by torture."

Merril gasped as fear spread across her body sprouting goose pimples and causing the hairs on her skin to stand on end.

"During dinner I was instructed to collect a particular item from Mr Blackshot's room and bring it to the study. The item was his doctor's bag. It contained his "kit" which consisted of many instruments of torture. I won't go into the specifics Merril as I assume you have enough imagination to understand what torture would involve?"

Merril was stunned and silent, she knew Dyrac and Cornelius were capable of many things, after all she was a willing donor when it came to Dyrac's need to feed on her blood. What her imagination was providing her with now was barbaric and, what she didn't know yet was, it was not far off from accurate.

Chapter 33

Verne watched as Merril moved the plaque on the inside wall of the folly exposing the opening behind it.

"What's through there?" he asked.

"Follow me Verne and watch your footing. It's a tricky ladder to negotiate and I'll tell you when we are nearing the bottom rung so you are ready," she replied.

Verne precariously followed Merril not even sure his rotund middle was going to fit through the hole that he found himself in front of.

They reached the bottom and Merril activated the gas lighting illuminating the passage way ahead.

"Merril, this is amazing, where are we going?" he asked.

"You'll see," she replied, "come on, we've got to hurry."

Kurt sat lifeless whilst Dyrac and Cornelius conversed at the drinks cabinet. Deep in conversation they were both unaware of the slight twitch in Kurt's right hand. Kurt was alive. Fading, and fading fast, Kurt still had a pulse. It was weak but it was there.

Kurt's consciousness was intermittent with his subconscious, flashing life events in and out of focus. His third eye fully active, Kurt experienced a vision and the foreseeing future events that would unfold at Wode House. In a state of comatosed delirium, Kurt's understanding of the real world versus the hallucinations he was having were blurring together seamlessly.

Verne made a mental map as he and Merril meandered their way through the passage way. Making a note of every turn, what they passed and what he could see in the ambient orange glow from the antiquated lighting.

"Here," Merril said, "stop." Merril went to press her face against the wall and appeared to be looking at something beyond when she quickly withdrew her face, turned and buried her face into Verne's chest. She was sobbing uncontrollably but her cries were muffled against Verne and even he barely heard her cry.

"What is it Merril? What were you looking at?" he asked instinctively putting his arms around her as if consoling a grieving loved one. He felt her warmth, her body against his and for a split second he forgot himself and what he was there to do.

"It, it, it's Kurt, Mr Lewis, Kurt. In there," she pointed not moving her face.

"In where Merril? Where are we?"

Merril stepped aside not raising her head and pointed. "Look for yourself," she answered.

Verne stepped forward and took a deep breath as he placed his face against the wall just as Merril did, having to crouch slightly as he did so.

"What the, is that, are you sure it's," he said stopping himself.

"It's him, what have they done to him Verne, why are they doing this? What do they think he knows or is hiding?" sobbed Merril.

"Merril," Verne was soft in his voice as he turned

to face her and with one finger under her chin he pulled her head up so she was facing him. Through tear filled, doe eyes she looked back at him. "Merril, I warned you what they were going to be doing. I told you they'd torture him."

"But," she sobbed, "look at him Verne. I need to get to him. I need to know if he's..." she couldn't say it but Verne knew she meant dead.

"Mr Gideon and Mr Blackshot are in there, and anyway it would take some time to get back to the house from the other side and interrupt them in the study."

Merril pointed to the hitched latch.

"Is that a? It is, it's a door isn't it?" asked Verne.

Merril nodded.

"Ok, well maybe they will leave soon and then we can go in together and check if he's..." Verne couldn't finish his sentence this time either.

Merril and Verne hushed one another as they both heard voices from beyond the wall. Dyrac and Cornelius were talking.

"We'll move him to the cellar for now," said Cornelius.

"You are joking right? If you haven't already forgotten we know it wasn't Kurt that was in the cellar remember?" replied Dyrac.

"Yes, yes, calm down man, but at the moment, just for tonight, we need to move him and the cellar is the best, and only suitable albeit temporary option we have right now. We can dispose of the body tomorrow properly." Said Cornelius.

Merril wretched silently and looked at Verne and whispered, "They are talking about him as though he is a lump of meat, like the carcass of an animal recently slaughtered at an abattoir. He was a human being Verne, he was my friend!"

Verne shushed Merril and they continued to listen.

"You're right, though it pains me to say," said Dyrac.

"I'm always right Drack, you know that," came the reply from Cornelius adding, "right, we'll need to get him on the floor and wrap him in the polythene. I've got duct tape in the bag so we'll make sure he is nice and secure, make sure nothing leaks, if you know what I'm saying."

Dyrac nodded and they both walked over to Kurt. Dyrac put his hands under Kurt's armpits and hoisted him in the chair slightly. Cornelius grabbed both feet and on three they lifted him off the chair and lay him down on the polythene. Cornelius decided to tape him up before they wrapped him to prevent his limbs from falling loose through the sheeting.

"Not so tight," said Dyrac.

"Not so tight?" questioned Cornelius, "he's dead Drack, he's hardly going to notice."

Cornelius bit down at the tape separating it from the rest of the roll after binding Kurt's feet together. Next he taped Kurt's legs just above the knees. Kurt's arms were placed across him, just like King Tut and all the mummified pharaohs were bound before being wrapped in bandages and placed in their sarcophaguses.

"Grab that end will you?" asked Cornelius pointing to the polythene sheet under Dyrac's feet. Dyrac passed it to Cornelius carefully making sure Kurt's bodily matter and fluids didn't spill out.

Cornelius secured the polythene around Kurt and unravelled the remainder of the roll of duct tape around him in a plastic/tape chrysalis. "There," he said, "cocooned, ready to be reborn in his next life," said Cornelius flamboyantly sarcastic.

"Shit, do we have to cover his face?" asked Dyrac.

"Seriously Drack," said Cornelius.

"Fine," came the reply.

"We'll finish these and then move him to the chapel in the cellar," said Cornelius lifting his whisky glass.

Merril looked at Verne and pointed indicating to move farther along the passage way. After a probably ten steps or so she stopped.

"We have to go to the cellar," she said to Verne.

"Did you not just hear them Merril, they are going to the cellar. Mr Gideon and Mr Blackshot, with Mr Lewis," emphasised Verne.

"Yes Verne, I heard them perfectly and that is why we are going there also. But not via the conventional way. Follow me," said Merril.

"Another door?" he asked but Merril did not reply she just beckoned him to follow.

Just before Verne turned to follow in the direction Merril was now walking a villainous smile formed on his face and there was deviousness in his eyes.

Chapter 34

After Abimilech's disappearance his wife Sarah slowly began to lose control. A once sweet and doting mother morphed into a bitter woman full of resentment blaming her daughter Idysha for her father's abscondment.

"You're wretchedness bore into him sucking the life from him," Sarah spat the words out addressing Idysha shortly after she arrived home from her boarding school. "Before you arrived," she continued pointing at her daughter, "I was his only reason for living."

"Mother, you don't know what you're saying. You're just upset," cried Idysha, "you were both such caring and loving parents. Remember the days we baked together? Remember the tin of trinkets you gave me telling me that it contained all your most precious things but the most precious one of all couldn't be contained in there because that thing was me?" She pleaded for consolation from her mother, for her mother to let her console her back.

"It was all just a daydream back then Idysha. I saw a change in your father once we sent you away for schooling. He was different, lacked patience. He was missing a cog in his mechanics causing him to malfunction, like a loose connection on a combustion engine, misfiring at the most inappropriate of times. I knew almost instantly it was because we'd sent you away and it was then I began to lose him.

Now where is he? He went on one of his expeditions with that ragamuffin he adopted, Dyrac, neither of them have returned nor has either one of them sent word. Just like that, disappeared off the face of the planet."

"Mother please," Idysha pleaded.

"You're intolerable, insolent and petulant child. You're dead to me," Sarah dismissed her only daughter, the only child she ever bore. It pained her so but she blamed Idysha. Sarah loved her daughter deeply but she loved Abimilech more and she could no longer bear to look at Idysha in the eye. For it was those eyes, the eyes of her baby girl; the ones that stared right back at her that reflected the mirror image of her fathers. It was this that cut through Sarah's heart.

Despite the calls from Idysha begging her to stop, to return to embrace her daughter which she so desperately wanted to do, Sarah carried on walking away not once looking back. Sarah left the side entrance of the family home and walked along the building passing a sundial. Just beyond that was a stone bridge that lead to an island of trees isolated in a small lake.

Idysha never saw her mother again.

"Merril!" exclaimed Verne.

Merril jumped, still in the dark and elusive maze of passage ways and still accompanied by Verne, snapping back into the fore.

"Merril," said Verne again, "is everything ok?"

"Everything is not ok," she replied, "but everything will soon be," she added vehemently.

Verne looked confused and a little uneasy. He knew more than Merril realised and for a fleeting moment he felt sorry for her and for what yet to come.

"Dyrac, what are you doing here? Where's Abimilech? Is he finally home?" asked Sarah startled at finding Dyrac standing blarzae, in the middle of the bridge.

Dyrac, now a man, gave no response but turned and looked Sarah up and down making her envelope her arms around herself in a self protective way putting up visible barriers that screamed, stay away.

"Answer me boy, well, where is he? Where have you been?" demanded Sarah.

Before she had a second chance, and in one swift movement, she saw Dyrac raise him arm and, holding a small cosh he struck down. Sarah fell in a slump to the floor.

Dyrac stood over a limp and lifeless Sarah. He wiped the cosh clean with a handkerchief returning it to his top jacket pocket. He scooped her up and slung her over his shoulder. He walked back along the bridge towards Wode House but veered to the right towards a small wooded area.

He turned back once to look at the house with an irksome smile.

"Drack!" Dyrac's flashback was interrupted by Cornelius.

"Christ Drack, where the fuck did you go to?" asked Cornelius trying to probe Dyrac's thoughts.

"Sorry Cornelius. Let's get on," he replied unlocking the door to the cellar.

"Getting him down here should be easier than

getting him from the study, after all we could just throw him down the stairs and then move the body to the chapel when we get down there."

"Absolutely not," said Dyrac, "Jesus Cornelius, we just butchered the man and he deserves some respect after what we put him through, despite the fact that he is no longer with us."

"You're too soft for this line of work Dyrac, that's why I usually go solo," said Cornelius.

"That's why you go solo?" mocked Dyrac.

"What's that supposed to mean?" asked Cornelius.

"You go solo Cornelius because you're a massive pain in the ass. You're an intolerable man, that's why I'm the only friend you have because," Dyrac added, "I'm just as intolerable as you."

They both chuckled acknowledging the accuracy of Dyrac's statement and sharing a moment remembering their long standing friendship.

Together they carried Kurt's body into the cellar. Cornelius still at the feet end was moving faster than Dyrac who was at the head end, and was going down the stairs first.

"Slow down you idiot else it will be more than Kurt's body that's down here, I'll fall down these stairs and split my head open when I hit the floor at the bottom," said Dyrac.

"Not a bad idea, I might speed up," added Cornelius giving Kurt's feet a gentle push, "then I can take Wode House for my own." Cornelius let out a fake laugh, like he'd just finalised a fool proof plan of world domination. An evil genius sitting in his imposing chair; looking down to his minions whilst stroking his cat in his evil lair.

"Very funny you bastard," replied Dyrac. "Ok, through here." He guided Cornelius and Kurt's body into the chapel. "Lay him down here for a minute."

"You know if anyone get's down here before we have disposed of Kurt properly he will be found," said Cornelius.

"We're not leaving him here but I can't do this whilst holding him," Dyrac replied heading to a cabinet in the far left corner of the chapel. He opened the door to the cabinet revealing a further set of doors inside.

"What kind of cabinet is that?" asked Cornelius inquisitively.

"It's something I had commissioned, I call it a Mysteriository. Things go in, but they seldom come out. That's not entirely an accurate description," said Dyrac, "but once inside the internal cabinet, items, be it valuables or people in this instance appear to disappear. There is a clever contraption inside that creates an illusion that the cabinet is in fact empty when the contents are actually there, just hidden from plain sight."

"That is a piece of fucking genius right there," replied Cornelius awestruck at the brilliance of the cabinet. "Where can I get one?" he asked.

"It's the only one, and will only ever be the only one," said Dyrac.

"Nonsense, who made it, I want to commission one?" asked Cornelius.

"It doesn't matter who made it, he and the plans have both been destroyed and I retained no copy of the schematic behind the idea nor do I recall the inner finer workings."

"Well shit!" exclaimed Cornelius, "at least show me how it works."

Merril stopped Verne suddenly in his tracks, almost to the point where he fell over her. "We're here," she said.

"The cellar?" he asked.

"The cellar Verne. Now listen to me very carefully if you don't want either of us to be killed, understand?"

Verne nodded and gulped simultaneously.

Chapter 35

With military hand signals, like those you'd expect to see a troop follow when in field combat, Merril indicated to Verne that they should move forward but quietly. She balled a fist and held it upright when they needed to stop and then with a quick flick of her fore fingers she indicated when it was clear to move forward again.

"We're not in Nam," said Verne referring to the military operation of the Vietnam War.

Merril scorned a look towards Verne that suggested he take matters seriously and obediently he nodded and followed her.

They both walked forward through the secret door leading into the chamber of curiosities. Verne was awestruck at the sights before him; objects, collectibles, artefacts and the macabre filled the room. He walked through careful not to accidentally knock into anything. Verne had to stop himself from gasping as he walked by jars containing preserved human body parts. He was used to seeing horrifying things but the thought of someone keeping hold of pieces of other, once living, human beings sat uneasy with him and his stomach churned and griped. A little bile hit the back of his throat.

Ball fisted Merril stopped. Verne almost walked into the back of her as he was distracted by the sights around and in particular an unusual looking box perched on the edge of a cob webbed, dusty shelf. The box was clearly oriental and appeared to be carved out of ivory, he thought on that and had a look around the room then changed his opinion. *It's probably carved from human bone*, correcting his own thoughts.

Merril softly clicked her fingers to try to get Verne's attention. He turned, "sorry," he whispered.

"Focus," she whispered in response adding, "wait here, DO NOT move," in an authoritarian voice.

Merril peered her head just enough into the open doorway to clearly see the centre chamber of the cellar. It was empty. She could see a flicker of light coming from the chapel and turned to face Verne.

"We're going to have to go through here. Keep close. Keep quiet. Keep to the side," she said.

Verne nodded not uttering a word. They began to move forward and Verne stumped his toe against the door as they walked through. He instantly grabbed his mouth stopping him from screaming and hopped around on his left foot. Merril waved her arms frantically in a 'DO NOT MAKE A SOUND' exclaimed mime.

They both composed themselves and continued forward.

They stood, backs against the wall side by side and listened. Verne was straining to hear what was being said and whispered to Merril, "how about we go either side of the door?"

Merril nodded and before Verne had chance to step a foot in front of him to move Merril was already on the other side of the door. Verne mouthed, "how did you get there so fast?"

Merril just smiled and shrugged, pointed to the chapel and then cupped her ear.

Kurt lay on the floor of the chapel still bound by

the plastic sheeting Dyrac and Cornelius had sealed his body in.

Dyrac and Cornelius were stood at the altar inside the chapel leafing through the large leather bound book that was resting on a table top gilded lectern.

"Stop!" exclaimed Cornelius, "It's that one."

"Are you sure?" asked Dyrac looking at the page Cornelius had just put his hand.

"I'm sure. I have done this before you know," he replied.

"Ok, well we'll come back to it tomorrow when we relocate Kurt's body." Said Dyrac leaving the book open on the page they were discussing.

"Yes and we will need the bottle," said Cornelius, "for the time being however, Mr Lewis, if you will?" With that Cornelius grabbed at the feet of Kurt and prompted Dyrac to get the head end again.

Dyrac and Cornelius placed Kurt's body into the Mysteriository. "He won't fit like this," said Dyrac.

"Give me a minute," answered Cornelius. Cornelius straightened Kurt's legs out in front of the cabinet placing Kurt into a seating position half inside the cabinet. "Hold here," he said to Dyrac holding out Kurt's feet.

Dyrac took hold of Kurt's feet stretching out his legs as far as he could holding them taut. With a crushing blow Cornelius struck at Kurt's legs just below the knees instantly breaking them. The sound reverberated around the chapel echoing the shattering cracks.

At the precise moment Cornelius struck Kurt's legs Merril peered through the doorway. She clasped her hand to her mouth as shock and horror filled her face. She watched as Cornelius twisted and turned Kurt's legs inwards at a right angle with his feet now parallel to the rest of his legs. Cornelius contorted Kurt and folded him, as easy as you would fold a piece of paper, so that he now fit snugly inside the cabinet.

Dyrac shook his head, "I'm sure there would've been another way," he said.

"Maybe," said Cornelius, "but we are running out of time Drack. Come on lets close this up and get out of the cellar."

Cornelius turned Kurt's body so he was sitting sideways in the space in the inner compartment of the Mysteriository. Dyrac closed the inner door.

Merril, urged back by Verne, whispered, "we need to get out of here, they are about to leave," and with that she beckoned Verne to follow her back into the chamber of curiosities. Verne and Merril headed through the room and were just closing the door to the secret passage way when they heard Dyrac's voice getting louder.

"In here," he said to Cornelius, "I swear I just heard something in here."

"Well unless Abimilech's risen from the dead I'm pretty sure it's a rat you'll have heard," replied Cornelius.

The door hadn't quite closed properly as Merril nervously held it too, as much as she could, without the latch catching and making a sound.

"It wouldn't be the first time that man has so called

come back from the dead would it?" said Dyrac.

"That's true," said Cornelius, "that man had a knack for disappearing presumed dead and then resurfacing again. Ok I'll look around with you."

They both entered the chamber of curiosities and had a quick glance around. The coast was clear and Dyrac was resolute with Cornelius's explanation that the sound he heard was probably just a rat.

"What's this?" asked Cornelius picking up an intricately carved and ornate box, "or should I say who is this?" instantly recognising that the box was carved from human bone.

"That, is a box Cornelius, a man of your genius I'm sure could've worked that out. As to who it is well, that was carved from the thigh bone of Ignatius Ptolemy."

"And," asked Cornelius, "who the hell is Ignatius Ptolemy?"

"Ignatius was, in his time, a prophetic cretin. He believed that Satan bore illegitimate children and sent them to earth to feast on the souls of the innocent. He was an eccentric, often critiqued for his fables depicting a demonic beast and it's thirst for power by drawing blood from pure and naive, orphaned children. He was condemned for his outlandish preaching back in 10 AD, or around then."

"And," asked Cornelius, "how is it you came to have a piece of his thigh bone, and how was it carved and why?"

"Cornelius," said Dyrac, "that story is for another time. For now, let's get back upstairs, have a quick nightcap and retire for the evening. Or should I say morning now," looking at his pocket watch.

Dyrac and Cornelius left the chamber of curiosities and Merril heard their footsteps going back into the house. She turned to look at Verne whilst pulling the door closed waiting for the click of the latch.

"That's quite enough the for evening," she said to Verne, "let's get back before they notice we are missing. I know a way to get to our quarters that won't involve us going back through the folly at this time." Merril knew the risks involved in leaving a door to the network of secret passageways open from the house side but there was no time to get back through the folly and into the house, let alone without been spotted by Dyrac and Cornelius.

Merril took Verne on another route along the passageways until they opened a doorway leading into what appeared to be some kind of walk in cupboard. After they both stepped through Merril pushed the door closed as much as she could. They turned and, after adjusting his eyesight from the dimly lit passageway, Verne realised they were inside a laundry room. Merril heaved a linen bin in front of the door way to obscure the fact that it was a door.

"Come on Verne, it's time to call it a night," she said.

Chapter 36

Merril didn't sleep all night. She lay on her bed staring at the ceiling. Each tick and tock of the clock grew louder and louder. The sounds appeared to go slower and slower like the long drawn out tempo of a metronome. Merril was conscious of every laborious second that went by and thought a different thought as each one drifted into the next. Her eyes were dry, burning and stinging, tiredness bore away at her that coincided with the curse of insomnia. She tried in vain to quantify, justify even, the actions of Dyrac Gideon that evening. She didn't think much on Cornelius, she knew little of him and knew even less of his line of work. Dyrac however, she knew him, or so she thought. She remembered memories which she had once forgotten, filed away and blocked out. She remembered the waif of a street boy her father came home with one day. Dirt ingrained into his skin giving his complexion an unhealthy hue, and smelling like a latrine.

Merril closed her eyes in a vain and futile attempt to fall asleep. No matter how much she tried, slumber evaded her. The harder she tried the more her mind spiralled out of control with thoughts of what had happened that evening, and of what was to come.

After what felt like an eternity Merril's morning alarm went off later than the usual working day. She had set it when she got back to her room in the early hours as she didn't want to waste her day off in bed. There was much to do, much to find out and it appeared the plans she had would be coming to fruition sooner than anticipated.

"So you're saying she knows but yet suspects nothing of what is to come?" asked Cornelius.

"That's correct sir. I did exactly as you asked and without much hesitation she took me through the hidden passage ways of Wode House. You were right sir, there's a whole mazed network of them. Not just one behind that painting," said Verne nodding his head to the large painting of the folly hanging on the wall of Chamber four. "And that, that in the painting, is how you get in. Although we did come back into the house through a different route. There wasn't enough time to get back through the folly and into the house without you or Mr Gideon spotting us."

"Another way in you say? Show me," instructed Cornelius.

"I'll check that the coast is clear of Merril and when I know it's safe I'll call for you sir," said Verne.

"Right you are, in the meantime I'll go and meet Dyrac in the study. We have quite a lot to get through today," replied Cornelius.

"You're telling me," said Verne under his breath.

Verne left Cornelius's room and headed back up to his own. He was on his way up to check Merril wasn't around when he passed her on the stairs.

"Day off right?" he asked looking Merril up and down as she stood before him dressed in her scruffy paint spattered smock dress and docs.

"Right," said Merril barely making eye contact with Verne.

"You ok?" he asked noting her abrupt and brusque

demeanor.

"Not really no," she said matter of fact, "but, I've got to get on. Personal matters."

"I'll bid you a good day then," Verne replied politely as he watched Merril slump off without uttering another word.

Dyrac stepped out of the copper rolled top bath and onto the soft sheepskin rug on the floor. He'd been in that bath over an hour and his skin had pruned. He was only kept warm by the open log fire burning away in the bathroom.

He closed the bathrobe around himself and made his way to the walk in wardrobe. He knew today was going to be difficult with top item on the days schedule being 'dispose of Kurt's body'. Later today he knew he had to face Merril.

Dyrac recalled Merril's first day at Wode House, how her face seemed familiar but he could not place where from. After all, she reminded him of someone from years ago. Not years ago in her lifetime but in his. She was youthful, still was, and he knew then he would enjoy feasting on her. He recalled the first time in her service when he tasted her sweet blood seep through his lips as he drew from her neck. Electricity soared through his body, exactly as it did that first time. He jolted himself and found he had managed to get himself dressed for the day completely oblivious to the fact.

He glanced at himself in the mirror and instead of the usual narcissistic admiration he felt for himself the reflection was of nothing but a feeble man, a degenerate, a vagabond. His reflection changed and what he saw looking back at him was no longer a man but a waif of a street urchin, filthy and unkempt but innocent. It was himself, aged six years old.

Merril had passed Verne on the stairs. She glanced back to see him turn towards his quarters when she stopped and crept back up them careful to miss the creaky floorboards on her way. She peered down the hallway and watched Verne go into his room. She swiftly made her way along the hall and entered into the laundry room where just a few hours earlier Verne and herself appeared from the hidden passage way. She took a second look out of the laundry room to make sure that all was clear. She inched away the linen blocking the doorway and pushed her fingertips into the gap pulling towards her as she did so. The door opened, she crouched and stepped inside.

As she turned to close the door behind her she noticed the sound of footsteps getting closer. Quickly she pulled the linen back and closed the door. Just as the latch took hold inside the hidden passage way the door to the laundry room opened. It was Verne.

"Blast, she must've closed it before she shot off," he said frustrated that the door to the passage was now closed, slamming the laundry room door behind him as he left.

Merril rushed off down the passage way and through the network of dusty corridors. She stopped only when she reached the wall behind the picture hanging in Cornelius's room. She stepped up onto the makeshift ledge and placed her face against the wall, her eyes just level with the mesh segment which, on the other side of the wall made up the window of the folly in the painting.

She couldn't see anything at first but soon saw Cornelius pacing, she heard the door to his chambers open and close and the feint voice of Verne. She couldn't hear what he said but whatever it was made Cornelius lash out in rage and he struck the side of Verne's face with the back of his hand. Merril gasped. Cornelius heard it but he didn't flounder nor did he give away that he knew she was there. Instead he played it to his advantage.

"You're utterly inept, you've failed me for the last time," he scolded a bemused Verne.

"Sir, but I, She..." he was interrupted with Cornelius placing his finger up to his lips.

"You'll make sure that it's done by nightfall, and let me tell you this," Cornelius's voice lowered and was barely audible, "...let....said and until....it's done."

The words were broken and Merril had no idea what had just happened inside the room but just before she could decide what to do next she heard Cornelius speak.

"I'll be meeting Mr Gideon in the study in twenty minutes, I know that his housekeeper is not working today so I'd be grateful if you could prepare a small bite to eat to be taken there," he said.

"Yes Mr Blackshot, I'll get onto it right away," replied Verne.

That was it, it was decided. Merril made a break for it and headed to the cellar.

Chapter 37

The cellar was more oppressive than usual but Merril put that down to the fact that Kurt's body was currently festering inside a cabinet in the chapel. The thought of all these souls being imprisoned in one way or another inside the cellar sent a shiver through her spine. It was macabre, it was desolate.

Merril was standing in front of the cabinet staring at the doors and wondering how she would unlock it. This wasn't going to be as simple as lock picking had become to her. The cabinet was an elaborately ornate piece. She'd never seen anything quite like it. She knew that the key to open the cabinet must be near and that there were limited places to hide one inside the chapel.

She had just about given up hope when she stubbed her toe against something on the floor. Her immediate thoughts were that she had kicked the edge of the altar however, she wasn't near the ends of the altar table and it would be strange to have a central leg. She kicked out her foot and her toes hit the hard surface again. She reached down and lifted the altar cloth finding a small casket underneath. She picked it up, "damn it, another lock," she said but smiled almost instantly. For this lock looked more forsaking. She almost squealed with delight after successfully picking the lock of the casket revealing the contents inside. She retrieved two keys. One was far too big for the lock of the cabinet but she kept it to one side. With the other she stepped closer to the cabinet and unlocked it.

Standing back she heard the internal mechanisms move and click until air escaped and dust broke away from the hinges. A small opening appeared from the middle of the front double doors.

Taking a deep breath she pulled the doors outwards. The cabinet was empty.

"How is it empty," she gasped asking herself. *How could it be? Where is Kurt? They haven't moved him already surely? Have they?* She thought. She was dejected but determined to find out what was going on.

Merril looked around for anything that would help lead her to where Kurt was. Her eyes were drawn to the large leather bound book propped open on the altar. She took a closer look tracing her fingers over the edges of the pages. She read out loud from the page that was open. The words weren't in English but she had no problem reading out what the text said.

Before leaving his room to meet Cornelius in the study Dyrac drifted in his own thoughts and went back to the time he first used his Mysteriository. He remembered how he was working with a travelling bazaar, a freak show of sorts. Reflecting on times he had his own side show. There would be the main event held in a large marquee, theatrical inside with a small auditorium of seats facing a small stage with forward facing gas lamps illuminating the performance unfolding.

There were three main attractions at Bartholomew's Bazaar of the Bizarre. Franklington the Magnificent was a giant of a man (inhumanly so). Franklington was almost eight feet tall with features befitting for someone of his stature. He'd grown up as any normal boy but soon into his adulthood his features began to change dramatically. He had enlarged hands and feet; coarsened, enlarged facial features; numerous small outgrowths or skin tags and he had a deepened and husk voice due to enlarged vocal chords and sinuses. He was pleasant enough but his condition gave him an unfriendly body odour. His family soon cast him out due to their lack of understanding. Nowadays the condition was known as acromegaly. Franklington was found wandering the streets of Shrewellsbury when he was picked up by Bartholomew and was instantly granted a contract. With nothing else to lose Franklington signed up. Not surprisingly he was headlined as the human Frankenstein.

Dyrac smiled remembering his friendship with Franklington, until he died of natural causes at only 42 years.

Franklington's performance was followed by the Begotti twins, Betsy and Lilibet. Siamese twins, conjoined at the head. They were in their early 20's when Dyrac knew them. The crowd would ooh and ahh, grimace and gurn as they walked on stage.

The main event however was that of Grecko the Grasper. Grecko had four arms. Thought to be a defect whilst in the womb and possibly the result of an undeveloped twin embryo, Grecko was born with an extra pair of arms. In addition to the additional arms he had a grossly disfigured face. He bore a similar resemblance to Ganesh, the Hindu God, son of Lord Shiva and the Goddess Parvati. And, like Ganesh, Grecko was known as the Remover of

Obstacles. He was a magnificent specimen and was a highly acclaimed freak as they used to be known before freak shows were banned.

Dyrac would occasionally watch the audience from back stage but after creating the Mysteriository by commissioning a man to follow his plans and bring it to life, he started his own side show at the Bazaar. The audience would often stop by before going to see the main show and Dyrac's reputation of being the vanishing man soon gave him fame in his own right.

He remembered the last time he used the Mysteriository before opening it again for the first time last night, since that dark day.

"But I swear it was just in here," said Imelda, "how do you do that?"

"It's magic," said Dyrac.

"Mr Dyrac sir, are you the devil?"

"The devil Imelda? Whatever makes you think that?" he replied.

"Mama says that magic is the work of the devil, are you the devil?"

"Dear sweet Imelda," Dyrac knelt so he could be at eye level with Imelda who, at the age of 7 years only just reached Dyrac's hip height, "I am no devil, but I am magic and this," he said pointing to the contraption before him, "is my Mysteriository."

Imelda gawped in awe, she smiled an innocent childish smile. Her naivety exuded from her as she giggled in delight. The birdcage and birds perched within it, that moments before had been placed inside the cabinet by Dyrac, had disappeared from plain sight.

"How did you do it?" asked Imelda whilst running

around the outside of the cabinet.

"A magician never reveals his secrets but, if you close your eyes tight and wish a hard wish, I can bring the birds back and you can keep them if you like?"

Imelda giggled, "really? Keep them for real? Forever?"

"You must promise to always look after them," he said.

"I promise," she replied. Dyrac knew that a child's promise was not a promise that was ever kept. Innocent enough when promised but seldom kept once the novelty had worn off.

Dyrac closed the cabinet doors and distracted Imelda with one hand whilst his other, free hand, pressed a series of buttons which in turn activated an internal mechanism of cogs and pulleys. A hidden cabinet contained within revolved and rested facing forwards. Once Dyrac felt a depressed button release and push against his fingertip he announced "Belugazah bizmelah." With a wave of his hands he unlatched the cabinet and opened the doors.

Imelda's eyes widened and a grin grew across her face. She heard the twittering of the birds inside and as Dyrac pushed the door open she oooed and ahhhed and clapped her hands.

"My birds, MAMA come see, my birds!" she shouted towards her mother who had been standing at the next stall along at the bazaar.

Imelda's mother turned and smiled towards her daughter, as she did she caught the eye line of Dyrac who immediately sunk into her gaze.

"Ma'am, Mr Dyrac Gideon and, my

Mysteriosity," he bowed, doffed his bowler hat and gesturing with his right hand introduced the item of furniture standing proudly next to him, simultaneously.

"Pleased to make your acquaintance Mr Gideon," she said raising her hand to greet him, "Miss Abigail Fauntleroy."

"Miss Abigail," Dyrac took her hand in his and pressed his lips against her gloved fingers, "the pleasure is all mine."

"Mama, mama," squealed Imelda, "look what Mr Dyrac can do. And he said he isn't the devil."

Dyrac blushed, "I'm sure your mama has plenty to be getting on with than to see such trivial tricks."

"Nonsense Mr Gideon," she said, "Please, indulge me."

"Can you make me disappear?" asked Imelda.

"Well, err, I suppose I...no...no it's too..." he was cut short with Imelda's enthusiastic retort.

"Please Mr Dyrac, plleeassseee," she said hanging on to the last please, in an almost begging desperate plea. Mama, please say it's ok?"

"Imelda dear please, stop bothering me and this nice man. Now wait here whilst I collect our tickets," said her mother looking at Dyrac in a 'do you mind just keeping an eye on and entertaining her for one minute' kind of way. Abigail Fauntleroy's attention to Dyrac's magical cabinet waivered.

Dyrac waved Abigail Fauntleroy off with his hands. He turned to Imelda and knelt down so he was eye level again, "you really want to try?" he asked, opening the doors.

"Oh do I ever?" replied Imelda hopping into the

cabinet.

Dyrac closed the cabinet doors and uttered out loud "Belugazah bizmelah!" He could hear Imelda giggling inside as he opened the doors and gasped, "Wow, I even amaze myself for the little girl has disappeared," Imelda was still sniggering and Dyrac smiled. "Let's see if I can bring her back ladies and gentlemen," he announced to a non-existent crowd. "Belugazah bizmelah!" Dyrac activated the mechanism on the side of the cabinet but there was no sound of whirring cogs or movement of the internal secret cabinet.

Panic stricken Imelda squealed from inside, "Mr Dyrac, let me out now, it's dark in here," she pleaded.

Dyrac, now also panicked, tried again to activate the cabinet's mechanism releasing Imelda but nothing happened. She was stuck and there was no way of getting her out without brute force. Dyrac thought on how long it had taken him to create such a masterpiece and, rather than raise the alarm, he simply pulled a lever to the side of the cabinet dropping a set of wheels to the floor. He wheeled the cabinet from its prime location and pushed it around the back of the main marquee.

Imelda was screaming inside but only Dyrac could hear her, knowing that they were screams of terror. In the hubbub of the bazaar the squeals of excitement and hustle and bustle of the crowds drowned out Imelda's cries. It wasn't long before her cries stopped through exhaustion. Little Imelda, unbeknownst to Dyrac, had passed out inside.

Dyrac knew he couldn't stay at the Bazaar any longer. He made his excuses to Bartholomew and, not being bound by any contract bid him a goodbye. Bartholomew was sorry to see him leave as Dyrac had been a hard worker and was always great at drawing an enthused crowd.

Dyrac set off on foot. From behind the marquee he knew he wouldn't be seen by anyone around the Bazaar and by now, even with Abigail Fauntleroy raising the alarm of her daughter's disappearance Dyrac knew he was far enough away to not be found.

A tear rolled down Dyrac's cheek and seeped into the corner of his mouth. He was back staring at his reflection in the mirror before him in his walk in wardrobe. That was the last time the cabinet was opened until he tried it last night successfully opening it. He was relieved when the empty cabinet opened as the decomposed corpse of a child would've taken some explaining to Cornelius. The three cabinets inside now contained a decaying Imelda and Kurt, with rigor mortis now setting in rigidly locking his folded remains in place. The third cabinet lay empty. *Room for one more* he thought.

Chapter 38

Without a second thought Merril tore out the page from the book and took one last glance at the empty cabinet. As she walked out of the chapel she heard a clunk followed by the scraping of wood and the screeching of a door opening slowly and eerily from behind her. She turned to see what made the noise and let out a scream. The once empty cabinet was no longer vacant and it was not occupied by Kurt. The horrific scene that befell upon her was that of a different body.

Merril realised that her scream must've been heard upstairs but rather than make haste and get out of there she found herself walking towards the cabinet.

Staring out of the cabinet was the decomposed face of a small child. It was dried and shrunken but it was unmistakably a child.

Reaching out Merril recoiled her hand just as quickly and wept. *Who are you, you poor thing?* She thought.

The child was curled in the foetus position. She was wearing clothing from times gone by, at least Victorian if not older. The hair, once in bunches with pretty bows still tied had continued to grow post mortem, that was evident given the straggly nature and unkempt style it was now in. A girl? The child's fingernails were curled and yellow, her skin leathery, taut and fragile was a deep blue grey. Where her eyes once were, a pair of crusted and shrivelled marbles stared back, almost like dried peas before being left to soak overnight to bring life back to them. Her hands, her tiny hands sat under her chin, in a self protecting way, tucked in and away from harm. Her burgundy dolly shoes were as bright and shiny as though still brand new and were patent, rather than polished.

This cellar is a sick mortuary full of death and pain, Merril thought. Not that any cellar should contain one body, let alone multiple bodies it was a far cry from a chapel of rest where those who had passed were prepared with care and attention ready for their loved ones to see them sleeping and to say their final goodbyes. It was a pit of despair. It was dark and oppressive and the more Merril had been down there it was clear the cellar was accustomed to being the terrifying resting place of tortured souls. She couldn't help but compare it to being like one of the circles of hell depicted in Inferno, the first part of three, of Dante's famous epic poem Divine Comedy.

It's just a crypt of horror, of death, an unforgiveable fortitude of benevolence.

Realising she'd been stood there too long and believing her scream would've been heard Merril quickly closed the cabinet doors whispering to the little girl inside she said, "I'll come back for you," before fleeing the chapel and running straight into the wine cellar. She grabbed the dusty, lonely wine bottle with a wax seal and ran through the chamber of curiosities through the hidden door she'd left ajar. After passing through a short while earlier she closed it with a click of the latch. Merril paused and caught her breath. She tried to stop the tears from falling down her face but she couldn't contain them and she slumped to the floor sobbed.

Dyrac was convinced he heard a woman scream but his mind was distracted with the delusion that it must be in his head. After the events of the night before, knowing what was resting inside the chest and recalling the thoughts of sweet Imelda. He shook it off not thinking there was any cause for alarm and brushed himself down. With a deep breath he left his room and made his way to the study.

Cornelius and Verne too heard a woman's scream and didn't dismiss it at all. "Find her," Cornelius instructed Verne, "and bring her to the study."

"Yes sir," replied Verne, swiftly turning on his heels and out of Chamber four. He knew exactly where to start his search for Merril, the folly.

Merril composed herself and wiped the tears from her cheeks. She picked up the items she collected from the cellar and wound her way down through the passageways. She reached the final corridor leading to the folly when she heard the scraping of the stone plaque echo down the tunnel. She knew it must be Verne coming for her when she remembered a concealed area inside the network of tunnels that Verne didn't know about.

She hurried back through the passageways and stopped near to the back of Chamber four and unhitched a well hidden handle stepping inside a small void. It was reminiscent of an old priest hole usually found in old principal Catholic houses. A priest hole was used to conceal the presence of a priest. After the ascension to the throne in 1558, Queen Elizabeth I passed a law prohibiting

Catholicism which led to legal persecution.

Merril remained perfectly still as the sound of footsteps grew louder, closer.

Verne must've been in the corridor for twenty minutes and his frustrations were audible to Merril. At one point he stood just inches from her and she struggled to hold her breath. She feared the sound of her breathing would lead to her being discovered. Verne moved off and she let out a huge breath exhaling until her lungs could deflate no more.

She remained resolute and held her position. Verne became ever more annoyed that he was failing in his task at finding Merril. The feeling of anxiety brewed and festered in the pit of his stomach, like a cauldron bubbling and spewing its contents. He thought of how to break the news to Cornelius that Merril was nowhere to be found causing a bilious heartburn pain pierce his chest. Sinking his head and clutching at his heart he gave up hope of finding her. As he made his exit through the folly he decided he was going to go to Merril's room before reporting back to Cornelius. After all, she'd need to get back at some point wouldn't she?

Chapter 39

Verne had found a tidy little hiding place tucked just behind a wardrobe inside Merril's room. The wardrobe overlapped a niche in the wall but was too big to fit inside the niche itself leaving a gap sufficient in size for Verne to squeeze into. He'd got through the door lock no problem. Verne had a particular set of skills which never left him after a period serving her majesty in the special armed forces until he was discharged on medical grounds.

Silently, like an assassin locked onto his target, he waited for Merril to return.

Merril had lost track of time whilst hiding from Verne. She had fallen back into a memory of her mother again. She realised that her final moments with her mother were somewhat fraught but she knew that there was a deep love there. Whilst her mother blamed her for her father's disappearance Merril knew that, in her past lifetime as Idysha her mother was her crutch and a pain pierced her heart.

She physically shook herself down casting her memories to one side. She spoke out softly, "Mother, soon we will be back with each other. We will all be together again, even Father."

Merril squeezed herself out of the spot she'd been hiding and stretched the cricks out of her back after seizing up being hidden and still for so long. She gathered herself together and made her way back to the folly to think about the next step she was about to take. She knew that this could only end one way and was prepared for that but she still shed a single tear. She didn't wipe it away she let it rest on her cheek until eventually it evaporated into nothing.

By now Verne's patience was wearing thin. *Where was she? Why hadn't she returned?* He decided he could wait no longer and that he'd have to go and speak to Cornelius who, by now, would be in the study with Mr Gideon.

Cornelius flew into a rage "WHAT DO YOU MEAN NOWHERE TO BE FOUND?" he bellowed at Verne as a spray of spit splattered across his face. Cornelius usually held his composure and immediately felt regret at his bitter retort in response to Verne's update on Merril. He thought fatigue may have exacerbated the tenuous strained exhaustion he was feeling and a knee jerk reaction was verbalised when previously he'd have taken a deep breath and projected his tone more appropriately.

Verne wiped his cheek and replied, "I've looked through the hidden passageways and I even lay in wait hidden inside her room but she hasn't returned and I didn't want to leave it any longer without giving you a sit rep."

"Sit rep? You're not in the military anymore Verne, Christ man. Find her. Do NOT return until you have found her, do you understand?" Cornelius emphasised his words annunciating each syllable. Verne was clear in his understanding and also a little pained by Cornelius's patronising tone. Before now they had a good relationship that was professional and polite. Verne knew his place of course but still, their relationship always had a familial nature to it too. It was in that moment that Verne knew any relationship they previously had, had been eradicated into insignificance and it was clear that he was just a minion to Cornelius, if that.

"Cornelius," said Dyrac, "calm down, she can't have gone far. It's unlikely she will have left the grounds. She will show up, if not today she will be ready to work tomorrow."

"What makes you so sure she is still around Drack?" asked Cornelius.

"That woman, no matter the disloyalty she has known, is a professional without fault. She honours her duties and takes pride in her work so, Cornelius, that is how I know she is still around. She's worked for me for fifteen years and she has nothing outside of this house."

Cornelius let out a grunt, walked over to the drinks cabinet and poured himself a whisky. The whisky was close to overflow when with a precise and intentional flick of the bottle Cornelius cut the flow perfectly as the honey coloured nectar reached the brim.

"Just a small one?" said Dyrac.

"Medicinal," came the reply.

"That's an awful lot of medicine Cornelius, you should take it easy. We both need clear heads today," said Dyrac.

"One of us needs a clear head Dyrac and," taking a sip from the glass wincing as the heat of the whisky caught the back of his throat, "that is you my friend."

Dyrac shook his head. "Listen Verne, be so kind and bring that food Cornelius asked you to prepare so we can get focussed and move on."

"Right you are sir," came the reply from Verne.

Verne was preparing brunch in the kitchen, it was too far past breakfast and not quite lunch time so brunch it was. He threw together a ploughman's platter but added some grilled mackerel to break the conformity of what would be expected. He made a huge pot of earl grey tea knowing that Cornelius would be unlikely to drink it but he knew Dyrac would appreciate the comfort that tea provided.

Separately Verne prepared a small shellfish cocktail with Marie rose dressing. It was one of Cornelius's favourites and one which Cornelius had commented was unlike any other he'd ever tasted before. He knew Dyrac wouldn't eat it as he made his immense dislike to the shellfish quite clear the night before at dinner. As Verne knew that it would only be Cornelius eating it he took care when adding the ingredients.

"Marvellous Verne, marvellous," announced Cornelius as he saw the spread Verne had prepared, eyes lighting up when he spotted the shellfish cocktail.

"You don't mind having all that to yourself do you Cornelius," asked Dyrac nodding at the separate dish with an almost greenish hue to his complexion indicating nausea at the sight of it alone.

"Why I insist," replied Cornelius.

Verne didn't know how long it would take for them to finish brunch so made his excuses and left the study offering his service at the ring of the bell.

"Yes, yes, Verne you go and do what you need to do and whilst you're at it, keep your eyes peeled for that Merril," said Cornelius.

"As you say sir," he replied with a courteous bow of the head. Verne left the study and a sudden rush of adrenalin soared through his body.

Chapter 40

The plan was unfolding and it was unfolding fast. Merril was anxious yet determined but first, she needed to figure out how to get the pythos from her room. She needed to get that and also find a new place to hide. She couldn't rely on the secrecy of the folly and the passageways now that Verne had revealed all. Then, all of a sudden like a flash bulb moment an idea sprung to the forefront of her mind. If she'd thought too long on the idea she would have dismissed it but there was no other choice and she knew that *they* wouldn't look for her there.

Merril headed back through the passageways emerging from the wall in the laundry room. She checked the coast was clear and scrambled to her room as though navigating an elaborately designed laser security system. Once inside she grabbed her tin and the pythos and scurried back along the corridor. She crept around almost stealth like and found herself outside Dyrac's room. She entered the room and immediately headed for the walk in wardrobe.

Sitting cross legged she opened her satchel and retrieved the page torn from the leather bound book in the cellar and the wine bottle with the wax seal. Carefully she tucked the pythos in the gap in her legs gripping it tightly as she placed her hands on the lid.

"It's time," she said.

Before Merril could completely open the urn she heard footsteps from a distant. She knew they weren't outside the room and looked up towards the ceiling Verne must be back upstairs she thought.

Verne was traipsing around his room with absolutely no agenda for the rest of the day except to wait for the service bell to ring but he knew he needed to do something and, given that motions were already in place, he thought of his actions. Instead of guilt and shame a distinct grin grew across his face. He caught a glimpse of his own reflection and noted that a proud evil genius stared back at him. The tension he had been feeling in his shoulders washed away and for the first time this weekend he felt relaxed. For a fleeting moment this disturbed him but almost as immediately as he felt a disturbance he also felt satisfaction and gratification.

"Now we wait," he said to himself.

"And we won't have to wait long," his reflection replied.

Verne decided to go on the search for Merril again but this time, as well as going through the folly he was going to check the cellar. If he couldn't find Merril, maybe he could find a clue to her whereabouts. Verne also had to see for himself whether Kurt was still in that cabinet. If he happened to find Merril too then it would be a bonus.

Verne was about to leave the side entrance in the kitchen when the service bell rang. His shoulders dropped as he turned and headed to the study.

"You rang," he said sarcastically.

"No need for the sarcasm thank you Verne," said Cornelius, "can you fetch a couple of bottles of red from the cellar? Dyrac, give him your key old boy."

"I don't think so," said Dyrac looking nervously at Cornelius.

"Oh dear fellow, don't be so worried. Verne here knows all about my job and what I'm hired to do. Isn't that right Verne?" he said slapping Verne on the shoulder.

"Quite right," he replied.

"Still," said Dyrac, "it's more about what I've got in the cellar."

"Fine," said Cornelius flamboyantly throwing his arms in the air, "then you go and get the Beaujolais," he added.

Dyrac didn't even flounder at Cornelius's remark. He simply left the study and headed to the cellar.

Dyrac had just retrieved two bottles from the rack when he heard a commotion upstairs. He ran through the house, not locking the cellar behind him in his haste to get to the source of the fracas.

Frozen stiff, right on the spot where he was standing Dyrac gasped "Cornelius!"

Merril thought against her next move then, as though trying to convince herself, she took a deep breath and opened the pythos.

An overwhelming chill engulfed her and simultaneously she felt a despair she'd never experienced before.

Chapter 41

The pythos shook from Merril's hands and fell on its side on the floor, rolling for a moment until coming to a sudden and complete stop. Merril clambered for the lid trying desperately to secure it back in place but she couldn't. Something prevented her from resealing it, an invisible and resistant force.

Merril heard a recognisable voice in her head. The words spoken echoed and she jerked and shivered. Goosebumps made the hairs on her body stand to attention and a feeling of blackness stayed with her.

She stared at the pythos waiting with apprehension for something to happen.

Dyrac stood in the centre of the crypt, hidden from view of Wode House and almost abridge the border of where the land owned by the proprietor of Wode House ended. It was a small crypt that had held the remains of a number of generations of the Gideon family, each having been cremated with their ashes being stored in their own respective vaults inside. The garden mausoleum was not at all elaborate in appearance. The walls were made of white marble which held well over the years. Small copper plated statuettes atop Doric columns at each corner had weathered forming a Verdigris coating, a tantalising bright bluish-green encrustation. The walls were bare except for the large carved lettering of GIDEON engraved into the pediment overlooking the doorway. Inside was a small chapel area, a place to remember and grieve. On the wall directly opposite the doorway was a series of small vaults approximately 1 foot square. The bottom row lay empty but the rest housed the ancestral line of the Gideon family.

As he stood there in the magnificent presence of the great family Gideon Dyrac dropped Sarah's body onto the marble floor, her head bouncing off as it made contact before resting against the coldness. He loomed over her and eyed up her whole body slowly, with a devilish smile on his face.

"Time to condemn you to an eternal hell. Unlike your predecessors you will not be afforded the luxury of interment to the grandness of this final resting place. Oh sweet Sarah, one day, after many years of the torture of your confinement, after you've had time to fester in the pits of misery and desolation I will come to set you free."

Dyrac opened the vault on the right, bottom row of the final resting places before him and retrieved an object from within.

He looked down at the pythos. It was a simply hand turned clay urn bulbous in the middle but tapered at each end with a slightly wider base than the top. It had two handles, one either side, fixed to the top and the shoulder where it bulged outwards. Whilst simple in design it was elaborately decorated with hand painted symbols and hieroglyphs depicting demise and destruction. There were representations of roman virtues surrounding the urn of which all appeared to suffocate under the hands of an invisible and powerful force. Salus (Security), Concordia (Harmony), Aequitas (Fairness), Clementia (Mercy), Libertas (Freedom), Felicitas (Happiness), Pax (Peace), Virtus (Worth) and Laetitia (Joy). The only one standing alone, was Spes (Hope), because without hope there was nothing.

It was a foreboding urn and was also Dyrac's chosen resting place for Sarah. Her soul would be extracted from her body in a ritualistic ceremony and would be encapsulated by the urn where, although without body, her soul would remain tormented for eternity. Eternity in so far that she would remain there without release or rest until such a time that the pythos was opened again. Sarah would not be alone in there, there was a malevolent force contained within which would feed on her soul and together, over time, they would combine.

Dyrac had found the pythos on one of his expeditions, he knew the instant he saw it what it was and what it contained. He recalls the mixed feelings of exhilaration and terror that consumed him all those years ago. For this pythos was the pythos. It was of course Pandora's Box. Depicted in history as a source of great and unexpected troubles, a present which seems valuable but which in reality is a curse. Evils fluttered within and mortal men suffered terrible fates over time as they tried, and failed to open it.

After locating the pythos and recovering it illegally Dyrac studied it over many years. Dyrac's reputation and wealth afforded him the luxury of being able to access archives of scripture through blackmail and bribery, theft, and the violation of holy and consecrated grounds; and by hiring the services of those hired to protect such historically valuable artefacts and documents.

Once Dyrac was confident he had mastered the ritual of opening the box without unleashing the evil contained within he would be able to store another soul inside. His intended was meant to be Abimilech but circumstances prevented this from being so and, as a consolation Dyrac decided that Abimilech's one true love would be the perfect tribute and as such set in motion a series of events long before he found himself standing where he was now, over her lifeless body.

Dyrac performed the ritual and recited the incantation which would secure Sarah Gideon's soul inside the pythos. He knew it was unsafe and unwise to keep the pythos at Wode House so he carefully placed it, and its new resident inside the chest which he had earlier put inside the crypt in readiness.

A wooden shipping container arrived at Wode House the next day. Dyrac had prepared a number of items he had collected over the years to be stored away. A sarcophagus from ancient Egypt, a variety of urns and tablets from the Mesopotamian period, scrolls said to have been taken from the Vatican archives and, as well as other items, the chest with the pythos inside.

The haulier was a long standing and trusted associate of Dyrac who extended a certain level of discretion and security to those who could afford the trusted associate rates. Money was no issue for Dyrac and he compensated the haulier well to ensure additional measures were in place to avoid revealing the whereabouts of certain items of interest that were stored. It wasn't necessarily souls that Dyrac was protecting, albeit in this case this was true, but his acquisitions were not always legally obtained and as well as authorities from around the world pursuing him, he also had underworld degenerates trying to intercept items as a target for the black market. Dyrac hadn't lost an item yet, although he had faced a number of close encounters. He certainly wasn't prepared to lose any going forward.

Decades would pass by before Dyrac would need, or see that chest again before Kurt would be instructed to bring it back to Wode House.

Merril thought carefully about her next move. If she released her mother's soul, and whatever else lay foreboding and unforgiving inside there would be no going back. The plan had changed continuously over the last 48 hours as recent and unexpected events at Wode House brought things forward at a much quicker pace than she wanted, or had prepared for. It had been some time since she performed a ritual of this enormity and she was out of practice.

The scar from the Karamabit on her thigh ached, an alarm went off inside her head. Carefully, she thought on what was about to unfold and, like a chess master, she planned each move with precision, poise and determination mapping out her plan of attack until she was confident of achieving check mate.

Merril broke the wax seal on the wine bottle and poured a few drops of the contents into the open pythos. She read aloud from the page torn from the book in the cellar annunciating her words with clear definition as a slight error at this point would change the incantation and the results could be more catastrophic and out of control than Merril needed.

An overwhelming sense of calm enveloped her and an eerie silence clung to the atmosphere like a forming fog swallowing the land in its path. Her hairs stood on end and as she exhaled a small cloud formed in front of her face like when warm breath hits the cold air. Instead of dissipating into the atmosphere around the cloud froze solid, stuck in time, like a pause button had caused everything to stop apart from her. She could freely move and rose to her feet whilst circling the still fog.

She reached out and pushed her hand downwards through it but it remained as though she was a ghost passing through a wall. She reached down to retrieve the page and picked it up with no difficulty so, physically, she knew she was still in the land of living.

In a flash the last few minutes rewound at a significant pace and, in what felt like the blink of an eye she was back on the floor, sat cross legged with a torn page in her hands. The pythos stood upright, sealed and silent.

Chapter 42

Dyrac and Verne stood over Cornelius' body as an omnipresent threat of doom encumbered them both simultaneously causing them to exchange silent glances. Dyrac pressed his fingers to his lips indicating to Verne to remain silent. Verne obeyed.

Dyrac tiptoed around Cornelius' body and slowly closed the door to the study. "We need to move fast and quietly Verne but I need to know what happened here," said Dyrac.

Verne nodded and proceeded to tell Dyrac how Cornelius grabbed at his chest and fell to the floor in a heap gasping for breath. Verne explained how he was unable to assist and despite calling out for help Cornelius died in his arms shortly before Dyrac burst into the study.

Verne was lying and despite Cornelius's and Dyrac's history committing violent atrocities against other living souls, he decided to withhold the true account of Cornelius's sudden death.

Cornelius's death was actually the result of Verne's deliberate and ill-fated preparation of the puffer fish element of his infamous seafood cocktail. Cornelius had been murdered. Verne arrived almost immediately after Cornelius began experiencing symptoms. Verne watched on as Cornelius grasped at his own throat trying to open his airways. Clutching at his chest and fighting for breath as his tongue and lips swelled. Cornelius's arms fell to his side as paralysis engulfed him. Verne stood and watched as a helpless and powerless Cornelius began sweating profusely. Weak and lacking co-ordination, as though inebriated he spurted bile which swiftly escalated to vomit. Cornelius projected a putrid gelatinous and lumpy substance onto the floor. With his pallor turning a purplish blue it was clear he was dying. Verne had a fleeting thought about aiding him but his body just stood there frozen, watching him suffer. Cornelius convulsed spasmodically and for a moment showed signs that he was lucid and regaining his composure. Then Cornelius coughed hard and took his final breath.

"Ok," said Dyrac, "so it's agreed?"

Verne was completely oblivious to what Dyrac had been conversing to him. He'd completely drifted into the recollection of Cornelius's death. So much so that he was reliving it moments later. Meanwhile, Dyrac had been talking to him the whole time. Verne had no choice, after all he did not want Dyrac to perceive him as insolent.

"Agreed," he replied not knowing to what he had just agreed to.

"Right, I'll gather some things together and meet you back here in half an hour. That should give you plenty of time to get these items from Cornelius's belongings," he said to Verne pushing a piece of paper into the palm of his hand.

During Verne's daydreaming he hadn't noticed that Dyrac had jotted a list of things on a piece of paper. He looked at the list and the colour drained from his face.

"Everything in order I assume Verne," said Dyrac.

"Err, yes sir, all in order," Verne replied holding the list to his temple in a salute, "in half an hour."

Dyrac left Verne in the study and made his way to his own room. Dyrac no longer felt the need to lock the study. Many of the secrets of Wode House were no longer secret but Dyrac had one more trick up his sleeve.

Merril, still sitting cross legged in front of the pythos knew she wasn't alone. She could feel an oppression fill the vacuum of space around her. It was unsettling and somewhat stifling, Merril reached for her throat nursing it as though she was suffocating. She jolted back into her consciousness as the sounds of distant footsteps grew ever nearer. She knew she needed to leave Dyrac's room before she was found.

Hurriedly she gathered everything together and, before she could turn and leave the room she saw the bedroom door handle turn. Swiftly she spun back to the direction from which she came. She looked around and noticed a small gap at the back of the walk in wardrobe. She was slender enough to hide in there and go unnoticed. She tucked herself in and furtively watched through a small gap in the veneer into the mirror at the end of the walk in wardrobe. The reflection bounced back the image of the whole dressing room and, as the door to the main bedroom was open she could also see the foot of Dyrac's bed.

Dyrac came into view and Merril held her breath for fear of being heard. He looked through to his walk in wardrobe and into the mirror. The reflection projected straight at Merril and it was as though he was staring right at her. But he couldn't be looking at her; he didn't know she was there.

All of a sudden there was an almighty explosion as shards of glass from the double bevelled mirror which both Merril and Dyrac were looking at shattered outwards.

"Shit!" shouted Dyrac ducking under his own arms jumping back from the shock of the mirror blasting into smithereens of its apparent own accord. At exactly the same time Merril let out a gasp. A black mist crawled across the floor from where the mirror once stood forming an effigy of a figure that clawed its way towards Dyrac.

Dyrac glared at the figure and almost as quickly as it formed it seemed to dissipate into the atmosphere around the room. Dyrac quickly looked from his left to his right, up and then down. He spun around on the spot trying to locate whatever it was he just saw. There was nothing there.

Remembering that he had to be back to meet Verne shortly Dyrac picked up his Karamabit. He traced it over the scars on his torso and, finding a space just above the right hip he gouged at himself. Blood coagulated and congealed around the fresh wound. A thick, solidified clump of clotting blood fell onto the floor squelching as it hit the ground. Dyrac looked down at the new rune he had just branded into himself; a vertical line with a triangle pointing to the right and sat in the middle of the line. It was the rune for protection and regeneration.

Chapter 43

Dyrac stared down at the shards of glass around his feet. Each of the pieces of mirror reflected back his own bemused face however; Dyrac wasn't alone in his reflection. Behind him, looming over him with head tilted as though facing toward Dyrac, stood a dark figure. The figure was unrecognisable to Dyrac and bore no facial feature. He turned his head to look at the figure but just as he expected the figure to enter his peripheral vision he saw nothing. He turned back to the mirror pieces and the figure remained.

Something dark and formidable wanted to consume him. He had to turn, he had to face whatever was there.

Dyrac took a deep breath in holding it as his lungs inflated. As quickly as he turned he exhaled. In that same moment a distorted dark mass thrust itself forward from directly in front of him and Dyrac was thrown to the ground blacking out instantly disappearing into nothingness.

Merril watched as Dyrac's head hit the floor. At the very same time the malformed manifestation seemed to vanish leaving its ubiquitous influence in the room.

Dyrac remained lifeless. Merril crept out from the void she was hiding and tiptoed over to Dyrac. As she got nearer she could see there was no rise or fall in his chest and she wasn't sure if he was breathing. She knelt down next to him and pressed her forefingers against his throat. It was feint but she felt a shallow pulse.

She left the room without once turning back to look at Dyrac and raced towards her own room.

Dyrac murmured as he began to come around. He placed his hand on his chest as he felt a pressure as though someone, or something, held him in a vice like grip. He opened his eyes at feeling nothing and looked around the room getting his bearings. He remembered the force that pushed through him and knocked him off his feet and, whilst the presence remained there was nothing in sight.

As he pushed his hands against the floor to get himself in an upright position he winced as glass pierced the skin causing his palms to bleed.

As he got to his feet he looked at his watch. He should've met with Verne twenty minutes ago. He grabbed the Karamabit off the floor which had fallen to the ground with him. He ran from his room and headed towards the study.

As Dyrac approached the door he slowed his pace and composed himself. He walked into the study and said "apologies for my lateness Verne," but Verne was nowhere in sight. "Verne?"Dyrac popped his head out of the study and looked up and down the hallway when he saw it.

Merril was panting after running to her room and after witnessing the events unfold in Dyrac's room. *Had I raised that thing from beyond this world? Was it Mama?* She thought. *There's no time to think Merril, you need to move,* her conscience quickly added.

Merril needed to get to the cellar and the only way

she could get there without being seen was via the laundry room and the secret door into the hidden passageway. There was no time, and absolutely no chance of not being seen if she was to go through the folly. Trying to work her way through the house would be impossible.

"Verne!" Merril screamed as she turned to face him having just closed the door to her room. "What are you..." Verne stopped her from talking, pressed his fingers to his lips and gestured to her to remain calm and not to make a fuss.

Merril nodded with her eyes alone.

"Cornelius Blackshot is dead," he said in a calm and composed tone, "I killed him. There isn't much time to explain but I want you to understand that I didn't betray you because I was ordered to by Mr Blackshot," Verne continued and Merril just listened intently.

Merril put her arm behind her back and reached for the handle of her bedroom door turning it and pushing it without taking her eyes off Verne the whole time. "In here," she said.

Verne shot a quick glance down the corridor behind him towards the main stairwell and followed Merril into her room.

"So, let me get this straight," Merril continued.

Dyrac was frozen to the spot outside the study as the apparition he'd encountered moments before in his room hovered at the end of the hallway in front of him. He couldn't take his eyes off it as he felt it's lifeless and faceless form seer through him. Right before his eyes the figure gained a more defined and human form. The identity of the silhouette was unmistakable but he knew it couldn't be. Only he had the resource and power to bring her back but there she was, his eyes were not betraying him.

"Sarah?" he whispered.

The black misty figure slithered stealthily towards Dyrac. Descending smoothly and continuously, effortlessly and without resistance. An eerie blackness filled the walls and ceiling as the figure drifted closer. Dyrac felt his chest compress ever tighter as it neared. His skin tautened sucking itself inwards exposing the protruding bones of his cheeks, ribs, spine and collarbone. He felt his face and as he lowered his hands he caught a glimpse of them. His fingers were boney and witch like, his hands had aged with liver spots forming on the back of his hands as though all the liquid in his body was being drained. His pallor was grey and his eyes bulged outwards as though being forced forward.

Dyrac shook himself and closed his eyes and immediately felt relief. If he could avoid looking at it he still had life. He felt for the study door and pushed his way through eyes scrunched tightly to prevent him from seeing it anymore.

Closing the door behind him Dyrac opened his eyes. It was not in the study with him and he didn't want to risk opening the door. He needed another way out. He walked towards the fireplace and looked in the mirror above the mantel. He watched as his face transformed from almost corpse like to one full of life and vigour.

He rushed over to the drinks cabinet and poured a slug of whisky down his gullet. No need for the formality of a glass, ice and water on this occasion. He shook the burning sting of the whisky off as he swallowed hard.

He looked towards the shelf where a hidden doorway led to an unknown passageway. *It's the only way out of here without going back out there*, he thought. Merril's secret may now be coming in as a handy escape route. Dyrac was thankful Verne's divulgence was detailed enough for him to now be able to use this alternative exit, if only he knew how to open the door from this side.

A turn of the study door handle startled Dyrac and he swiftly turned, staring straight at it, urging it to not open.

"If you're with me Verne then we need to go now and you need to understand your place in all this. You need to be able to walk away and never look back when the time comes," said Merril.

"I'm with you Merril," he replied.

"Well, first things first, we need to get into the cellar," said Merril.

"Laundry room," Verne said.

"Laundry room," she replied.

With that both Merril and Verne set off out of her bedroom both fully aware of their roles in Merril's plan and both fully aware that one of them, maybe both, may not make it out of Wode House alive.

The handle of the study stopped turning and Dyrac fumbled with the books on the shelf looking for a catch, nothing. He headed over to the desk and opened the drawer. He retrieved a silver letter opener and made his way back to the bookshelf feeling his way around the edge of the shelves. He felt a slight draught brush against his fingers and forced the letter opener along the edge pushing it until he felt a click. He jimmied the blade up and down and it gave way opening enough for his fingertips to grip. He pulled towards himself and the door opened an inch. Reaching through he pulled again this time the door opened revealing a void. He looked through into blackness. *It's the blackness or,* looking back to the study door, *that blackness,* he thought.

Dyrac opened the doorway fully and apprehensively stepped inside. He didn't know where the passageway would lead, or what he would find along the way but he needed to get to the cellar and he knew, from what Verne had said, that there was a doorway into the cellar.

Going into the unknown Dyrac walked forwards breathing deeply.

Chapter 44

Kurt lay motionless and broken in the Mysteriository cabinet. Hidden from view he was folded to fit into a compartment that made up one of three chambers in a complicated mechanised storage unit. In another was the body of a once full of life, and an innocent little girl. Rigidity now set in and her once perfectly fitting and pristine clothes were now bedraggled and hanging off her decomposed skeleton. Her beautiful golden locks of hair now tatty, brittle and dusty grey. Her rose tinted plump cheeks now sunken and shrivelled drawn into the sockets under her cheekbones. She was no longer the beautiful Lady Imelda Fauntleroy. Now a long gone memory whose precious quips and childlike glee had been forgotten when her Mama died of a broken heart just a few months after her disappearance.

The final chamber lay empty and waiting, as though it's purpose was yet to be fulfilled.

Merril and Verne checked the coast was clear before stepping foot inside the cellar and into the chamber of curiosities. Merril walked over to Abimilech and stroked his cheek softly, "Papa, I'll take you with me," she said.

"Sorry, did you say Papa?" asked Verne looking a little repulsed at the sight of Merril stroking this mummified man's face.

Merril ignored Verne's line of questioning and continued through the cellar to the central chamber. She looked towards the long narrow chamber which contained the now empty chest and back across to her right to the wine cellar from which she had retrieved the lonely dusty green bottle with wax seal.

Then, looking straight ahead Merril stepped one foot in front of the other, confidently and directly. Walking towards the chapel Merril undid the flap on her satchel taking out the torn page from the book that sat upon the altar.

She looked immediately towards the Mysteriository as she entered with Verne hot on her heels looking all around to make sure they weren't being followed.

"Holy shit," he exclaimed, "that's a....it's not Kurt, it's a...." mouth agape he couldn't form the word.

"a girl," Merril completed his sentence.

"Who is she?" asked Verne.

"I don't know Verne but we need to somehow get her and Kurt out," said Merril.

"Kurt? But Kurt isn't in there, look Merril it's a little girl," said Verne.

"It's got another compartment Verne," said Merril.

"Another compartment?" Verne questioned, "How do you know?"

"I saw it move, well, I stand corrected. I heard it move when I was in here earlier and when I turned to look back there she was," said Merril.

"But how? Where? There isn't room?" he asked.

"I'm guessing it's bigger on the inside," said Merril, "It's got some sort of mechanism that switches the internal components to reveal another chamber."

"It's genius is what it is," said Verne.

Merril looked disconcerted and Verne immediately retracted his comments, "I'm sorry Merril, it's disgusting is what it is," he said.

Merril opened the book on the altar and flicked to the section from where she tore the page and returned it. She flicked through the book a little more and found an envelope with a broken wax seal. She unfolded the envelope and took out the document inside. She gasped.

"What is it?" asked Verne.

"I'm taking this with me," replied Merril, "I'll explain as we move Verne, and move we must. We'll need to come back for them later," she added nodding her head in the direction of the Mysteriository.

Verne gulped hard and nodded back to Merril. They both raced towards the chamber of curiosities and passed by Abimilech with Merril briefly touching his arm as they did so.

They left the cellar and headed through the maze of corridors and down some steps leading underneath the small lake emerging up the stairs on the other side and out through the folly hatch.

Moments after Merril and Verne left the cellar Dyrac entered. Carefully he edged through the doorway adjusting his eyes from the darkness he had been in as light from the small window leading to the grounds of Wode House infiltrated the dusty cellar, illuminating eerily a number of collectibles Dyrac had acquired over the years.

Dyrac stopped at the side of Abimilech and spat in his face smiling with utter contempt for the man.

As Dyrac walked through to the chapel he stopped dead in his tracks as he noticed the Mysteriository was open and not on Kurt. Dyrac's immediate determination for the task at hand left him and standing inside the open chamber of the Mysteriository was little Imelda. But she wasn't dead!

Imelda held out her hand towards Dyrac beckoning him to come nearer. Dyrac edge a step forwards and stopped shaking his head whilst closing his eyes as though brushing off some sort of hallucination that he must be having at that moment. Dyrac watched as the apparition before him remained and beckoned to him again. This time Imelda spoke out.

"Mr Dyrac, sir" said the apparition, "where are my birds, can you bring them back?"

Imelda stepped out from the Mysteriository carefully holding herself steady with one hand as she stepped down onto the floor. She looked towards Dyrac again and back to the Mysteriository.

"I've been in there an awfully long time Mr Dyrac haven't I?" she asked.

Dyrac never uttered a word. Imelda stopped and turned to look at the cabinet and as her eyes caught sight of her own rotten corpse slumped in the chamber she let out an ear piercing screech and rushed towards Dyrac open arms and straight through him.

Dyrac slumped to his knees arms open wide as though to catch the little girl but she was gone and only a dusty haze was left in between him and the Mysteriository. He looked as it settled and there, slumped inside the chamber was the body of Lady Imelda Fauntleroy.

"I'm sorry," Dyrac said.

Merril stopped in front of Verne holding up the

document she'd taken from the envelope in the altar book.

"It's my father's will," she said.

Chapter 45

Merril handed Verne the satchel keeping hold only of her Karamabit. Inside the satchel was the pythos and Verne had one job.

"I'll meet you there Verne," said Merril.

Verne nodded and embraced Merril tightly, "be safe," he said.

Merril breathed Verne in and the security that his embrace gave her. She held onto him momentarily before pulling herself away and headed back into the folly hatch down the steps of the ladder into the corridor below. She waited to hear Verne move off and as his footsteps grew feint she carried on.

She didn't illuminate the passage ways, instead she independently turned the gas on each lantern to on as she passed hurriedly to avoid breathing in the gas that escaped with a hiss through the system.

Dyrac got to his feet and, still shaken from his encounter with Imelda, he trembled to the chamber of curiosities.

He walked over to where Abimilech was once housed in a Perspex casing but he was gone. Dyrac shook his head knowing he must be seeing things and he looked swiftly around the room. No-one else was there other than him. *Your mind is playing tricks on you Dyrac,* he thought. But it wasn't, Abimilech was gone.

Dyrac decided he needed to face the blackness that was left in the hallway by the study. He must confront whatever this formidable force was that was causing him to hallucinate. He made his way out of the chamber of curiosities to the central chamber of the cellar where the stairs leading the kitchen ascended to his right.

With trepidation but determination he took a step forwards and was halted in his tracks almost immediately. Standing before him, just a few feet away but between him and the stairs stood Abimilech.

Abimilech towered over Dyrac's frame. Dyrac wasn't in the least bit slight in stature but Abimilech was a foreboding giant of a man in life and it appeared, in death also.

"You can't be there," said Dyrac trying to convince himself this was another hallucination, "I was there when you took your last breath" he added.

The figure in front of him loomed towards Dyrac and whispered, "you mean when you took my last breath urchin."

Dyrac gulped hard and braced himself maintaining his position anticipating an attack from in front.

"I will pass you Abimilech," Dyrac said surprising himself with the confidence and direction his tone projected.

"Little Dyrac Gideon," said Abimilech, "you will yield. Maybe not to me but, before the day is out yield you will."

Dyrac shuddered as he felt that shiver you get when someone supposedly walks across your grave. When all the hairs on your body stand to attention and you feel a chill in the air as it brushes against your skin.

Dyrac took a step forward, Abimilech grew in magnificence. Dyrac stopped.

"What do you want? What can you possibly want from me?" Dyrac asked.

"What rightfully belongs to the Gideon family," replied Abimilech.

"Everything here belongs to me!" shouted Dyrac, "the bricks and mortar, your body, your soul, they all belong to me!"

Dyrac waited for Abimilech to respond but instead of uttering another word blackness filled the room behind Abimilech. It was encroaching towards Dyrac and he felt the air being sucked from the room. The cellar shook violently as though a small earthquake in the distance was feeding and building itself up to a catastrophic crescendo. Dyrac tried to hold on but there was nothing to hold on to. He fells to his knees again and tucked his head in between his legs like a frightened small boy.

The shaking became destructive. Dyrac heard wine bottles crash from their shelves exploding their contents like a torrential river of claret rushing through to the central chamber. Jars containing curiosities shattered against the floor and body parts that were once preserved sloshed around in the blood red lake that Dyrac now found himself kneeling in.

Like the biblical plague where God turned the Nile into blood, Dyrac was engulfed with terror. He pleaded and begged Abimilech to stop announcing that he would put good all that he did wrong but the chaos continued.

Dyrac knew if he was to emerge from this unscathed he must move. He got to his feet with all he had left. He took his Karamabit in his right hand and swooped down hard in front of him towards his threat. The Karamabit stopped only when it his own thigh piercing his flesh and spilling his own blood. As his blood pulsed out of his leg he found himself alone in the cellar with no evidence of the scene he just witnessed.

He sharply looked around and could see the curiosities in their rightful place, the wine bottles were back on their racks neatly stored by vintage. He looked through to where Abimilech once lay in a Perspex case and there he was, still dead.

Dyrac's mind was being tormented. Some unforgivable force was to blame and he could come to only one conclusion. He turned to where his back was facing and walked into the narrow chamber where the chest Kurt had brought to Wode House lay peacefully.

With a key he had affixed to a pocket watch chain on his waistcoat Dyrac unlocked the chest and opened it with a back draft of air thwacking him in his face and knocking him off his feet. Dyrac peered into the chest. It was empty!

Dyrac knew instantly that the pythos had been opened. It could be the only explanation for all that had happened since he was in his room. The only possible rational reasoning of the events that were unfolding, the hallucinations, apparitions and the mental torture he was experiencing. But who opened it and how. Verne certainly wouldn't be able to manage such an incantation and Kurt and Cornelius were both dead. This left only Merril.

Dyrac felt a penetrative pain in his leg and he looked down. He could see that the gash in his leg from the Karamabit was deep and blood continuously poured out. In bringing down the Karamabit he had exposed a complex network of severed nerves and shredded muscle revealing the bone beneath.

Dyrac grimaced as he took his belt from his waist and made a tourniquet to stem the blood flow. Dyrac had a thirst for blood for sure but never his own and never in this quantity.

He took a couple of steps keeping an eye on the tourniquet. It was working, the bleeding had stopped. He walked towards the stairs of the cellar and began climbing. He turned the handle on the door at the top and walked into the kitchen. Looking down the hallway to the study there was no blackness waiting for him this time. He decided to look for a first aid kit or for something that would act as a bandage.

Merril pushed the doorway from the hidden passage into the cellar and walked through. She stopped to look at Abimilech and she lifted the Perspex case exposing him to the air. Merril half expected the mummified remains to turn to dust as soon as the air hit him but he stayed in the same state that he had been in for many years.

"Come with me now Papa," she uttered as she bent over to lift him from his resting place, "we've got work to do."

Before Merril had chance to remove Abimilech from where he lay she heard a commotion from overhead. *Dyrac is in the kitchen,* she thought.

Changing tact quickly Merril raced into the narrow chamber and dragged the empty chest into the central chamber. She ran into the chapel and lifted the body of a small girl from the cabinet and gently placed her inside the chest. As she covered Imelda with fabrics taken from the chamber of curiosities she whispered, "we are going to get you out of here, we are coming back for you. For all of you."

Merril went back into the chapel to retrieve Kurt. She had one problem. How did the mechanism work and how was she going to get to him?

Chapter 46

Verne walked along the side of Wode House around the back and away from the building. Looking back he noticed that where he previously saw a splendid house that any architect would be proud to have their name against having intricate beauty carved into the sandstone walls, what he saw now was in dark contrast to the magnificent grandeur he arrived at just a few days before.

Wode House looked abandoned. As though decomposing in its surroundings that appeared unkempt and overgrown. Verne knew this couldn't possibly be the case as sufficient time had not passed for it to be so. Yet, right before his eyes the house echoed within its own history as though it had chosen solitude for itself. The walls appeared to crumble and the house was nothing more than a silhouette of a previous existence. The wind whistled through the surrounding trees with what sounded like feint screams calling out for help.

Wode House looked bleak and dreary as though ghosts had been awakened. The walls blistered with a time-warp forgotten and the way the sun sat in the sky, a heavy sepia tone encumbered its very being. The old mansion glared back at Verne with dankness and repulsion.

Verne shuddered and brought his gaze back to the path he was taking. He felt the satchel resting against his side and pressed it as though reassuring himself that the contents were still in place.

After walking a little further the Gideon family

crypt came into view.

Unlike Wode House the crypt looked beautiful. As though respectfully looked after and lovingly nurtured. The ground around the crypt was neat and tidy and the brilliance from the white marble exuded a halo of light around the outside in an aura like majesty.

Verne stopped momentarily outside the crypt and took one last look back towards Wode House. It was barely visible with the distance and tree line obscuring it from full sight. Verne sighed heavily and despite all his inner being willing him to return for Merril he sat dejected, and waited as instructed.

Verne peered inside the satchel and noticed an unusual urn. He was tempted to look inside but something prevented him from doing so and he fastened the satchel back up securely. His instructions were clear and they did not include him touching the contents of Merril's bag.

All Verne had to do now was wait.

Dyrac fumbled around the kitchen knocking various items off shelves and worktops, crashing into furniture as the pain in his leg irradiated up to his head. He clutched at his head with his Karamabit still in his hand and with his other hand he tautened the tourniquet around his thigh.

Finally he found a first aid kit. He flung it onto the kitchen table spilling the contents. He grabbed at a sealed packet of bandages and tore it open with his teeth. He quickly bound his wound as tightly as he could bare. A rush of adrenaline relieved him as he spotted a large brown sea though jar with a white child proof locking white top full of its contents. Dyrac wrestled with the lid and spilled the contents into his mouth chewing the tablets as he reached for some sort of receptacle to put water in to wash away the remnants. He grabbed a small vase next to the Bristol sink in the kitchen and, without checking if it was clean turned the faucet to on filling it. He guzzled the water as the tap continued to run refilling it to quench a thirst he also felt in abundance.

Dyrac looked back at the jar. The label read:

Naproxen 500 mg
Ms Merril I Gideon

Before Dyrac could read any more of the label he spat the left over contents in his mouth across the sink spraying the window sill and splattering the window with flecks of tablets.

"Gideon!" he exclaimed, "how dare that girl use my..." he cut himself short.

It was a pivotal moment. Cogs clicked into place, the jigsaw pieces finally start making sense, the final piece of the puzzle had just locked in revealing its secret.

"Idysha!" he shouted.

"Yes," came a reply.

Dyrac turned swiftly to find Merril facing him at the cellar door.

"But you...you can't be...you died?" said a shocked Dyrac. "You've been working for me for..."

"15 years Dyrac," replied Merril, "and all along you had no idea who I really was."

Dyrac tried to form words but his mouth moved and no sound came out.

"You did not hire me because of my credentials,

satisfactory references nor because I came highly recommended. You hired me because I wanted you to hire me."

"But..." Dyrac shifted uneasily unable to bare weight for too long on his injured leg.

"But nothing Mr Gideon," said Merril, "I needed to wait for the right time. I needed to make sure everything was in place before my true identity was revealed. I know you suspected and I know you found evidence that fed on your suspicions but it is only now, at this moment that the realisation of who I actually am has hit you. Am I right little urchin?"

Dyrac gripped the Karamabit hard, "yes," he replied.

"I know what you did to my father Dyrac. I know what you did to my grieving mother. I know she saw through you for what you really are; a vile cretin. Something that you would have your servant scrape from the sole of your shoe if you trod in it."

"I'm your brother," said Dyrac.

"You're no brother of mine," said Merril as she walked around the large kitchen table running her finger along the top, "a brother of mine would not have killed his own!" she spat with venom as she spoke.

"Merril, it's me..."

"Quiet," she shouted, "I want to explain how this is going to end. And it will end Dyrac, I can assure you of that.

By now you'll know that mama has been awakened, oh yes I know about the Pythos and yes, it was me that released her."

"Then you'll know that..." said Dyrac.

"Oh I'm quite assured that no harm will come to me," said Merril confidently and morose. "Mama has unfinished business you see and, now the truth has been revealed to her it's you she is after Dyrac. Not me.

I wonder has she sent any of the others to see you?" she asked noting Dyrac's facial expression shift, "Oh she has, father was it? Or maybe the little girl in your cabinet, yes I know about her. Who was she Dyrac? So young, so innocent. What could she possibly have done to aggrieve you so brother?" Merril taunted Dyrac.

Dyrac tried to compose himself and, with the painkillers starting to take effect he stood tall, "so Merril, where do we do this?"

"Recognise this?" asked Merril holding up her own Karamabit, "quite apt don't you think that a family blade should be the thing that destroys the only family each of us has left?"

Dyrac held his Karamabit in front of him. His right fist was clenched over the handle with the claw like blade protruding to the right and pointing downwards. "I recognise the workmanship and the steel," he said.

Merril struck down hard with the blade whipping the air with precision proving to Dyrac that she knew how to handle the weapon and how to use it.

"Well then," said Dyrac, "do we bow to each other before first blood is drawn?"

Merril nodded.

They both stood on the same side of the large kitchen table facing each other. They stepped closer and as they both bowed their heads Merril stopped and before Dyrac had chance to straighten he felt the blade of the Karamabit puncture the flesh between his collarbone and neck. Dyrac howled in agony but gusto encouraged him on and he raised his head and glared through the top of his eyes towards Merril.

Dyrac lunged himself forward and swooping his hand across his body the tip of the claw sliced through Merril's mid riff. Blood pooled into her clothing but she didn't falter.

The pair of them urged the other to take a shot but both were apprehensive about their next move.

Merril noticed that blood was pulsing from Dyrac's new wound and she knew it wouldn't take much to bring him down.

Chapter 47

Dyrac was weakening but he tried not to let it show. He could feel the blood loss affecting his coherence. His delusions were infiltrating his senses and standing in front of him he could see Merril poised and ready to strike down with her Karamabit. He also saw Abimilech standing behind her towering above everything filling the void in the room. His mere presence weakened Dyrac more than he wanted to admit, *still in death you control me,* he thought. At the side of Merril stood Sarah. She was pristine in appearance, and unlike at the time of her death was in one piece. She looked Dyrac up and down before grimacing eerily as she felt her arms and legs nodding in acknowledgement of his thoughts.

Dyrac remembered when he took Sarah to the crypt the day he took her life. Before he broke her neck with his bare hands Dyrac had rendered Sarah unconscious as she grieved over the death of her husband, Abimilech. Dyrac had appeared before Sarah in the grounds of Wode House and, as she lay slumped over his shoulders he carried her to the family mausoleum.

After ending her life Dyrac repeated the words:

I condemn your evil to an eternal hell,
Evermore your soul contained.

At the same time he performed a satanic ritual dismembering her and encapsulating her tortured soul to an eternity of pain and suffering. The very same pain and suffering the Gideon's had bestowed upon him from which he could not escape. Her soul was drawn from her lifeless body and was contained within the pythos condemning her for perpetuity and unforgiveness.

After dismemberment he set aside Sarah's limbs and drained the blood from her body siphoning it into a green glass wine bottle. After containing her blood inside with a cork he dipped the end of the bottle in hot wax forming an air tight seal. The bottle bore no label.

He decapitated the head from the body and set it upon a spike which he had placed inside a white waxed pentagram on the floor of the crypt. Each triangle point contained a different symbol representing various pits of hell. He decimated her remains burning her limbs and torso until nothing but ash remained. Sarah's ashes were poured into the pythos along with her soul.

In the days following her untimely and barbaric death Dyrac travelled with the pythos to Cambodia where, during an archaeological dig at Ankor Wat he planned to bury the pythos in the temple. Only he would ever know of its true location and, with the dig nearing its end he was confident Sarah would not be found. Not until the time came where he needed to summon her. A time would come, for that he was sure, where Sarah's penitence would come to fore and she would obey his command. A command she used to hold over him.

When the time came, Dyrac sent instruction to an ally in Ankor Wat to retrieve the pythos and ship it to him in a chest by boat where he would have the chest collected and brought to Wode House. That day came when Kurt was instructed to deliver the chest to Wode House and store it in the cellar.

Only Dyrac knew of the true contents of the chest and he knew that the time would come when he would need Sarah's help. He'd been sent the last will and testament of Abimilech Gideon detailing that the rightful heir was his only surviving child Idysha Gideon albeit Dyrac thought she had died his suspicions were confirmed as events began to unfold at Wode House.

Dyrac's only hope was that Sarah would be as bitter over the last will and testament as he was, for Sarah was still surviving after Abimilech passed away and the will showed complete disregard to her existence. He would use this as a form of manipulating the soul of Sarah Gideon now trapped inside Pandora's Box to aide him in his endeavours to take full control over the rights to Wode House and the Gideon family name.

Dyrac's plan never came to fruition as he now found himself barely clinging to life and standing in front of the sister he thought died long ago.

Chapter 48

Dusk was setting in and the moon was illuminating the sky transcending fuscia and violet ribbons broken only by the occasional cloud. The moonlight cut through the kitchen window and the reflection of the Karamabit blade highlighted Merril's hostile eyes.

Merril thrust her hand in an upwards motion from the side of her waist puncturing Dyrac in the groin with the cutlass like hook of the blade. She yanked backwards as the blade eviscerated Dyrac's scrotum tearing his flesh piercing his upper thigh like a butcher hanging a carcass on a meat hook.

Dyrac crumpled in a heap to the floor in a pool of his own blood dropping his Karamabit far out of reach. The gushing was uncontrollable and Dyrac knew his life was ending. Merril straddled Dyrac's body and retrieved her own bloodied Karamabit. She raised it to her face as she peered into his eyes and with her tongue she licked the blade clean then wiped the side of her mouth with her finger as though catching a delicious morsel of food before it fell to the ground.

"You never were worthy of the Gideon name," said Merril.

Dyrac couldn't speak. He tried but there was no energy to muster the words and he had little left in him to try to berate someone. He could feel his body going into shock as any blood remaining inside him was pumped to his vital organs in a vain attempt of survival.

The smell of gas began to permeate around the

kitchen bringing Merril to the fore and remembering she had to get Kurt, Imelda and her father out of the cellar. She had little time, she knew that but before she left the kitchen she needed to make sure Dyrac was not going to follow. All too often she'd seen the impossible become possible and she needed assurance as well as finality that this had ended tonight.

Merril pressed her fingers inside the wound she had inflicted and Dyrac whimpered. It was the only sound that he could manage a slight murmuring indicating the excruciating pain he was in. His eyes pleaded with her to finish him but she wanted him to suffer and, a part of her wanted to watch.

She knelt down next to him and pressed her face against his, she could smell the aftershave he wore that stirred a fluttering inside of her. She pushed her neck against his lips and said, "drink from me Mr Gideon, one last time."

Dyrac didn't move his lips. Merril looked at him straight in the eye and he turned his gaze away from her.

"So, you can't bring yourself to look at me anymore when once you couldn't keep your eyes from me?" she said.

Merril pushed herself to her feet in a fit of rage. She walked over to the kitchen sink and opened the cupboard beneath retrieving a bottle of hydrochlauric acid which she kept to remove heavy lime deposits from the pipe work. She slowly walked back over to Dyrac with the now opened bottle and sadistically said "I'll give you the benefit of not watching yourself suffer," and she poured the contents on his face dousing his eyes instantly blinding him.

The intensity of the burning acid against his face took Dyrac's mind away from the extreme agony he was in elsewhere.

Merril looked down at Dyrac who began to convulse. He was gurgling and choking on his own blood stained vomit and he was struggling to breathe. It sounded as though he was drowning as he spurted and grabbed for air.

Merril watched as his eyes bubbled and effervesced out of his face and then nothing.

Dyrac was dead.

Chapter 49

Merril felt no remorse as she bent over Dyrac one final time and picked up his Karamabit. She tucked his and her own blade into her top and headed towards the cellar.

A slight stir in the background caught Merril's attention. It was a sound like something heavy was being dragged through mud. A sludgy sloshing, very quiet but obvious. Merril turned to see what, or who was there.

She stared into the darkness of the kitchen and only shadows gave way in the light of the moon. She brushed it off as her imagination playing tricks on her then she saw it. Something moved.

"Who's there?" she shouted.

Verne stepped into view.

"Verne," said Merril, "you scared the..."

"I scared you?" he replied looking at the scene of the massacre before him. "What the hell happened here?"

"There's no time Verne, you were supposed to wait, you were never meant to come back," said Merril angrily.

"You'd been gone so long, I couldn't leave you with that maniac," he said pointing to Dyrac's lifeless body.

"I can handle myself," she replied.

"I can see that," said Verne with a hint of terror in his voice.

Merril had a maniacal look about her.

"Verne, are you going to help me or not?" she

asked.

"Well I'm certainly not going to not help you if that's what will become of me," he said still in shock.

"It's not as though you haven't killed anyone Verne," said Merril.

"Yes but..."

"There are no buts Verne, now get a grip and come and help me," she interrupted.

Verne followed Merril trying to avoid stepping in anymore of the aftermath of the encounter between Merril and Dyrac. As he reached Merril at the entrance to the cellar he stopped her.

"Merril, you're hurt," he said looking down to Merril's waist.

"It's nothing Verne, just a scratch. I've been through much worse, trust me," she replied.

Merril opened the cellar door and they descended into the central chamber. The smell of gas was bordering unbearable as they both gagged.

"It's the lanterns in the passageways," said Merril, "that is where the smell is coming from."

Verne didn't question he just followed Merril into the chapel.

"We need to get Kurt out of here," she said.

"Do you know how this contraption works?" asked Verne.

"No," said Merril, "but I have a key that may help."

"A key?" he asked as he turned to see where Merril had walked to.

Merril turned holding aloft an axe that she found under the stairwell, "the key," she said.

"Right," said Verne.

Merril hacked away somewhat delirious with enthusiasm. The sides of the Mysteriository collapsed revealing the other chambers and Kurt fell to the floor.

"Kurt," said Merril, "here Verne, help me."

Verne shifted nervously towards the cabinet kicking away the axe under from Merril's side.

"Grab his feet," she said.

"His feet and his head?" asked Verne as Kurt was still in a folded position rigor mortis having set in.

"Whatever Verne, just lift on three, 1, 2, 3," said Merril heaving Kurt from the other end.

They placed Kurt inside the chest and covered him with the remaining fabrics Merril had put to one side.

"Now Papa," said Merril.

Verne gagged, "you mean the mummified man in that box in there," he nodded towards the chamber of curiosities.

"Yes Verne, the mummified man, do you think you can cope with that?" she asked noting Verne's greenish hue.

"After you," he said directing Merril to go first.

After carefully moving Abimilech to the chest Merril closed the lid shut.

"And how are we supposed to move this chest now it contains three people?" asked Verne.

Merril disappeared into the wine cellar and re-appeared wheeling small squared piece of wood set on four casters. "They used to use it to move crates of wine with ease," she said placing in next to the chest, "We just hoist the chest onto here and simply wheel it along through the passage way," she added."

"And at the end, when we get to the steps?" asked

Verne.

"Well, we'll make a pulley," said Merril looking around frantically, "with this," she said holding up metres of rope she just happened upon in the chamber of curiosities.

"Not quite thought this through have you?" he asked.

"Well I hardly had much time Verne, I didn't know I'd be removing three bodies from this bloody cellar tonight did I?"

"Ok, ok," he said trying to calm Merril down, "so are we doing this?" he added.

"Together," said Merril.

Merril opened the door to the passage way.

"We can't use the lighting," she said to Verne.

"But it's pitch black in there," he replied.

"I'll guide you Verne, I know these hallways well enough that we don't need the lighting," said Merril.

The passage was hauntingly sinister. Verne peered into the passage looking both to his left and right, it was do dark he couldn't see anything from beyond his nose.

"I can't do this Merril," he said at the same time helping Merril through the doorway with the chest in an effort to convince himself that he could.

They hauled the chest in silence through the passage. The only sound was that of the caster wheels scratching along the wooden floorboards lining the floor of the corridor.

The concept of time was beyond them as they trawled along, Merril counting the steps in her head so she knew when to turn and change direction. Eventually, after what felt like an hour but had only been five minutes or so, Merril spoke.

"Here," she said, "stop here Verne we are at the steps leading down under the lake. We should be able to slide the chest down the stairs and then it's a short walk to the ladders to the folly."

"Merril," asked Verne, "say we manage to get this chest into the folly how are we going to get it through that small hatch in the folly wall?"

"Don't worry Verne the chest can remain inside the folly until I come back for it," she replied.

"You're coming back," asked Verne.

"I need to come back, it's my home, my family are here and I want to finally lay them to rest with our ancestors in the crypt where you were meant to be waiting. Hang on, Verne, where's my satchel?" she asked recalling that Verne didn't have it with him.

"It's in the crypt," replied Verne.

"You left it unattended?" she asked.

"Yes why, it only had an old urn inside," he replied.

"That's not just an urn Verne, that's my mother," said Merril, "and she's not quite..." she stopped herself from saying anymore.

"Your mother!" exclaimed Verne, "Well, I'm pretty sure she isn't going anywhere Merril, she's in a vase in a bag," he added.

"Verne you..." Merril stopped herself, "you're quite right." It would be too much to explain to Verne the force that Merril's mother had now become and that Merril herself had unleashed the evil within Pandora's Box. She made a mistake trusting Verne with it.

The chest slid easier down the stairs than Merril

and Verne anticipated and they quickly moved on towards the ladder at the end of the passageway. When they arrived Merril ascended the ladder.

"Wait here Verne, I'll go to the top, sort the rope and then with you as anchor we will hoist the chest up into the folly."

"You want me to wait down here, with the dead people?" he asked.

"Yes Verne, don't panic they won't bite," she paused before adding, "hard," Merril sniggered to herself.

It took some doing but Merril and Verne managed to haul the chest into the folly. Merril smiled as she lay herself across the chest embracing it as though she'd just been reacquainted with a long lost relative.

Chapter 50

Byron Bryson opened the back door of Bryson & Sons.

"Morning Joel," he said to the newspaper delivery man, "crazy news about Wode House isn't it?" he added.

"Alright Byron, I know. To just go up like that, and all those bodies," said Joel.

Joel dropped a bound pile of newspapers at Byron's feet. The headline read:

WODE HOUSE UP IN FLAMES

Byron tore open the bundle of papers and removed the top copy reading out loud.

"Five fire appliances from Clifton Fire Station were called to tackle a blaze at Wode House in the early hours of this morning. A huge fire caused extensive damage to the 500 year old building as flames and smoke billowed from the roof of the renowned manor house.

The fire has now been largely contained however, a few pockets of fire remain which crews continue to work on to extinguish.

Speaking at the scene Chief Fire and Rescue Officer, Peter A Smith described the scene as 'a sight like no other he had ever witnessed'. Peter A Smith had been in the fire service for 25 years and he was nearing retirement. 'A number of bodies were recovered from the main house which were not identifiable at this stage. Further bodies were found in the crypt away from the fire. The police are treating Wode House as a crime scene at this stage with a number of pathology experts being drafted in to examine the bodies that were found in various states.

Up to 70 percent of the property was involved directly in the fire which is believed to have started in a maze of tunnels underneath the building.

The focus at this stage is to prevent the fire from spreading. Local people are urged to remain away from Wode House with cordons having been set up on the outskirts of the perimeter of the grounds.'

Wode House was completed in the early 1500s and was of historic importance. The Gideon family had been in residence for its full duration. It is believed that the owner and occupier, Mr Dyrac Gideon was in the property at the time the fire broke out. No survivors have been reported and the fire appears to have ravaged the building.

A press conference has been scheduled to take place at 10:00am with Chief Fire and Rescue Officer Peter A Smith and the Chief of

Police James Colton
providing an update with
the public interest in
mind."

"Shit," said Bradley. Byron's son appeared from the back door of the shop, "Kurt was there. Do you think he was in the fire?"

"I don't know Bradley," said Byron, "let's hope to God he wasn't."

"Whatever happened there, I'm sure we will never know the full truth behind what happened at Wode House," said Joel.

Verne reached up to grab Merril's arm for help as he neared the top of the ladder. Merril reached down but instead of pulling him up she reached for her Karamabit and sliced at his arm inflicting a gash through Verne's wrist. The Karamabit was so sharp the cut almost severed his hand from his arm. Verne screamed recoiling and falling back down the shaft. With a thud his body struck the floor and he was rendered unconscious.

"I'm sorry," Merril's voice echoed down the shaft and along the passage way under the lake.

Quickly Merril opened the chest and pulled Abimilech from inside. She stepped through the folly hatch. Before securing the stone plaque back into place Merril ignited a flare which was housed in a small tin at the entrance to the hidden tunnel. It was kept for emergencies should the lighting ever fail. It never did. She dropped it down the shaft.

As fast as her legs could carry her Merril, with

Abimilech held close, ran along the bridge and passed the back of Wode House. As she raced along the bridle way, adrenaline fuelling her speed, a series of explosions reverberated in the background.

A torrent of water sprung from the lake as the tunnel below exploded. The flare ignited the gas lighting system Merril purposefully left on and just like a well timed pyrotechnic display the lamps blew one by one.

When Merril was a safe enough distance away she turned and watched just as the windows of Wode House exploded outwards and the building became engulfed in flames.

The twilight sky was now shielded by a veil of darkness as the smoke swallowed up the whole sky. Fierce fire could be seen lapping out from the windows. With an almighty crash the roof caved in a huge fireball. The fire grew gentler, almost playful as it consumed the might of Wode House.

Plumes of black grey smoke wound around the building like a serpent devouring everything in its path.

She began moving again at a walking pace. As she arrived at the crypt she turned to see dirty flakes of snowy ash shower the scene and settle on the ground.

Merril entered the crypt and lay Abimilech next to the urn containing her mother's ashes. Merril wept, her sobbing was silent. She wiped the tears from her cheek and she took both Karamabits out from her top. She lay one on top of Abimilech's chest and the other, her own, she held in her hand.

"It's over," she said and with one swift movement she slashed across her own neck immediately falling face forwards over the body of her father. Her blood seeped into the dried mummified leathery skin of Abimilech and oozed into the seal of the pythos.

Together again, for the last time.

The End.

Printed in Great Britain
by Amazon